the Maltese
Dreamer

the Maltese Dreamer

A NOVEL

CATHERINE VERITAS

*This book is dedicated to the Beautiful Mystery
of ancient Malta*

And to Beauty-Makers everywhere

Acknowledgements

My deepest thanks to James Tucker—who loved the Goddess in me before I knew Her
Laurel Kahaner—who en-Couraged me to write
Martha Morrison—who modeled the art of a creative life
Author Elinor W. Gadon—who introduced me to ancient Malta

I thank the many friends, family, readers and critique-ers who have loved me and supported my journey, in the United States, and in Malta. Particular gratitude goes to Riley K. Smith for my wonderful cover, Charles Borg of Malta for his beautiful photo of the Sleeping Goddess, and H.O.Charles for my fine map of the Maltese Archipelago. Special acknowledgements go to Susun Weed of the Wise Woman Center, Woodstock, New York, and Jerome Berman of the California Museum of Ancient Art, whose lectures and works expanded my mind and enriched this writing.

Preface

❧❧

The Temple Culture of ancient Malta, which flourished for a thousand years (from 3600 BC to 2600 BC) left behind dozens of magnificent and extraordinary megalithic temples. The architecture described in this novel, the geographic locations, and the general history, are true to the region. I have taken some liberties, such as transposing the spirals from the altar at Tarxien to the altar at Ħaġar Qim, and using some modern place names. The quoted mythical texts are translations of the Canaanite tablets found in the ancient city of Ugarit, and the love poem lines are from the "Song of Songs." The statues, spiral altar, and shell necklace can be viewed in the National Museum of Archeology, Valletta, Malta. Beyond these details, this is a work of fiction. Consult a professional wise woman herbalist before using herbs to treat health conditions.

Name pronunciations:
Nuriya—pronounced "**Noor**-ee-a"
Ilobaal—pronounced "**Ee**-lo-ball"

Temple pronunciations:
Mnajdra—pronounced "Im-**Nai**-dra"
Ħaġar Qim—pronounced "**Ha**-jar **Eem**"
A Glossary can be found at the end of this book.

Contents

∽∿

1.

Healer's Apprentice

☉⊘

Malta, 728 BC

Nuriya balanced a pot of water onto the cook-stones then stood, opening her arms wide, as if embracing the whole of the Great Mediterranean Sea. Yonder, merchant galleys sailed, slicing through turquoise waters toward far-flung ports of call. Nuriya closed her eyes and let the sea wind lick the sweat from her skin, dreaming of the handsome seafarer she would one day marry, who would sail her to Tyre, the homeland she had never seen. Together they would find her father, and she would at last be welcomed into the bosom of her true family.

She opened her eyes to see Korba climbing the hill from Mnajdra, the ancient temple that was the healer's passion and devotion. An empty waterskin swung in front of the healer as she bent to her walking stick; her apron was smudged with rust-red ochre. Nuriya turned, ducking into the cool of the dwelling she shared with her teacher, taking a moment to breathe in the fragrance of drying summer herbs. She stepped through to the back storeroom, a shallow, dry cave, which had been Korba's only dwelling before a neighbor helped her build the thatch-roofed anteroom and wooden door. The storeroom held baskets of vegetables, berries, and seeds stacked alongside jugs of honey wine and bowls of grain. Nuriya selected a handful of dried mushrooms, two turnips, and picked up a bowl of soaking grain. She went back outside to stir barley into the cookpot and cut vegetables for their pottage. Korba arrived, humming softly, and began washing at the basin.

Moments later a high, thin cry turned their heads. "Heal-er!" A boy was racing toward them, down from the Standing Stones temple, another ancient, abandoned sanctuary further up the hill, crying, "Fetch the healer. Hurry! My sister's hurt!"

Korba identified herself and calmed the boy enough to determine his need, then directed Nuriya to heat fresh water. Nuriya moved aside the cookpot, replacing it with a smaller medicine pot, then gathered the supplies Korba requested, wrapping herbs and a waterskin into the healer's traveling kit. When steam rose from the medicine pot, Korba removed it from the heat, mixed in crushed, dried, poppy flower-heads, then cooled the mixture enough to pour it into a watertight bladder. Soon they set off, up to cliff trail and east on the port road, then following the lad inland through terraced farm fields. The healer chanted prayers as she walked a steady pace while the boy fretted and tried to hurry them. Nuriya carried the supplies and gathered fresh plantain along their route.

They found the boy's young sister resting under a makeshift lean-to, a small bit of shelter from the summer sun. A group of men could be seen swinging scythes in a nearby field. One broke from his work and approached them. His expression was grim, for one moment his children had been playing next to him as he drove a heavy-laden ox-cart, and the next moment his daughter was pushed off and into its path, her foot crushed under a turning wheel.

Nuriya sat down next to the girl to see what comfort she could offer while the healer assessed. She glanced around first, hoping to see the child's mother, but neither boy nor father were looking for anyone else to join them, and neither was the child. She was gazing up at Nuriya, her expression pleading and scared. Nuriya resisted the urge to look away, to close her eyes, to not see the child's pain, an all too familiar struggle in her role as the healer's apprentice. She gently smoothed brown locks that tangled across the girl's forehead, feeling the chill of her skin, even in this heat, noting the tear tracks that marked her cheeks. Another familiar sensation rose in Nuriya, the pressure of her own emotions building inside her chest. She breathed a tight breath and took hold of the girl's hand. Petite, clammy fingers clung to hers. Nuriya felt an immediate kinship with the child and at that moment, more than anything in the world, she wanted this child to be well. Korba had taught her how to pray, and though she did not know whether the Great Mother heard her prayers or what She chose to do with them if She did, Nuriya silently and fervently prayed the words she was taught: "Great Mother, source of all life, guide my hands and my heart to bring your healing to your daughter."

The girl's name was Tian. Korba greeted her by name then asked, "Does it hurt a lot?" The child gave a vague, slow nod. "Can you move your toes?" The girl responded by turning a confused and glassy gaze back toward Nuriya, as if seeking an answer in her.

Korba felt the pulse at Tian's forehead and temples, closed her eyes for the space of a breath, then moved to carefully unwrap the crude and stained bandage. She poured from her waterskin, rinsing parts of the foot, water trickling into a bloody puddle, revealing what had clotted and what had not. Korba pushed herself back to standing and addressed the father, "Where is your dwelling?" The man pointed to a reed roof peeking out above a nearby hill. "I need to get Tian out of the sun. You carry. We'll follow."

The man hesitated a moment then nodded, awkwardly picking up his daughter and leading the way, clenching and unclenching his jaw with each and every step.

The rubblestone field hut was a chaos of unwashed pots, mats, and clothing. The boy hurriedly made a place for his sister and Korba used a mound of bedding to prop up Tian's legs. She left Nuriya with the child and went to find embers in the ash-filled fire ring, pulling out her two medicine cook-bowls, and setting to work.

Nuriya had lived with the healer since she was as young as the child before her; now Nuriya was almost fifteen, almost a woman. Over the years Korba had taught her how to gather herbs and prepare medicine, how to massage away pain, and how to hold her hands over injury with healing intention when touch was not appropriate. Nuriya held her hands now over the swollen mass of Tian's foot, trying not to picture the bones, broken and twisted under the damaged flesh. It hurt her that such pain existed, that this tender child should suffer. She tried to remind herself, as Korba often did, that the power which grew Tian from an infant into a bright young child was the same power which could, perhaps, heal her mangled foot.

When it became too difficult to think healing thoughts, Nuriya stroked Tian's hair and hummed a lullaby. Korba came in, handing her a jar, and went back out. Nuriya pried open the stopper, dabbing a finger into the sweet bee nectar. Cradling Tian's head, she made up a song, "Honey, honey, sweet little girl, a special, special, bee made this just for you," and enticed until the listless child sucked honey from her finger. Then she offered more.

Korba came in again, felt Tian's forehead, looked deeply into her eyes then handed Nuriya the medicine bladder of steeped poppy-heads. "Two sips," she said and Nuriya nodded, propping Tian's head higher. The healer returned shortly with her two medicine bowls. She rechecked Tian's eyes then spoke directly to her, "Tian, I'm going to examine your injury now." She moved to carefully test the ankle, holding Tian's heel in one hand and her lower leg in the other. She thoroughly cleansed the injury with medicinal tea, reopening the wound as little as possible. Tian squeezed Nuriya's hand during the procedure, whimpering a little but not drawing her leg away. Korba examined the distortion in the foot but there was too much swelling to see how many bones were involved. She applied a mash of plantain leaves and honey, wrapping the foot with more leaves, and securing them with cloth. Turning her attention to the father, Korba said, "I will show you how to make her medicine. Who will help you?" Korba was gently prying into the family situation, for everyone on Malta, save the odd exception of she and Nuriya, lived in family clans, not in isolated field huts, and no explanation had been made for the absence of Tian's mother and kin.

"No one."

"Well, come along. And you'll need to make crutches, too."

It was late in the summer's long afternoon when they packed up, Nuriya wishing to stay, gazing back at Tian, her one wadded, mess of a foot propped next to its perfect partner. The healer told the father she would be back the next afternoon. "If there's trouble, fetch me sooner. A flag on the post says I'm home. I'll leave word with Bon in Wied Filfla if I'm away." The father offered to pay in wheat "when the harvest's done," and the healer said that would be fine.

They walked home with Nuriya brooding moodily, staring at the ground a few paces in front of her. By the time they reached the fork in the trail, between the temple Mnajdra and their dwelling, the sunset was a red-orange glow over the western cliffs. Nuriya retied the welcome cloth and turned toward home, but before she took another step, Korba placed a hand on her shoulder. "Talk," Korba said.

Nuriya faced her teacher, pursing her lips, and stalling. "I'm sad," she burst out finally, with a tone more angry than sad.

"Tian's foot?"

"That. And everything. That her mother's not with her. That she'll walk with a limp when her foot heals. Why couldn't we do more?" Nuriya whined.

"It's time for Tian to rest and for Great Mother to do Her part."

Korba was deeply devoted to the Great Mother, and believed that all healing outcomes, indeed, all of life, rested in the Great Mother's hands. But Nuriya was not eased by such words, and she suffered until every patient was well. She didn't want to hurt Korba, the most respected healer on the island, but she felt so helpless and frustrated and useless that she didn't want to hold herself back as she usually did. "If the Mother is so great, why does She let these things happen?"

Korba held her gaze for a long moment before answering evenly, "It is not given us to see through Her eyes." That was as much retort as Nuriya might expect and she turned to stare out toward the sea. The bright stars of the Scorpion poked through the twilight, the red heart and pinchers. Temple Mnajdra was a majestic silhouette against the fading light. "I know you wanted to do more," Korba continued. "It was hard to see Tian hurting."

Nuriya bit her cheek to suppress another reply she would regret.

"Will you make offering in the morning? You'll feel better."

Nuriya nodded, to appease her teacher, and they walked the path home in silence.

At dawn the next day, Nuriya's first thought was of Tian. Then the questions flooded in: How much pain was she in? Were the herbs working? What if Korba waited too long to adjust the bones? Without a word, she dressed and followed Korba to the garden. The healer picked a sprig of plejju mint and a handful of beans, saying, "Bring an offering, Nuri."

The towering rosemary outside the garden wall caught Nuriya's attention. She snapped off a blue-green sprig, thanking the stately plant. They walked down the rocky slope, absorbed each in her own thoughts. The sea this morning was the color of slate and the great clouds resting above the horizon were outlined white gold with the sun they veiled. Mnajdra looked stunning, her limestone glowing pink with the dawn light.

Every morning for the past thirty years, Korba had brought an offering to the main altar of this ancient building. Nuriya grew up accompanying Korba to her daily morning prayers, though recently she accompanied her less and less often, for she found herself squirming at the healer's emphatic devotion to her God. This morning, Korba spoke a restrained few words of prayer then stepped back, saying, "Tell Her what is in your heart, Nuri. Ask Her for help."

Nuriya felt a moment's irritation even now but she was so full of feeling for Tian she could hardly breathe; she had to speak to someone! Despite her cynicism, she trembled as she set the rose-mary sprig between the water bowl and the statue of the Goddess. She closed her eyes, moving her lips in silent prayer. "Please don't make Tian suffer. Help her heal, if you can. I want the swelling gone and her foot to be well. Please, if you can do this." After a few moments, Nuriya opened her eyes. The altar looked quite lovely— the painted bowl, the plump statue of the Goddess, the rosemary sprig with its gallant blue flowers sitting atop the altar that Korba was painting with ochre spirals. Nuriya's eyes still stung with un-shed tears, but she did feel less agitated.

As she tended the chickens and fetched the water, Nuriya carried her concern for Tian like a stone in her gut. Sometimes it pushed itself, unbidden, into her throat and her jaw would tighten with the effort to push it back down. She joined Korba later, mending mats indoors, out of the summer sun, and in that quiet activity, the images came again—the mangled foot, the brave little girl. She couldn't wait to return.

It was not the busiest time of year for the healer; summer herbs had been gathered and put up to dry or infused into oil, and when the last of the beans were picked, the garden would lie dormant until the first fall rain. Any time was time for birthings or broken bones, but no new trouble sought them that day, and after a morning of mending, the healer and her apprentice set off to tend their patient.

Tian was lying inside the hut with her injured foot elevated. Korba unwrapped the bandage and examined the foot, commenting, "good, good," and "not yet." After changing the poultice the healer directed Nuriya to clean the outdoor fire ring while she had a private chat with the girl.

Later, Korba met Tian's father as he came in from the fields, speaking sharply, "Your daughter needs her mother even if you do not."

"It's not your business."

"Your affairs are not my business, but your daughter's healing is." Korba gave new instructions, making them a good deal more complicated than necessary, and muttered annoyance under her breath for much of the walk home.

While Nuriya was at chores the next morning, neighbor Bon stopped by to see if they needed anything from market. Korba put a packet together for him to deliver to the spice vendor, Kepi, then gladly accepted his offer of an ox-cart ride to Tian's.

When they arrived, a woman with chestnut hair and sorrowful eyes was there to greet them. It was she who gave Tian her cherub features, and Nuriya reproached a pang of jealousy even as she noticed Korba's gratified smile. Already Tian's mother had cleaned and aired the room, hung clothes to dry and was mending tunics.

The swelling of the foot had diminished considerably, and the distortion of its shape was clear to see. Korba warmed her poppyhead brew, adding honey, and Tian drank it while her mother held her, murmuring soothing encouragements, and singing softly until she slept. Korba whispered instructions to her apprentice then poured her concentration into manipulating the delicate bones. Even sedated Tian cried out, "Mommy, mommy," and Nuriya had to use both hands to hold her leg down. Finally, Korba nodded that she was pleased with her result. She poulticed and splinted the foot, then the women went outside to talk. Nuriya stayed with Tian, glancing out as often as she dared through the open doorway, straining unsuccessfully to hear the women's whispered, heart-to heart conversation.

That evening after supper, Nuriya faced out to sea, listening to the crickets beckon the night. Small animals skittered in the dried grass and a breeze rustled her hair. Evenings had once been a time of teaching for healer and apprentice but these days Korba took up her pipe after supper and retired early. Nuriya enjoyed the drunken, darting dance of the bats then watched the first stars reveal themselves—the blue Pearl, the orange star of the Herdsman, the red heart of the Scorpion. Gradually those first lights became immersed into the magnificent starry array; there would be no moon tonight to dim their radiance or their number. Thinking of Tian curled into her mother's arms, Nuriya turned her head toward the east, the direction of port town. Nuriya had lived there once...she had a family once...

Nuriya's father had been the assistant to the Overseer of the Dock at the Phoenician colony at Marsaxlokk Bay. Phoenicia was a land of five kingdoms on the far eastern shore of the Mediterranean Sea, bordered by the Kingdom of Israel to the south, and

Assyrian Empire to the east. The Phoenician settlement at Marsaxlokk was called a colony, but the only Phoenicians living there at that time were the Overseer, the dozen men who served as dockworkers as well as guards for the two warehouses, a good-natured family that ran an inn, and Nuriya's own small household.

Nuriya's mother died during a pox epidemic that spread, with devastating effect, throughout the entire Mediterranean basin. Nuriya had lived with the healer ever since, for her father had returned with his Overseer to their home port of Tyre. Nuriya tried to keep alive her few memories of her father, his handsome, long face and dark-lashed eyes, the way his voice rumbled when he was angry. Whenever she saw a particularly elegant merchant ship, she would imagine that the captain looked like her father, and she often dreamed of marrying such a man, who would take her to Tyre to find him.

In the ten years since Nuriya lived at port, everything about the Phoenician colony had changed. Hundreds of people resided there now. There were worker's barracks (they used to live in camps), warehouses, and rows of dwellings for market workers and crafts-men. There were two taverns besides the inn, a meeting house, and a residence for the Phoenician Magistrate. Merchants per-suaded to stay year round had built homes and even brought their families. A market bustled every day during the trading season, and every fourth day throughout the winter. And last spring, a Tyrian war ship, boasting a very impressive purple sail, had been stationed there.

People from all over the Mediterranean passed through Malta now: Libyans from Africa, Elmyans from Sicily, men from Ibe-ria, and from all the kingdoms of Phoenicia. The common tongue at port was the Canaanite language of Tyre, the varieties of peoples each speaking their uniquely accented versions. Nuriya loved being at port on market days, hearing the language of her youth and the accents from faraway places. She loved the flashes

of purple and red cloth, the smells of foods spiced with her childhood memories, the clink of scales, the calls of vendors, the
trinkets from all around the Great Sea.

When Nuriya was young, Korba took her to port often, walking half the morning to get there, so she could mingle with the
innkeeper's children. Afterward they would watch ships from the
west unload tin and silver into the warehouses while galleys from
the east offloaded wine and oil, then stacked precious ingots into
their hulls to transport to Tyre. As Nuriya grew up, however,
Korba seemed evermore reluctant to spend time at port.

In case the canny healer could read her thoughts, Nuriya
moved to a rock down near the signal post, resting her chin onto
her palm. How would she find a husband to take her to Tyre if
Korba whisked her away whenever a sailor looked at her? The
fruit vender's son gave her free figs, and the way he brushed her
hand made her giddy, but he wasn't a sailor and she doubted that
he or his father would ever be able to buy their passage home.

Nuriya went back to gazing at the stars, seeking out the
Wanderers, those privileged stars which moved independent
of the design of the night. Behind her in the sign of the Fishes,
the Wanderer called Bright Star of Wisdom shone brilliant
and distinct, and before her, the Beauty Star slung low in the
west. Nuriya liked to imagine that her mother lived inside the
Beauty Star, her favorite star in all the night sky. She spoke
aloud her mother's words for I love you, "Ana bahhebek," and
imagined her mother twinkling back to her, "Kesi Nuriya, ana
bahhebek."

When Nuriya awoke the next morning, she immediately noticed that something was different. The moodiness that had
shrouded her for days was gone. Even her eyes felt different. In
the faint light seeping through the doorframe, the rock wall
before her looked like it was breathing, coming close, receding,

close again. She wondered if she was still dreaming and closed her lids, feeling the tranquility of sleep calling her back.

"Sleeping late this morning are we?" Korba asked in her semi-stern voice as she shook out her sleeping mat, already dressed in customary apron and tunic.

"Good morning, Korba-ma," Nuriya greeted using her term of endearment. "I feel . . . interesting today."

The healer pushed wayward hair from her face and peered down with a quizzical smile. "Very nice to hear it, my sweet, but you still have eggs to collect before it's too hot." Korba turned then and pushed open the door. Summer heat poured in. "And we need a haul of water this morning," she stated to the day as she stepped out into it.

Nuriya didn't mind the reminder of her duties this morning; it was just her guardian's practical manner. But, she lay back with a sigh, she would take her time in getting up just this once.

Korba had already placed her temple offering and had water warming on the fire when Nuriya stepped outside, pulling her shift over her hips. She bent over the healer's silver hair to kiss her crown. "Thank you, love," Korba said with a note of surprise.

Nuriya popped back inside and out again with a bowl of dried berries and two mugs, half filled with herbs steeped the night before. Korba added hot water to each mug, and the two break-fasted companionably, healer and apprentice, foster mother and foster daughter.

Nuriya gathered eggs to a chorus of indignant squawks then shooed the flock out to find their morning scratch. The chick-ens mostly stayed inside the rubble-walled yard, but she checked several times a day if she was home, to make sure none were touring the countryside. Their water topped, she hopped up to sit on the wall. The sun was heavy upon her head, already washing color from the landscape. Nuriya lingered on this wall nearly every morning. The last few days all she could think about was Tian but this morning she squinted out toward Filfla, the tiny uninhabited island, reliving her childhood dream of visiting its terns and seals as her first stop on an adventurous journey to Tyre.

A galley with a milk-colored sail and a brightly painted eye of Osiris rounded the bluff, sailing west. Surely this ship boasted a handsome, dark-lashed captain, and just as surely it sailed for the great city of Carthage, where wealthy men built homes as large as temples. Nuriya imagined crowds of women at the markets in Carthage, wearing beautiful robes, with servants fussing over them. She patted her unkempt hair, picturing it braided atop her head and on her chest the heavy jewelry of a high-born lady. A surge of longing rose in her heart, tugging her dangerously back toward blue. She jumped to the ground, brushing off her wistful thoughts like so many crumbs.

She called to Korba that she was going for water and headed uphill with an empty jug and a thick carrying strap, picking her way rock to rock, round bunch grass and dried thistle flower. She had a feeling she was being watched and looked around, but there was no one she could see, not even a falcon overhead. She shrugged and ran the rest of the way, dropping down, panting, at the rim of the cistern.

Her heart jumped to see two eyes peering.

Nuriya caught her breath, chiding herself for being silly then contemplating her own reflection, wondering what people saw when they looked at her, why they looked twice. Korba and she were obviously not related, so that was something. Korba was a hand-span shorter than Nuriya, with silky, silver hair that hung past her shoulders. Her eyes were dark and perceptive, like mouse eyes Nuriya thought when in an ungenerous mood. Korba's face was tanned to leather from years in the sun, but even sun-browned her skin was lighter than the color of Nuriya's fingertips. Nuriya's summer color was that of roasted carob and her hair, the black of kohl. Her face was wide through the forehead, different from other Phoenician women, and her eyes were just too large. The Egyptian vendor called her 'Miut' and Nuriya cringed every time she heard it because Kepi was likening her to Bastet, her beloved cat Goddess.

Nuriya frowned. Even if she had a proper gown she would never be mistaken for a merchant's wife. All her musings these days ended with this same dropped heart. She would always be an outsider. Not that she wasn't grateful to Korba, but living here, with no mother, no father...just an old woman for company. Her throat got tight. Her reflection, distorted from the puckering that precedes tears, was plain ugly. A tear splashed the dark water and ripples fanned out. When the surface cleared, her face reformed. Still ugly. Another tear splashed her reflection at the place where her brows bunched close, making her blink. It felt like something touched her there, and began to cut, wedging inward. Sharp! Her hands flew to her face and she rolled from the rim. Behind Nuriya's eyes were flashes of light, each flash a jabbing knife. She had the vague awareness of the sun burning overhead and of an ache deep in her belly, but overwhelmingly she was paralyzed by a violent show of lights. Finally, the lights abated, leaving throbbing head pain in their wake.

The sun was approaching its zenith. Nuriya dragged herself into the private shade of the carob tree and sat with her back to it, waiting for the pain to go away. How she longed for her mother to be with her, her real mother! Korba had taught her that whenever she was hurting or lonely she should pray to the Great Mother, "Who was the Mother of all things," but that would never comfort like flesh and blood, like Tian's mother, holding her so sweetly.

A breeze whispered around Nuriya's ears; she was glad for that comfort at least. The pain in her head had dulled, but she still felt unsteady, like she couldn't walk if she stood, like she was teetering even as she sat. She reached her hands to rest them on solid ground and had yet another strange sensation—it was as if the earth rose up as a spirit and entered her body. Her legs filled with density as if made of clay, and they felt enormous, like the statues of the Great Goddess. The sensation spread throughout her body until Nuriya felt mighty with it—she, the motherless child, felt like a Great Mother. There was a heat too, deep and low inside her, like an ember burned there, and in her mind's eye she watched the ember burn a path into the ground. It was strange, but it was wonderful—her body like a mountain, her belly like a volcano. Nuriya wanted to stay that way forever—part earth, part fire...not the always-wanting woman-child...only earth, only fire...

Then the pain returned. A hot knife hacked as if to split her head, to break it apart. She wanted to smash herself into the rocks, and had the tiny, ironic image: the healer's apprentice, dead from headache.

In the next instant, something equally improbable happened. Just when she thought she could not bear the pain, Nuriya saw her mother before her eyes—her real mother, as she was on the day she died, vivid and beautiful, kohl-smudged eyes red from crying, forehead wet from fever, skin drawn from illness and pocked with sores. Her mother gazed with such love and sorrow that Nuriya was overwhelmed with a longing greater than any physical pain. She willed with all her heart to reach out to her mother and take hold. Suddenly what was inside, moved out, and Nuriya didn't have a moment to react, because what moved out kept on moving, and took her witnessing with it. She fell upward, into swirling blackness.

"Welcome back, daughter." Korba spoke the words the moment her apprentice opened her eyes.

Nuriya tried to smile. "I'm thirsty," she croaked.

Korba brought the waterskin to her lips. "How do you feel?"

"My eye..." she trailed off. "What happened?" She sat up and found the back of her shift crumpled and red-stained. "Oh, no," she groaned.

"It won't be the last time you stain your tunic, Nuri," Korba said. "Welcome to your womanhood. It's a holy day for you." Korba kept her tone light but she was worried. It had been years since Nuriya last had a seizure and Korba was troubled to think that her first *moon time* could have caused them to return.

When Nuriya had been gone too long, Korba went looking and found her, her body tremoring and eyes unseeing, under the carob tree. Korba ministered to her, holding the points on her forehead and feet, and praying for her safe return. Now the sun was high in the sky, roasting them through the deep shade of the carob. A breeze might bless them soon if they were lucky. "Do you feel well enough for me to get a clean tunic?"

Nuriya nodded, but reached out as Korba pushed to standing. "What happened?"

Korba pulled the waterskin off her shoulder and handed it over. "We'll talk."

When Korba returned with two bundles, she asked again, "How are you feeling?"

"My head feels like it's full of rocks."

The healer opened one bundle and handed Nuriya a small vial of oil infused with lavender flowers then began rummaging for her pipe, saying, "And I have mint to smoke."

"Just the lavender, please," Nuriya replied grumpily as she rubbed the oil into her temples. Korba helped her pack a girdle with lamb's wool and adjust it around her hips then shook out a fresh shift. "What happened?" Nuriya asked again as she settled the shift over her girdle.

Korba hesitated, lips pursed.

"Tell me."

"You had a seizure."

"Why?"

"Do you remember when your father brought you to me?"

"No."

"Your mother died of the pox and you were very sick."

"I know that. My father couldn't care for me. You asked if I remembered it," Nuriya said irritably.

Korba continued, carefully choosing her words, "Your fever caused you to have seizures." She would not, could not, tell the whole story. Nuriya's father brought her to Korba, not for treatment, but for exorcism. With no priest on the island, he had sought out Korba, who was called "the witch of Mnajdra" by the men at port. Korba explained to him, repeatedly, that her seizures were a result of illness, not spirit possession. The man was an idiot and a fool, and Korba scowled, remembering. She had initially been sympathetic for what must have been a terrible ordeal, but came to understand that the man was more concerned about his reputation than the wellbeing of his child. He left his daughter with Korba, visited her one time, then departed the island without coming back for her.

"It happened more than once?" Nuriya asked uneasily.

"Yes."

"How many times?"

"Six, or eight." Korba spoke like it hurt her to say.

"Eight? How come? Was I still sick?"

"You had seizures after you were well."

"Why?" she whined.

"It seemed...maybe when things upset you. I always thought if you would talk about it, it would help. Do you remember anything at all this time?"

Nuriya did remember. She remembered seeing her mother and losing her in a vast, swirling darkness. She didn't want to speak it. She shook her head and stood; the headache was no worse standing. For distraction she nudged the other bundle with her foot. "What's this?"

"Something that I saved for you for just this day."

Nuriya dropped to her knees. "What is it?"

Korba took a leather pouch from the bundle and proffered it.

Anticipation and trepidation mixed in the younger woman. "Go on." The healer dipped her head but held Nuriya's gaze.

Nuriya set the pouch on her knees and unfastened the cords to reveal a tangle of gold, silver and ivory. "Oh," her breath whooshed out. With exquisite care she picked out a bracelet of ivory beads, the symbol of the ankh carved into the largest. "I remember this," she whispered, seeing the memory of her mother stirring porridge over a brazier, the ivory beads adorning her slender wrist. She lunged toward Korba, squeezing her tight. "I miss her," she said, trying to control the quaver in her voice. It was something she had not said out loud for a very long time.

"I know, dear."

Nuriya took a breath, sat up, and then pulled from the pouch a tarnished silver chain. Hanging from one link was a swirling silver snake clasping a blue stone of lapis lazuli. The design was startling. She studied it, set it aside and pulled out the last item, a gold bracelet, each end forming the shape of a woman. "I remember the bracelets," she said, slipping the beads around her wrist and the gold above her elbow. "But I don't remember the necklace. Was it my mother's?"

"I imagine so."

"Where did you get them?"

"Your father gave these as payment. I kept them for when you became a woman."

Nuriya picked up the snake and turned it over. Symbols were etched into the flattened back. "Did you see this?"

Korba nodded. "It looks Egyptian."

Nuriya's skin pricked. "I wonder what it says."

"I know whom you could ask."

Nuriya made a face at the comment then confided, "My mother could write like that."

"Oh?" Korba tried to sound nonchalant, but this was just the kind of thing that fascinated her.

Nuriya did not elaborate, but she was seeing it in her mind: her mother drawing symbols on her hand with kohl, telling Nuriya to wash off the marks, and bidding her to drink the wash water. Nuriya felt strange remembering it, and for a moment was afraid she might tumble out of herself again. "I miss her," she said again to break the tension.

"Of course," Korba said gently. "Now let's see that beautiful necklace on you." She slipped it over Nuriya's head.

"How do I look?"

"Beautiful as the Goddess. Your mother would be proud."

Nuriya felt exquisite wearing her new adornments. As she twirled and curtseyed before the healer she became keenly aware of her guardian's absolute plainness, not only her lack of adornment but her life devoid of any luxury. "Korba..."

"Yes?"

She tried to put on a brave face. "My father said these were payment. Maybe we should trade them."

"Absolutely not. As far as I am concerned these are gifts directly from your mother to you." Korba spoke with sternness but there were tears in her eyes. "You, Nuri, are the daughter I never had, and I am proud of the woman you have become." She patted Nuriya's arm and looked away to the horizon, struggling with rare emotion. When Korba turned back, she said brightly, "When you're ready we'll go for a bath. Then we'll have ourselves a feast."

They stopped by the dwelling for a rabbit snare and collecting basket and as they made their way across the slope below Mnajdra, Korba set the snare in one of her most reliable locations. She would not let Nuriya help because the feast was in her honor. They wound down a steep trail to the sea; their bathing spot was a small protected cove bound by perfect sunning boulders.

After they bathed Nuriya stretched out, feeling relaxed and dreamy, with only her girdle for clothing. Korba hunted for mussels then found a place to lean back and watch the sea birds dive through the shimmering aqua and silvery white. They both dozed, lulled by the gentle, steady slap-slap of water on rock.

It was late afternoon when they headed back and while they climbed the trail, Nuriya pondered the dream she'd had of a beautiful woman, wearing the necklace of the silver snake, standing in a room of polished stone.

Korba quickened her pace as soon as she spotted her snare and she began to sing a prayer chant. She snatched up the hare, unwound its noose, and drew her knife without altering the rhythm of the chant. She brought the animal to a flat rock and cut through the underbelly, leaving the entrails for the foxes. She laid the hare on top of the mussels and began to praise it as they continued home, thanking it for feeding Nuri on this first day of her womanhood, saying that its blood and meat would nourish her all the days of her life. Korba cooked at Mnajdra's fire ring, chanting or praying all the while, the hare over the fire and the mussels wrapped in seaweed, nudged into the coals. Nuriya was so altered by the events of the day that not one complaint about Korba's continual praying entered her mind. Their feast was delicious.

Korba gave her apprentice the next day to herself so that she could "ponder the miracle of blood," but what Nuriya spent the day pondering were the gifts from her mother and the dark, handsome man who would one day admire them on her.

Despite her aversion to the Egyptian vendor, Nuriya did want to show Kepi her jewelry and so, two days later, as soon as the eggs were collected, the women started out. The morning was cooler than it had been of late, with puffs of cloud roaming the sky like herds of freshly washed sheep. The women walked steadily but not hurriedly along cliff road toward the grotto, then inland along Wied Filfla until they reached the well-worn village track. They passed terraced hills and fields of emmer wheat, through the

oak grove and up to the fishing village situated above the magnificent three-lobed Marsaxlokk Bay. By mid-morning they were on
the far side of the bay, the Phoenician side.

The market was bustling. Close by the fork, where the wide alley
split off and sloped down to the docks, sat a scribe with his shekels,
scrolls and scales. He was a government official who answered to
the Magistrate. Farmers lined up in front of him with carts of wheat
or barley in season and afterward sat on the low walls on either side
of the dock alley to compare their take. Next to the scribe wagons
of wine and olive oil were brought up from the warehouses, and
sometimes a cart of luxury items such as glass vials or ivory plaques.
Down the street could be found merchants of fresh and salted fish,
alongside vendors offering almonds, fruit and dates. There was a
merchant who traded hemp cloth, and another who traded only
the fine purple wool of Tyre and soft-colored Sidonian linen. Locals
spread blankets piled high with carob pods and pulled wool while
their children ran roughshod up and down the lane.

The women headed straight to the spice vendor's stall. Kepi
was an enormous woman, broad and tall, sitting like a queen
upon her reed-covered bench, presiding over her spice bowls
and the less identifiable items that were her trade as the market's only amulet maker. Her hair was henna dyed, for surely it
would be white by now, and she wore an expression that let you
know she thought quite highly of herself. Kepi was fluent in
three languages, her native Egyptian, Canaanite and Maltese.
She clucked her tongue over Nuri's jewelry, saying, "Tell me,
Miut, who was your mother?"

"I don't remember her," Nuriya said, squirming under Kepi's
intimidating visage.

"What was her name then?" Nuriya looked toward Korba but the
healer shook her head. Kepi picked up the snake. "Very fine," she
purred. The vendor's own arms were armored wrist to shoulder
with hammered metal and colored beads. "I wonder how a woman

with adornments as fine as these ends up here." Pity and curiosity mingled in her tone. "Ah well. I knew you were one of ours, Miut."

"But..."

"Korba never met your mother," Kepi cut her off, casting a glance toward the healer, challenging her to deny it. "And I tell you, your mother was Egyptian." She turned back to the necklace, saying, "I am glad the Nubian King conquered the delta lords, but how many were tossed out before he succeeded? Look at me." She threw her head back and cackled.

Kepi relished her own story, though it had nothing to do with Nubian Kings or delta lords. In order to take a younger wife without returning her dowry, Kepi's husband had accused her of infidelity. Rather than move in with a son-in-law she despised, Kepi took as many treasures as she could stitch into her ample robes, packed up her spice trove, and found the first passage out of Memphis. She spent two years on Crete before making her way to Malta. The weather suited, she said, and the men left her unmolested.

Who would be bold enough to molest Kepi? Nuriya asked herself whenever Kepi repeated that particular comment. "I wanted to know about the writing," she ventured, for this was her reason for showing Kepi the jewelry.

The vendor fixed Nuriya with a haughty stare. "I am a clever woman but that doesn't mean I was taught the symbols." With an imperious "hmph," she held the necklace away from her eyes and squinted. "Maybe I can recognize something..."

"Nuri's mother could write," Korba said and Nuriya shot her a stricken look for boasting her private memory.

"Your mother could write?" Kepi sounded galled. "Miut, you must know who she was."

"I don't," Nuriya stammered.

Just then a man approached the stall seeking an amulet for his wife and Kepi turned the force of her attention toward him. Korba gave Nuri's arm a squeeze. "Go on. I'll talk to her."

She found a place to sit away from Kepi's stall in the shade of the meeting house, putting the bracelets back on and tucking the necklace inside her tunic. She wished they hadn't come; Kepi always upset her. With practiced skill she shifted her focus to the people around her. Yonder a well-dressed servant argued with the cranky fish merchant. Nearby, a dockworker wove through the crowd carrying a heavy keg, his dark skin gleaming in the sun. A soldier strode by in the opposite direction, and Nuriya let her eyes be drawn to the rhythm of brawny thighs. Just then a door opened beside her and a group of men poured from the meeting hall in animated conversation. They turned toward the docks without giving her a glance. Some of the men wore cloaks, even in the summer. They did it for show, and it did impress. The one with the distinctive headdress was the Magistrate—he wore a coil of knotted cloth atop his head. His moustache and beard were neatly trimmed and he carried himself with an air of inapproachability. He was taller than all his entourage save the young man, said to be his son, who strode at his heel. Only one of the men was a local. That was Erdu, the translator, distinct in his lighter coloring and stockier build. Erdu wore a miniature version of the Magistrate's headdress and people grumbled that he fancied himself Phoenician now. Nuriya looked after them feeling exceptionally dowdy. It was time for a new tunic at least. She looked across at Korba and Kepi, their silver and henna heads pressed close. "Talking about me," she supposed. Korba waved her over but Nuriya shook her head. The healer disentangled herself and crossed the street. "I told her to be more gentle. She gets too excited. Come." Korba extended her hand. "We need to talk to Coroli about the summer honey."

It was time for the summer harvest and a few days after their market visit, Korba and Nuriya took offerings of dates and flowering mint to two nests they would harvest the next morning. "My pets," Korba called to the bees, "I'll be back tomorrow for your sweet nectar." Honey from wild bees had been Korba's survival and salvation when she first moved into the cave above Mnajdra as a young widow, with no family on the island to call her own. Korba ate honey, traded honey, used honey for medicine and to make wine. The healer loved everything about the bees but Nuriya did not. Nuriya had been stung numerous times and had not forgiven the bees for it.

All that evening Korba sang harvest songs from her youth, about abundance and generosity, and all for the bees. The songs were in Korba's native dialect, similar to the local language of Malta, and eventually she coaxed Nuriya to join her for a verse or two:

> Winged blessings, humming peace
> Offering food, offering sweet
> Winged blessings, humming life
> Gifting healing and gifting delight.

The next morning they took embers in a clay bowl, and boughs of rosemary and sage, to an oak behind the Standing Stones Temple. The nest was in a crag where a large branch split from the trunk. Nuriya got the herbs smoking underneath and Korba chanted until she felt the time was right, then she reached into the nest bare handed to harvest a portion of combs. It always frightened Nuriya but Korba, in blissful rapture, never got stung. They harvested a second nest in the ravine beyond the cistern.

Nuriya set up catch pots near the fire ring and kept herbs smoking all day to discourage other interested parties. She filled and sealed ten pots that Bon had brought them then boiled the combs. By lamplight she poured honey infused water into two large amphoras, mixed in must from their previous batch of wine, and sealed the jars.

Nuriya was up with the sun the next morning, picking out insects that snuck into the pot of combs, then stoking the fire; she'd melt half the wax for salve and press the rest into a pot for a future use. As the combs heated she sat back to ponder the dreams that had filled her sleep with winding paths and winged beasts.

Just as Korba returned from her offering, a woman scrambled up the hill from where she left her cart at the fork. "Are you the healer?" she asked Korba nervously.

Nuriya covered the fire while the woman, with eyes to the ground, described her need. Her husband had lain in pain since the morning before, it was hard to pass water and there was blood in his stream. Nuriya froze where she knelt by the fire ring because a sharp pain was pressing behind her right eye. While Korba gathered supplies, Nuriya tried to breathe out the pain. She feared what might come, a blinding headache, or a seizure. In light of the woman's distress, however, she managed to pull herself together and not say anything to Korba.

The woman, Caron, drove her cart fast and spoke not a word en route to her husband's clanland near Tarxien. Nuriya could see that she was with child. It bothered her that the woman seemed more withered than fecund, but she put it out of her mind for she needed all her energy to keep her fear of flashing lights at bay.

Caron's husband, Borg, lay on a sleeping mat in a small hut amongst a collection of ten or so other dwellings. He was on his side with his face pressed to the ground. Blessedly, the instant Nuriya entered the small dwelling and her attention shifted to him, her head pain eased.

The first task of the apprentice was to bring comfort while the healer assessed and prepared medicine. After a brief exam, Korba motioned Nuri to work with light massage and then went out to the hearth. Nuriya silently recited the invocation: "Great Mother, Source of all life, guide my hands and guide my heart to bring Your healing to Your child." Korba had taught her to refer to every patient as "child" even if they were older than she. Nuriya was aware of Borg's wife in the doorway behind her, watching with unnatural intensity. Again she put the woman out of her mind and rested her hands onto Borg's back. He flinched, but she kept steady. Without pressing, she molded her hands to the shape of his muscles, and moving slowly, pausing at each new place, she willed her hands to be a comfort to him.

With sudden vengeance, the pain returned behind her eye. This time she was sure flashing lights would come. She pressed her fists into her eyes sockets, her fingernails digging into her palms. *Help me!* she prayed to any who might listen.

There was a tiny click at the base of her skull, like a bone adjusting there, and the intensity of the sensation abated. She took a breath, in and out, checking herself. The pain was gone, no flashing lights; all that remained was a feeling in her eyes.

Relieved, Nuriya reminded herself to her task, but when she looked at Borg's back, what she saw was something completely strange. She blinked. And blinked again. What she saw was the image of a rock, small and sharp edged, in a too tight place. Borg groaned. Oh my—she was seeing inside Borg's body!

The healer came in with a mug of goatvine and parsley root. "Korba," Nuriya sputtered, wanting to tell her. Korba handed the mug to her while saying, "Borg, Nuri will give you medicine to help you pass water." The man's eyes darted to find his wife. Caron nodded, and through gritted teeth Borg raised himself to the cup. After he drank, Nuriya caught Korba's attention, but couldn't find words. The healer nodded and went back out. Borg lay down resignedly.

The image of the rock reformed before Nuriya's eyes. She was wondering what to do, when she noticed an ethereal substance moving through Borg's body and collecting around the stone. Sharp edges began to soften and the walls of the passage began to relax. It's the medicine working, she thought. How strange that I can see it—and how wonderful.

Then a different image pressed into Nuriya's mind. Something dark, like a heavy cloak, covered over the beautiful healing she was watching unfold. The darkness was tainted with desperation and fear. Instinctively Nuriya tried to push it back but her effort had no effect. She felt choked and suddenly she wanted to cry. This is too strange, she thought and forced herself to stand. Caron's eyes flicked toward her and immediately back to her husband. "Keep watch," Nuriya said needlessly, as she passed outside.

Korba looked up from her perch by the hearth with a quizzical expression. The clanswoman she had been speaking to stepped away. "I need to talk to you, Korba," Nuriya said. "Something's wrong with my eyes."

"Sit." The healer cupped Nuri's face and looked into her eyes. "Dilated, but equal." She reached to check the pulse at her wrist.

Nuriya shook her head in frustration. The dark cloak was still before her vision and now disturbing images overlay it: Borg holding his distraught wife; bloody cloths in a hole. Nuriya pulled her hand from Korba's. "Something's wrong with Caron."

Korba's hands remained suspended in air. "What do you mean?"

In an instant Nuriya understood. "It's her pregnancy."

"Caron told you she's pregnant?"

"She didn't have to say it." The healer frowned. "You have to check her, Korba."

"I don't know if she'll let me. She's so worried about her husband."

Nuriya felt her way into her words without fully comprehending them. "He fears it will be worse this time. Her sickness is part of his sickness."

Korba contemplated her apprentice a long while then gazed toward the open door. She moved the steaming pot from the hottest part of the fire and went in to see the couple.

Shortly, Caron came outside with the healer. "You will heal him?" Caron asked anxiously.

"Your husband will be fine," Korba assured. "Can you see that his pain is already less?"

"Yes," she admitted plaintively. "Thank you."

"Caron, I want to talk about your pregnancy."

The woman clutched her belly. "Are you a witch?"

"No, Caron. I'm a healer. I want to help you keep this baby."

Caron shot a glance around the yard, meeting Nuriya's eyes then dropping her head and pleading, "I don't want anyone to hurt my baby."

"You are pregnant then?"

She nodded, without lifting her head. "Can I check my husband again?" she begged.

"Of course," Korba said. "Then let me help you."

When Caron came back out, Korba told her apprentice to watch Borg. "Just be near if he needs anything."

Nuriya nodded. The darkness had receded to the periphery of her vision. She went to sit in the doorway and stationed herself facing out.

Korba and Caron went into another dwelling for the exam. When they came out they made a bee-line straight to check on Borg and Nuriya moved back to the hearth. "Will the baby be all right?" she asked when Korba joined her.

"The baby has taken hold, but Caron is very depleted. She miscarried four times, and the last time she bled for many days."

"You'll give her dock root?"

"Yes. And what else?"

"Bramble. And any green she can find."

"Good. I think Borg's through the worst of it, by the way."

Suddenly, like a wind extinguishing a new flame, Nuriya's energy went out of her. She sat abruptly, her eyes unfocused and she sank her head between her knees.

When she lifted her head, Korba put a hand under her chin. "I have three patients on my hands now," Korba said.

"I'm sorry," Nuriya whined, panting.

"Nonsense. You did good work. I need to get you home."

She poured Borg's second medicine into a mug and went to see him.

Caron came to bid them goodbye before a kinsman took them home. "Thank you, Mother," she said, bowing her head before Korba.

"You are welcome, child. Come when you are out of medicine for your husband. I'll have yours waiting."

Korba put Nuriya to bed that night fussing over her like when she was a child. Nuriya was exhausted to her core, just let me sleep, her only thought, but Korba chattered on, oddly elated. "I am proud of you, Nuri. You saw the pregnancy when I did not. You need some nourishing herbs like Caron. Are you comfortable?" Nuriya hadn't told Korba half of what she'd seen but at this moment she hardly had the energy to breathe. She willed herself to shut out Korba's well-intentioned fuss and fell deeply and soundly asleep.

Nuriya slept late and awoke hungry. She was eating cold porridge when Korba returned from Mnajdra in a bubbly mood. "Tell me," her teacher plunged right in. "How did you recognize Caron's pregnancy? I was misled by her depletion." Korba was ever eager to learn, even from her own student.

Nuriya took another bite, chewing as she spoke, "The way you taught me, I guess. What I didn't tell you is that I saw your medicine working."

"Good. What did you observe?"

"I saw the stone, and after Borg took the medicine I saw the stone dissolving."

"Wait. Nuri. Say it again. You *saw* into Borg's body?"

"I think so."

Korba's enthusiasm instantly changed into concern. "I am an herb woman," she said sternly. "I don't know about seers."

Nuriya ladled water into her bowl, puzzled by Korba's reaction. She swirled the water and drank.

Korba was tapping on her chest. She dropped her hands and

spoke with unusual force, "You must go to the temple and pray about this, Nuri."

"I wasn't trying to see," Nuriya stammered. "It just happened."

"Seeing is a gift from the Mother. You must seek Her guidance."

Nuriya felt deflated. She had thought that seeing into Borg's body was exciting, despite the head pain and the near-fainting, and she was looking forward to telling Korba all about it. But Korba was making her feel like she'd done something wrong, like she'd used some herb she wasn't supposed to touch. She put her bowl away and headed deliberately toward the chickens.

"I'm serious, Nuri. You must pray about this," Korba called.

Nuriya did not want to pray about a strange way of seeing. She didn't know if she even wanted it to happen again, but Korba continued to pester her until finally Nuriya demanded to know why she was so bothered. The healer admitted that on Lipari, where she grew up, there lived an old woman who could *see* into the body and tell a person what was wrong. That same woman also held loud conversations with people who were dead and was generally so bizarre that everyone avoided her unless their circumstance was dire.

Nuriya tried to make light of Korba's words. She patted her teacher's arm, saying, "Don't worry, Korba-ma. No matter how bizarre I get, I'll still know how to make a mean poultice." Korba didn't laugh, but she did stop pestering her.

A few days later Bon took the women and their honey pots to market. Nuriya did her best to avoid Kepi, but the vendor left her stall, tracked them down, and demanded the story about her mother writing on her hand, extracting every vague detail. No, her mother said nothing out loud, Nuriya told her, and she had no idea what the symbols meant. Kepi dragged her back to the stall and began rummaging through baskets. Nuriya was silently pleading Korba's intervention when Kepi turned on her, brandishing the statue of a man with the head of a jackal. "This is for scorpion bites," Kepi declared. She clicked her long, curling fingernails on the base of the statue. "Do you see these symbols? You pour water over them to cast its spell. I want to know," she aimed a curling nail at Nuriya, "what spell your mother made for you." Then she pulled the snake from under Nuriya's tunic, turning it over and muttering, "Bird...vulture? Arm? No. Snake? Ach. Is this what she wrote? Wait..." the vendor struck a pose and spoke in a mocking imitation of Nuriya, "You don't remember." They parted company with Nuriya feeling shamed and vowing to never speak to Kepi again. Even Korba was taken aback by her friend's rough manner.

The women were nervous as Nuriya's next moon time approached. Every morning since her first menstruation, Korba directed her to chew a handful of soaked milk thistle seeds and drink a strong tea of sweet vervain. They hoped it would be easier than the first time, and it was, only a small headache and a little cramping.

The most urgent focus in those days of late summer was getting Caron healthy. Indeed, she flourished under Korba's guidance and Borg never ceased grinning at his wife's increasingly round and rosy condition. Whenever they visited Tarxien, however, Borg's father appeared briefly to scowl at them. Korba chuckled the first time she saw him, telling Nuri that Grof had been calling her a "witch" ever since he was a boy.

Borg expressed his gratitude to Korba in every way possible, including coming out to Mnajdra to help carry mead jugs and repair shelves. Gradually he wore down Korba's usual reserve and Nuriya saw the old healer was growing genuinely fond of him.

While Borg and Korba visited, Nuriya worked on making new tunics. Korba had bartered a length of undyed wool, similar to that they currently wore, but it was new and clean and Nuriya loved working with it. The healer also bartered a drape of luxuriously soft Sidonian linen and gave it to Nuri as a womanhood gift. Until she knew what to do with it, however, she set it aside and worked with the wool. While Borg chatted, Nuriya sewed, the extraordinary circumstance of their first meeting hanging about like the memory of an unsettling dream, with the bizarre lady seer from Lipari haunting the background. And though Korba had stopped pestering her, Nuriya sometimes caught the look of questioning worry on her teacher's face.

2.

Hawk

☯☯

The Phoenicians from Tyre were famous for their many festivals and two were celebrated at the Malta port—the garland festival at the first full moon of spring and the harvest festival at the autumn equinox. Korba complained that festival days were just a time for men to get drunk but that did not daunt Nuriya's excitement; she anticipated the event for days.

This year the autumn festival began with the handsome crew of the warship parading down the market street, led by the Magistrate, the raucous crowd parting neatly before him. The warriors were elegantly uniformed in helmet and cape. Their swords and shields and the bronze plates sewn to their stiff leather vests, gleamed in the sunlight, dazzling the eye, and making Nuriya swoon with excitement. The men stopped in formation before the shrine to the Goddess Astarte, lit copious amounts of incense then paraded up ladders and gangways to the deck of their warship. Cedar planks from the forests of Lebanon formed the hull of the sleek ship. The banner of Tyre, a white crescent against a purple sky, flew above, while the deadly bronze-tipped battering ram was hidden below water level.

Korba and Nuriya trekked with the crowd up the bluffs near
Ta' Silġ to watch the ship row into the bay and demonstrate
impressive maneuvers of speed sprint, stop and reverse, spin
and turn. The captain called orders from the stern platform, his
mate blew the brass horn, and the soldiers swung their battle
axes or held them overhead in a menacing display. Nuriya
whooped and hollered with the crowd while the men passed
wineskins.

Next came the contests. Dockworkers hoping for a warship
placement would compete hard all day in rowing races and en-
durance tests. As the crowd cheered with greater and greater
abandon, Korba and Nuriya left the bluffs. Back at the market it
seemed that everyone from the island and half again more were
there. Nuriya had to yell to be heard, "I want to watch the
sword fights." Just then a barrel-chested man with a very long
beard grabbed the flesh of her rump, winked to her scandalized
glare and strutted back into the crowd. Korba started to follow
him then changed directions, grabbing her young charge and
pulling her into Kepi's stall.

The vendor put them to work without a second thought.
They measured from spice bags and handed out oatcakes laced
with saffron and Nuriya, caught up in the fun and pace of the
day, forgot her vow not to speak to the vendor. When there was
a lull in traffic, Kepi gave Korba and she, each, a small but precious gift—a cloth-wrapped, brown lump of poppy-tears.
"Strong medicine from Egypt," Kepi told them. "The juice of
many poppy flowers is in each one. For pain, for sleep, this is
much stronger than the dried flower-heads you brew." They
thanked her, then Korba offered to take Nuri to watch the foot
races.

The contests for locals were at the west end of the market on
the fork of the road toward the fishing village. When they arrived, a burly farmer from Dingli was being awarded a wineskin

and laurel wreath for winning the heavy stone carry and they were setting up for the throwing contests. The foot races would come after. While Korba took the opportunity to do an impromptu consultation with farmer Frer's pregnant wife, Nuriya took her own opportunity, and daringly slipped in with a group of revelers heading down to the docks.

In front of the warehouses, in an area usually piled high with amphoras and grain sacks, a dense ring of spectators surrounded two combatants. Sunlight glinted off shields and off the belt of silver discs worn by one of the combatants as they circled, parried, and swung dangerously sharp blades. Nuriya flinched with every slash and clang then gasped when one soldier nicked the other's forearm, while the crowd cheered all the louder at the flowing of blood. The wounded warrior kept his attention full on his opponent as they locked swords, menacing into each other's faces. They parted, and then they were swinging and clanging once more. The crowd roared, as the warrior with the silver belt knocked the other, with the bleeding arm, off balance. The tripped soldier turned his blade down to signal surrender while the winner mimicked a motion to sever the knee. Nuriya's heart filled with pride as the champion bowed before them, and added her cheers to the raucous cacophony. Although the warrior's face was mostly hidden by his helmet, she thought his eyes most handsome.

Angry shouts could be heard as two men began arguing over the settlement of a wager. The crowd began to undulate, some surging toward the commotion while others edged back. A crack to the jaw sent one gambler flying, bringing down a swath of bystanders. A boy flew backward into Nuriya, tumbling her and a white-haired gentleman into the contest arena. In the next instant, Nuriya was flying again as the champion scooped her up from the dirt and swung her back to her feet. He did not pause in his work, moving on to hoist the old man and extend his hand down to the boy, but for Nuriya, that moment of swinging in those strong arms was the most exhilarating sensation she'd ever experienced. She looked around, dazed, as the champion joined the other warriors in fanning out among the spectators, settling them and moving the gamblers off to one side. When the warriors reassembled in the contest arena, Nuriya edged to the back of the crowd, then craned her neck to watch the champion address his next opponent. He stood tallest among all his compatriots and Nuriya realized with a thrill that he must be the Magistrate's son. Finally she tore herself away and hurried up the alley.

Korba was scanning the crowd from the center of the fork. "We are leaving now!" Korba said in a manner that broached no discussion. Nuriya promised herself that next year she would have a different chaperone.

Korba pulled her young charge through the outskirts of another cheering crowd as one of their favored sons was being awarded the prize for the first foot race. They got jumbled into the commotion but Korba doggedly pushed on until they found themselves in a pocket of space among their neighbor Tul's clan.

"Neighbors, celebrate!" Tul called. Hawk, their russet-haired son, wearing a laurel crown, was balanced precariously on his uncle's shoulders, his friends helping to support his weight. Korba raised her free arm in a determined salute and trudged on.

"Hey!"

Nuriya turned in time to pull from Korba's grasp and catch the laurel crown sailing through the air. She was delighted that she caught it, and thrilled to be a part of the games. Korba waited impatiently for her to extend the wreath back to their wobbling neighbor, while Hawk playacted that he couldn't reach and almost fell. "Hawk, Hawk, Hawk!" friends and family chanted until Tul's son grabbed his prize, and Korba resumed her headlong march home.

Five days after the autumn festival, Zac, a youngster from Tul's clan, scrambled up to Nuriya, who was working outside next to the fire ring, and began dragging her back the way he had come. "Hawk's hurt! Come on!"

"Zac, wait. What happened?"

The women got the story from the boy as they gathered supplies and quickly set off. The young men were riding the bull they called Jimi, challenging each other to prove themselves daring. Hawk held his seat when Jimi crashed through the pen to the cheers of onlookers, but then they were off into the rocky hillside scree. Jimi slipped, Hawk fell and the big animal trampled him. Korba made the invocation as they hurried along.

Hawk lay where he fell, as no one had dared move him. Like the other young men he wore only his loincloth. He was twisted onto his right side exposing torn skin and a dark bruise across his left lower ribs. His thigh was bent where it should not, and he was obviously in pain, but more so, he was embarrassed by his predicament. "I'll live," he reproved his mother hoarsely as she fretted and babbled her concerns.

Nuriya knelt by Hawk's head as Korba began the assessment. Although his coloring was correct, Nuriya thought his name was better suited to someone more compact, for even as a boy Hawk had his father's broad shoulders. Only once had she seen him use his size to advantage. She was harvesting roots a few years back when a group of boys approached. One of them began chanting, "Black girl, orphan girl," and other boys joined in. Before they repeated the taunt a second time, Hawk had separated from the pack and tackled the rhyme leader. A circle formed around the brawling boys and Nuriya raced home. She couldn't call Hawk "friend," he rarely said even "hello," but she would always be grateful to him for that.

Hawk's brows bunched together his gray-green eyes as he attempted to smile into Korba's frown. The skin of his broken leg was bleeding, but of more serious concern to the healer was the injury to the ribs. The movement at the site was unnatural, the bones denting inward with each in-breath.

Nuriya knew what Korba was worried about. Healer and apprentice often discussed the workings of the body as they dispatched each part of the rare goat or pig given as payment. More importantly Korba had seen for herself the position of the organs when she had the opportunity to examine a man killed by pirates.

Before the Phoenicians established themselves at Marsaxlokk Bay, there had been a slew of pirate attacks at the fishing village as sea-roving bandits entered the harbor to stage ambush on passing merchants. The pirates would raid the food stores of the island folk if they wished and would take a woman or child captive if they caught one. It was for this reason that the Maltese made room for the Phoenicians when they sought to establish a port-of-call, for they were fair in their dealings and there were trained warriors among them.

But in the years before the Phoenicians, the locals defended their own the best they could. They built a wall on the sea side of the village and organized night patrols, local men arming themselves with homemade weapons. When pirate raiders approached one night and met with armed fishermen, they made an example of them. They mutilated the bodies of the two they killed, a third escaping with a gash in the back of his leg. Korba had been tending a birth in the village and was called to treat the injured man. After staunching, cleaning, and binding the wound, the healer went to inspect the dead. Loitering near the first, she wished to wipe away congealing blood and probe under the exposed coils of intestine, but there was a strong taboo against handling the dead unless kin. She moved to the smaller of the two. He was a boy really, not even a man. What drew her to the gruesome sight was the center of the boy's body. The mutilating gash revealed not only his torn stomach, but also the ocher pouch and underneath, the head of the blood-colored sac. It answered a question Korba had as to the position of these organs. She had seen a man die from a kick in the ribs; at first the man seemed well, but then he lost all strength and died in the night. He had bled to death, with the bleeding all on the inside.

If that type of injury happened to Hawk, could she stop it? The healer fingered the vial she wore round her neck that held the tincture she used to stop bleeding after childbirth. "Hawk, you have a broken leg and broken ribs," she stated the obvious. "Are you in a great deal of pain?"

"Just a scratch," Hawk croaked. "Jimi landed like a flea."

Korba almost smiled. "I'm concerned about the injury under the ribs, Hawk. I'm going to give you medicine to slow your blood." She unstoppered the vial. "Under your tongue." She tapped a few drops into his mouth then rummaged in her apron, pulling out strips of white bark. "This is willow. Chew it and keep it in your cheek." She pointed her apprentice to the ribs, "Work there, Nuri," and then moved to the fire Tul had made for her nearby.

Nuriya sat by Hawk's side. "I'm not going to touch," she said. "If the pain increases let me know." She held her hands over the injury site. An angry heat radiated up from where the bones sucked inward. She glanced toward Hawk's face and saw that he was looking at her with a kind of awe. Pain delirium, she thought.

Hawk spoke to her gravely, "I know you will heal me. Thank you." He crooked a half-smile then closed his eyes.

Nuriya was taken aback; she truly did not know if they would heal him and she felt a familiar flare of anger at the limitation of herbs and prayers. She closed her eyes, feeling grim, and experienced a quick wave of nausea and knot of tension behind one eye that rapidly focused into a piercing point. She squeezed her eyes as hard as she could and as mysteriously as it had come, the sensation abated. Like a wind blowing away fog so that she could see far, her eyes felt clean and sparkling, like new.

She turned her attention back to her patient. A section of two ribs, the width of a large fist each, had broken free. Nuriya could picture the hoof of the frantic beast crushing the bone to the breaking point. She needed to know the damage underneath. Without stopping to think, her vision began to snake its way between the broken ribs, witnessing, under the bones, frayed tissues like shredded cloth bathed in blood. Tiny vessels oozed blood and others spurted in rhythmic patterns. Fascinating...but horrifying. There was too much blood! The thought came: "more shepherd's purse tincture," and she turned to tell Korba but all she could see in that direction was confused color and splotchy darkness. She turned back to Hawk—she could see clear again—but all that blood!

Within the gruesome scene, it felt like something waited...for her. Me? You want something from me? Hawk's words reverberated inside her mind: "I know you will heal me." She had to try.

She focused on one tiny, lacerated vessel and imagined sealing it off. It was the same as holding her hands over the body with healing intent but...this was crazy...she was inside his body. Maybe it was a trick of her mind, but the vessel seemed to respond. Something changed, and less blood seeped. "Slow, soothe, seal," she prayed and focused on another tear. Again, in the image before her eyes, the amount of blood steadily diminished.

She cast around then for the source of Korba's real worry—the blood-colored sac. There it was, under where the ribs grated raggedly on each breath. It looked to be intact and she felt a moment's elation. Then with horror, she saw a large vessel leading from the sac oozing out thick life fluid. It's leaking! Hawk could die! Stay calm, she told herself roughly. Focus! She tried to ignore the impossibility of what she was doing and think only of her intention to seal the tear, ignoring—then forgetting—everything else.

Suddenly Nuriya's attention shifted to Hawk's ribs. She didn't decide to change focus—the area she was working on simply faded and the ribs became clear. The broken edges were sharp—with every breath there was potential for further injury. The pieces needed to be brought into line and rejoined to the rest of the bone. Some kind of binding needed to grow fast. Nuriya imagined weaving a web around the bone, strong and flexible, like a spider binds its dinner, over and under, web of silk, web of light, holding the bone like a tender new babe. The image before her was exquisite, and even her hands glowed with the same light as the web she wove.

Eventually and gradually, the trance lifted, and Nuriya saw her own familiar hands hovering steadily over Hawk's side. His eyes were closed; he was sleeping maybe, or concentrating. Korba was kneeling beside them, holding two bowls with bandages draped over one arm. When Nuriya met her teacher's eyes, she witnessed something profound. She saw the great depths of Korba's caring and her absolute commitment to being of service. Korba waited for Nuriya to move, and she did so reluctantly, for it was rich to see her teacher so clearly in this way. She took one of the bowls while Korba bent over Hawk's side. Korba's head snapped back and Nuriya could see over her shoulder that Hawk's ribs were nearly smooth, barely indenting on each breath. The healer reached for the vial around her neck and held it out to Nuriya, silently asking, the moment between them like the ringing of a bell, the teacher offering the decision to her apprentice. Nuriya nodded, and Korba turned to tap more shepherd's purse under Hawk's tongue.

The elder healer patted the herb mixture around the ribcage, being extremely careful with the area of fracture. "I want you to do the wrap," she said to Nuriya. Then to Sema, Hawk's mother, she said, "We need a lamp and more blankets, and send Jute to me. I need her to fetch something."

Nuriya soaked the bandage in medicine and draped it over the herb mash with Hawk watching calmly. Sema watched also as Nuriya worked the cloth around her son's ribs. She whispered to Korba worriedly, "I know you trust the girl, but don't you...I mean...should she be..?"

"She's the one you want tending to the ribs. She's more gentle than I."

"Yes, but..."

"Sema, I love your son. We will do our best for him."

"Yes," Sema said and retreated to fetch the blankets and call her daughter.

When Nuriya finished the wrap, she found Hawk staring at her. Rather than look away, as she normally would have, she let herself be drawn in, as she had with Korba. The color of Hawk's eyes reminded Nuriya of springtime rosemary and inside them she witnessed Hawk's kindness and his esteem for her. Then as if in a dream, she saw him walking toward her, his hair lit from behind, his stride long and confident, a smile upon his face. Nuriya knew in that instant that Hawk would heal, and that he would walk without a limp.

Hawk looked away and the vision was broken. Nuriya suddenly felt faint. She was kneeling but she felt as if she was going to fall over. "Korba," she called reaching backward.

Korba was at her side instantly. "I'm here." The healer looked into Nuriya's eyes. "You're done now. Come." She settled her apart from the others and said, "Rest. When I'm ready to set the leg I'll let you know."

Nuriya lay back on a patch of dirt, one rock pressing into her side and another into her thigh, feeling disoriented but immeasurably happy. She'd had a true vision of healing! She knew that Hawk would heal, and that she had helped. She gazed up into the cerulean sky, feeling very, very pleased.

Korba roused Nuriya after the sleeping draught she administered to Hawk had taken effect. She told her apprentice to watch how she felt for direction and told Tul to hold his son's hips firm. Tul asked with rough reluctance, "I don't doubt that you can do it, Korba, but shouldn't I do the pull?"

"His body will find the right place if I guide it," the healer replied. She pinched Hawk's ear, testing his depth of relaxation, then said, "Hold calm, Hawk. We're going to fix your leg." Hawk made a sound like a question rising up from the depth of a dream as Korba straddled his leg. "Great Mother," she said, "lend me Your hands." She grasped his knee and pulled with fierce and controlled strength. There was a scraping sound, not too loud, but sickening nonetheless and the thigh eased straight. "Nuri, pad the leg. Lift the boards. Good. Pull the ties, not too firm." Nuriya put her hands on either side of the completed splint and Korba slowly released her pull. "Think healing, girl. Help those bones mend."

After a time Korba drew Nuriya away from the others. "What did you do over there with the ribs?"

Nuriya was wondering herself, what was real and what her imagination. "I wove a web, I think. I don't know."

"Daughter, the Mother is working though you in mysterious ways." She turned to her friends. "Sema, Tul, it's time for me to get Nuri home. We'll check Hawk in the morning. Two sips if he wakes but no more, and fetch us if you have need."

Bravely holding back tears the entire time, Sema could hold them back no longer. Tul took his wife into his great arms and said over her shoulder, "Thank you, Korba. We'll see you tomorrow."

Korba lay awake long after Nuriya had fallen to sleep with a grateful smile on her weathered old face.

Nuriya awoke the next morning remembering how her hands had glowed with healing light. She felt in such a brilliant mood that when Korba asked her to join the offering, she agreed. At temple, her teacher prayed out loud, and as usual Nuriya listened with half an ear. "Great Mother, thank you for Your healing to Hawk through Your daughter, Nuri. I pray that Your gift to her will be a blessing to many. I am old, Mother, and soon my apprentice, my beloved foster daughter, will take my place. I thank You for bringing her to me and I ask You to guide her all the days of her life."

Korba turned to Nuriya, her eyes shining with pride. Whatever Nuriya was going to pray flew from her mind. Of course Korba was aging, but she was healthy still, and who said she wanted to take her place? She faced the altar and silently begged, please don't let Korba get old too fast. Then she pushed away that unpleasant thought.

The women visited Hawk after breakfast. His friends were already there and made a party of moving him to the farm house. That day and each day after the bruising on his ribcage was smaller. On the fourth day Hawk greeted them standing on his good leg, leaning over a pair of fine crutches. "I know you are eager to be getting about, young man, but I want no weight on that leg," the healer admonished.

"But, Korba, I was going to hike to port today. They're giving out prizes for a three-legged race."

"No weight," Korba repeated, ignoring his jest.

"Yes, ma'am." Hawk feigned contrition then sought Nuriya's eye and winked. It flustered Nuriya and she pretended not to notice.

Late in the day Bon brought his wife to see the healer about a cut on her arm that wasn't healing well. After Korba thoroughly cleansed it, she let Nuriya lay her hands over the area with healing intention. No special sensation came, other than a peaceful feeling for her and the patient. That was fine, but Nuriya was eager for her gift to come again.

A few days later while the healers were stripping leaves from herb stalks, they saw two children in a donkey-cart racing to the fork. One jumped out and ran toward them, screaming hysterically.

Scarcely had the women gathered supplies and mounted the cart when the children set off at breakneck speed. Korba pleaded with them to slow but such frenzy gripped them that they would not. Nuriya huddled around her teacher, placing her body between Korba and the cart rails, and thus they raced all the way past the Dingli cliffs and down a steep slope near Rdum to a compound packed tight with people.

An imposing man swept out of a small hut and strode straight toward Korba. "My brother needs healing. See to him."

Korba matched his style. "Boil water. I'll need it."

The man's face twitched. He snapped his fingers and a woman stepped forward. Healer and apprentice stepped inside the hut without witnessing their exchange.

A mid-aged man on a low pallet in the center of the room appeared to be in the prime of fitness though his wife lay stretched across his body, as if barring him from movement. The woman sat up when the women entered and pointed to her husband's chest. "There! A demon enters there and makes terrible pain and terrible sickness."

Korba addressed the man, asking what ailed him, but his wife answered for him, "The demon won't let him work. Every time he goes up to the field, it strikes him. It gives him pain and makes him faint. He must stay indoors all the time. It doesn't come to him here." Korba felt the man's pulses, checked his pupils, and against the protest of his wife, asked the man to sit. The healer put her head to his chest and listened to his heart and breath.

Nuriya did not have a clear view as Korba examined him. She focused her eyes on the diamond of hairless skin below the man's rib cage, the shallow rhythm of stretching and sagging there. Aversion welled inside her. So eager she had been to witness her hands glowing with the *gift*, but she felt none of that now. Despite that her role was to stay and comfort the patient, she followed Korba outside to the hearth, knowing she did not want to touch the man and doubted his wife would let her, anyway.

The headman strode toward Korba. "Will you cast out the demon?"

"Your brother has a weak heart," Korba replied.

"Can you not cast out a demon?" the man challenged.

"There is weakness in your brother's heart," Korba repeated. "Medicine will make his heart stronger."

The headman seemed to grapple with his temper. "Are you certain?" he asked.

"Yes."

"Will he work again?"

"Yes. He will take medicine for five days. Then he may work again as long as he takes medicine every morning."

"Try it then," the headman snapped.

Korba turned to Nuriya. "Go inside and tell them I am making medicine for his heart. I will bring it when it is ready."

Nuriya obeyed, not wanting to protest in front of the intimidating headman. The wife eyed her warily as she re-entered the tiny space and sat opposite. "The healer will bring medicine for your heart," Nuriya said. She did not want to look at either of them while she waited, so she closed her eyes. That's when she felt it—the momentary dizziness, the spot of pain behind her eye. No, she begged inwardly. Not now. But she knew what was coming. Her head squeezed painfully tight and she dreaded what would follow. She felt the clearing in her eyes—and then she *saw*.

Inside the man was a thing clenched like a fist, wanting to harm, wanting to maim. She jerked back and tried to shut her eyes, but they were already closed. She opened her eyes and still she saw the grotesque gnarl. The image was frightening but she forced herself to think rationally. Could she help? Korba's medicine would make the man's heart stronger, but if she could loosen this angry knot, his heart might be completely well. She focused her mind to imagine the comfort of a loving touch, and then offering that touch to the man. As if responding to her thoughts, he turned toward her. Nuriya was shocked to see the unconcealed contempt in his gaze. Suddenly, the man grasped his chest, his contempt turning to panic as the fist exploded inside him. His face blanched pale, then yellow, then vomit hurled out toward Nuriya, splattering her hair, and face, and dress. The woman screeched and Nuriya grabbed her head as pain hammered inside it. Korba rushed in. "Your black girl brought the demon into my house!" the woman was shrieking. "Make her go! Make her go! Make the demon go!" Korba saw Nuri's distress but she could not tend to her; the man was clutching his chest, struggling to breathe, his face streaked with vomit, his eyes and veins bulging. Korba grasped the back of his head and massaged with firmness down the vein at the side of his neck. She massaged the bulging vein, one, two, three, four hard strokes, before the man's grip loosened. Korba slipped her hand under his and massaged hard over his chest. The pain went out of the man's face and he sank back to his mat.

"Get her out. Get her out!" the woman shouted as Nuriya clung to her head like it was shattered. Korba dragged her apprentice through the doorway. The mood outside was hostile. The healer pushed through the silent, glaring kinspeople toward the empty cart. "Stay here. I'm going to finish the medicine."

A crowd of onlookers, mostly children, gathered around Nuriya as she crouched by the cart, trembling with pain and humiliation. When the pain lessened, she stood, and her gawkers stepped back. No one offered a means to wash. She stumbled to nearby bushes, grabbed handfuls of brush and scraped vomit from her skin and shift. Then she approached the hearth. "Korba?"

"It must wait."

Nuriya huddled next to the hearth, freezing cold despite the warmth of the day. These people didn't want her here. The angry man and his angry wife didn't want her here. But here she had to wait, for Korba to finish her work. Leave me, leave me, leave me! she demanded whatever it was that made her see inside that man. Her grand and fanciful dream—of healing powers and hands glowing with light—she banished it now.

It took several rejections before Korba found someone willing to talk to her. The healer taught the woman what her medicines were and how to administer them. "I should check him again, but I will come only if you, personally, send for me." The imposing leader reappeared then commanded the child cart-drivers, "Take them away. Go. Now!" No mention of payment was made.

After being jounced and jostled all the way home, Nuriya stood facing Mnajdra, fuming. "I do not want to see what a person should not see," she declared.

"Tell me what happened."

"I saw a knot inside him and I tried to loosen it. That's all."

"We don't know what came before in that clan, Nuri. It seems..."

"I don't want to know," Nuriya interrupted. "I don't want to see, and I don't want to know!"

There was a pause before Korba spoke again, "I have said you must ask the Mother to guide your gift."

"This isn't a gift!" Nuriya shouted. "If the Mother thinks this a 'gift'," she yanked the fabric of her soiled shift, "I tell Her, 'No!' I want no favors from Her!"

The affront in Korba's face made Nuriya want to scream. What boon had paying homage to the Great Mother ever yielded

Korba? What Korba gleaned from life she did with her own hard work. But it wasn't her intention to disrespect her teacher. It was Korba, as always, who knew what to do; it was Korba, as ever, who maintained dignity in the midst of crisis. Nuriya was humbled by her, regardless of how simplistically she imaged her God.

"Healing is dirty work, daughter," Korba said icily. "Vomit and feces are part of it."

"Don't you think I know that?" Nuriya asked. It wasn't just the vomit that distressed her. It was the man's contempt and his wife's accusation. It was wanting to help and have it go all wrong. They would always remember the black girl who "brought the demon into the house." Now the man wouldn't take Korba's medicine, his heart would get worse, he would probably die and she would be to blame.

Heart-sick herself, Nuriya trudged home while Korba went to Mnajdra to pray. As she scrubbed her stinking body, and washed her soiled shift, she thought about things. She understood why Korba said everyone avoided the woman on Lipari who could see into the body—because she was a freak! Nuriya didn't need one more way to make her different. She'd had a beautiful experience of healing with Hawk and then a terrible experience today and no way to know whether she would help or make things worse. Right then and there she disavowed any special powers of healing or sight. She put all desire for a "gift from the Mother" (she spat the words in her mind) behind her. How could she have been so stupid as to believe she had been favored? She deliberately stowed away the snake necklace and the bracelets in case they were associated with her strange sight—she didn't want to think about any *mother* just now.

Soon Nuriya realized she would also have to avoid Hawk in order to not be reminded of her short-lived gift. "Go check him, Nuri," Korba urged a few days later.

"You saw for yourself he's fine."

"He likes you, you know."

"I don't want him to like me. He looks at me like I'm a holy ghost."

"Just go."

Nuriya did not.

The healer handled discussion of the man in Rdum by end-lessly reviewing the ways to treat heart conditions. She tried to get Nuri to speak of her hopes and fears about healing but Nuriya persuaded that all she wanted was to be an excellent herb healer. Korba knew there was more to her precocious charge than herbs and continued to pray on her behalf that the Mother guide Nuri and reveal her gifts slowly, as she was able to integrate them.

Two moons passed with no mysterious visions and blessedly, no headaches. Nuriya did her best to be an attentive and sub-missive apprentice and Korba rewarded her by letting her conduct the exams herself. Nuriya described what she observed, Korba confirmed or queried further, and together they planned treatment. Before long, the healer sent Nuri on her first solo calls—only to clans they knew well, a precaution for her safety as a woman and to avoid any ignorant response to her ethnicity.

By the time the rains came in late fall, Nuriya had treated a variety of conditions on her own, even setting a broken arm, which she did expertly, though she wished she'd had Korba's help for it. Nuriya remained vigilant, especially if working alone, for any sign of head pain that might herald a change in vision. She was not sure what she would do if it occurred, but she hoped vigilance would ward it off.

By the time of the longest night, the weather turned chill. Lung conditions and old injuries flared, and for a while, the healers were called out every day, traveling together or singly, for this was the first year that two clans could be treated at once.

One winter morn Hawk showed up at the cistern as Nuriya was lowering the bucket. "I was just passing by," he said. That was a lie, and she didn't take the bait. "My leg's good," he tried next. Nuriya glanced to see Hawk hopping and wobbling to keep his balance.

"I'm glad," she said repressing a smile and lifting the bucket over the rim.

"I'll get it for you!" Hawk jerked forward to take the bucket and pour into the waiting jug. He lowered, hoisted and poured; and one more time to full.

"Thank you," Nuriya said politely.

Hawk stoppered the jug. "I have something for you—I mean—I will have..."

Nuriya put her hands on her hips and tried for patience. Hawk was pleasing enough to look at—she liked how the overcast sky highlighted his rosemary eyes, and how his sheepskin cloak complemented his auburn mane—but she could hardly tolerate his childishly awe-struck expression. Hawk scuffed a sandaled foot and looked down. "Payment, I guess."

"Korba works that out with Tul," Nuriya said, dismissing the subject, and bent to hoist.

"Wait." Hawk reached to stop her. She straightened and he managed to hold her gaze. "I know what you did for me."

This was not a topic that Nuriya was ready to discuss; in fact, she was very much trying to keep it from her mind. She nodded, smiling tightly, and crossed her arms across her chest.

"Do you want me to carry the jug for you?"

"No. Thank you."

"I'll let you know when it's time."

"What are you talking about, Hawk?"

"The calf."

"What about the calf?" she asked, relieved at last to shift from this blundering attempt at conversation into a healer's focus.

"Blaki's pregnant. I'm giving you her calf."

Now astonishment washed through Nuriya. Clans on Malta were lucky to have one working animal amongst the whole of them. "That's too much."

"I know what you did," he said plainly.

Hawk's clan was unusually rich in animals. Besides goats and sheep, they had a donkey, and Jimi, and a small herd of oxen they bartered to farms that didn't have their own. Hawk had taken charge of the animals four years before and in acknowledgement, he was given his own calf the spring of his fifteenth year. Now he was offering Blaki's first born to Nuriya.

"Korba doesn't like to keep animals," Nuriya stammered, but she was already thinking of how having their own transportation would dramatically improve their lives.

"I'm giving it to you."

"I don't know what to say." Then, she gave in to the enticing possibility and delight blossomed across her face. "This is very fine of you, Hawk."

Hawk blushed. "You sure you don't want me to carry that?"

"No, thanks. I've got it."

Hawk grinned through his blush then turned, breaking into a zany, zigzagging run, mended leg and all.

3.

Descent

◎◎

It was a particularly wet winter and the healers often returned from calls with their hair and clothing drenched through. After one bleak spell of rain three days straight, they were cautiously optimistic with the thinning clouds and the strong south wind on the morning of the fourth. Indeed, by noon of that day Nuriya was out dancing in sun patches.

Their first call came shortly after. Three children from one clan were down with fevers and swollen throats, and in waiting out the rain their conditions had worsened. The healers loaded their kits with extra remedies to strengthen family and neighbors.

When they reached the cliff road, they paused to wait for a donkey cart that raced toward them from the direction of port. A middle-aged Phoenician man pulled his donkey to a stop, jumped from the bench and ran straight to Nuriya, pleading that she come to port to tend his dying wife.

"I could go with him," Korba offered.

"Of course I'll go," Nuriya said. She was flattered that the man had asked her in particular. She checked her bag to make sure of her supplies, brushing away a moment's misgiving. She could do this; she had trained for this.

The man spoke non-stop as he hurried his donkey. He was a market worker named Vylat. He described, through tears, his wife's suffering, how she neither ate nor drank but only cried in pain. He couldn't bear it. He knew she was dying, but not like this! He told Nuriya what a good wife she was, about her loyalty in coming with him to the colony, about their courtship in Byblos, about the forests where he grew up. Talking about his youth lessened Vylat's distress and Nuriya relaxed enough to enjoy the beauty of the day. Majestic clouds towered over the landscape. Light sparkled from waxy leaves and rocky crevices offering their caches of raindrops to the sun. The spicy scent of clover filled the air as young stems were crushed under the cart wheels. By the time they reached the outskirts of the port, however, the man was complaining bitterly about his mother-in-law. She was miserable and meddlesome and did not take to strangers. She thought the healers were evil and forced her own remedies on her daughter; maybe that was what was killing her.

It was market day and the road was clogged with people and carts. The man cried in frustration between his lewd curses. He managed to turn up a side alley and raced along a row of close packed dwellings that paralleled the market street. He halted the cart, jumped out and motioned Nuriya to follow. She did her best to compose herself before entering the low doorway.

An old woman was kneeling in the center of the room, wailing at the top of her capacity, adding green herbs to a brazier of glowing coals. Pungent smoke filled the small space, overpowering the scent of sickness. There was an altar before the brazier where a variety of small birds had been sacrificed.

Abruptly the wailing stopped. The woman turned to face Vylat. Her eyes were glazed but the emotion in them was unmistakable rage. "You left her! You left my daughter! She is dying because of you! How dare you bring a stranger into my home!" To Nuriya she shouted, "Leave us, witch. You will not kill my daughter!" She raised a bony finger and pointed out the doorway. Nuriya dumbly turned in the direction she pointed before a thin cry pulled her attention to the pallet at the back of the room. "Look what you have done!" the old woman shrieked.

Vylat went to his wife, clasping her hand, kissing it, and speaking hoarsely, "My love, I brought the healer to ease your pain."

The old woman screamed, "You will not let her touch my daughter."

"Meera. Do you want the healer to help you?"

The ill woman mouthed, "Yes," with a look of desperation on her ravaged face.

Vylat kissed her hand, repeating, "My love." Then he stood and turned to his mother-in-law. "This is my house, mother. The healer will be allowed to tend Meera."

"She will not defile my daughter!"

Vylat steeled himself then soundly slapped the old woman.

She caught herself, her anger giving her strength. "How dare you beat me in front of my daughter!"

"Leave us, woman!" Vylat's hand was at the ready to strike again.

The old woman hissed and went back to her altar. She picked up a dead bird, dripping blood over her palm, and raised it to the ceiling, screeching, "God Melquart, why do you forsake me? I am your faithful one! Astarte, strike down this man as you destroy all your enemies!" Vylat waved Nuriya to the bedside as his mother-in-law continued to name and implore her Gods. The young healer forced herself to move through the barrier of sound and smoke.

Kneeling by the sick woman, Nuriya no longer heard the commotion behind. Meera was indeed gravely ill. Her face was gaunt and her shoulder bones looked to pierce her skin. Heat burned her brow and her pulse raced weakly. "Water," Nuriya said to Vylat, pulling blankets off his wife. She took the softest cloth from her bag and wiped Meera's brow ever so gently. She squeezed water drops along cracked lips, and the woman opened her mouth to receive them, though her grating breath and wide-eyed look of terrible pain continued without abating.

"Where does it hurt?"

Meera struggled to mouth words then gave up and began to fumble with her loose shift. Vylat helped to lift the cloth. Below the ribs on the right, her abdomen was grossly distended, webbed with swollen veins, the skin oozing in patches. "It started there," Vylat said with a look of unbearable impotence. "Now she hurts everywhere—her bones, her back. Please don't let her suffer like this, please help." Nuriya's compassion for the man returned tenfold. She handed him the cloth. "Cool her brow. I'll prepare medicine. Is there another cook fire?"

"You will use this brazier," Vylat said, then he shouted at his mother-in-law, "Mirde, move!" He got up and forcibly placed his hands on Mirde's shoulders. She screamed obscene oaths but allowed herself to be moved to a bench. She was obviously losing her mind. Vylat stoked the embers and placed three pots next to the brazier before returning to his wife's side.

Nuriya set out her supplies avoiding the bodies of the dead birds. Her hands were shaking and tension pulsed at the back of her head. She studied her medicines: willow and poppy heads would take long; the poisonous henbane seeds-although Korba used them with skill, Nuriya was terrified to attempt it; and the small brown cake from Kepi. That seemed the right choice, but how much to use? Sick as Meera was she'd have to be careful.

She stirred honey into warming water and used her knife to scrape bits off the resinous cake of poppy-tears, coaxing it to dissolve, then adding mint and more honey to cover bitterness. Closing her eyes, she took several long, counting breaths, stretched her neck and tried to ease her mind. She scooped a small cupful of liquid and added a splash of water to hasten cooling, fretting over whether she was diluting it too much. She started another pot to heat; she'd know better how to dose after observing the effect of this. She took the cup to Meera's side and pulled a fresh cloth from her bag. "Vylat, I'm going to give Meera medicine now." The sound from the bench intensified, but Mirde did not interfere. Nuriya soaked cloth in the liquid and tested it for temperature. "Meera, this is medicine for pain." She squeezed a few drops onto her lips. At first it drizzled down the woman's chin, then registering what was needed, Meera opened her mouth like a bird asking for food. Her throat caught as if she would drown on the small sip, but her mouth gaped for more. Nuriya offered several swallows then paused. Meera sank back, exhausted from the effort. The sound behind them had decreased to a low keening, the old woman rocking forward and back on the bench, her arms hugging her sides, a dead bird smashed to her tunic.

Meera's eyes were half lidded. There was a slight slowing of the pace of her breath, but she continued to struggle for air and her pulse raced too fast. After a time Nuriya said, "Vylat, I'm going to make something stronger. I must tell you that once she sleeps, she may not wake." She wanted him to understand that this was the time for saying goodbye.

Vylat nodded and clasped his wife's hand.

Suddenly, the old woman was upon Nuriya, smacking her head and back as if she were a dog. Nuriya crouched, using her arms to ward off blows. Mirde was screaming and Vylat was shouting and struggling until he had his mother-in-law bound in his arms. "I have no choice, Meera, forgive me." He wrestled Mirde to a side door, pushed the woman in and latched it behind her. There she began again her wailing cries, accompanied by kicking and cursing. "Please, healer. I'm sorry for my mother-in-law. Please, help my wife."

Meera looked grotesque in her fright, struggling with small ragged breaths. Nuriya couldn't bear it if she died like this, in a panic. She put her hand on Meera's forehead. "Be easy, Meera. I'll make your medicine now."

She asked Vylat for wine and went back to the brazier. She scraped a generous amount of poppy into the warming wine and added one henbane seed. As she stirred, she chanted one of Korba's prayers under her breath, "Mother earth, Mother sky, Mother sea..." became, "Mother, mother, mother ..." but Nuriya wasn't chanting for the words; she was chanting to keep her own panic at bay. She forced herself to think of the healing she wanted to happen: Relieve Meera's suffering. This is what you are here to do. Soothe her pain. Make her last breaths gentle. She refused to think of Mirde who continued to wail and kick at the door; maybe later she could do something for her. Nuriya scooped poppy wine into a mug, blew over the surface, and willed it to be what the woman needed. "Meera, this will help you sleep," she said and the woman parted her lips to receive the promised oblivion.

Eventually Meera's breathing calmed. Her eyes softened and became glassy. A hint of smile twisted her ravaged face and she took on an otherworldly look, eyes flickering behind closed lids. She slept that way as Vylat and Nuriya watched. Day turned to night and Meera did not wake. Even her mother waited in silence. Embers burned low in the brazier, Vylat got up to light a lamp; still they waited.

Meera's hand flickered in her husband's and she forced her eyes open. Vylat bent over her, murmuring, "Meera, I love you." Sad, luminous eyes gazed into his for a long time then sought Nuriya's eyes over her husband's shoulder.

The young healer instantly wanted to turn away—but she could not. Meera was needing—demanding something from her. Don't want from me, Nuriya prayed. Let the herbs take you. But Meera continued to stare, locking Nuriya to her gaze. An echo of head pain tickled behind Nuriya's eye, and a hint of fear followed. Her thoughts began to scramble. Let yourself go, Meera. I have nothing more to give you. I cannot take this from you. Still, she remained trapped in the woman's gaze. Then, in a flash, Nuriya knew what was needed. She opened her mouth and these words came:

"The heart of the Mother is as wide as the sky
And as deep as the sea.
Her heart will swallow all your sorrows
And forgive every lack.
She loved you before you were born,
And She welcomes you back,
Into Herself."

Nuriya had listened to Korba at many deathbeds over the years but this was the first time she had spoken this prayer and she was humbled to witness the effect of her words. She watched as Meera, guileless as a child, teetered between hope and fear, fear and hope, until with a movement of thin, cracked lips, the dying woman mouthed, "Thank you."

Her eyes sought her husband's then and Vylat struggled to hold her gaze and not cry. "I love you, Meera," he whispered fiercely. Then closing her eyes, Meera breathed her last, and returned her life to the force that called for it.

After a long, silent moment, Vylat broke into deep, sorrowful wails and Mirde joined from her locked room. Nuriya backed away, quietly packed her bag and stumbled out into the dark alley, gulping in cool night air. A man and a woman, alerted by the mourning cries that the long wait was over, moved past her and entered the dwelling. Nuriya's work was finished. She had done what she was asked to do.

If the healers completed treatment late, they would sleep where they were and arrange transportation in the morning, but tonight Nuriya was desperate to get home. The day had been overwhelming and she wanted to spill her heart to Korba. She moved down the alley, past yellow trickles of lamplight leaking through window coverings, looking for an opening onto the market street. She found a passage between two buildings and turned. The Wanderer called, the Golden Teacher, shone in an open patch of sky with thin clouds veiling the surrounding stars. The half moon would set before she got home, but if she circled around the oak grove, this would be enough light to find her way.

During the day, the market street had been filled with spice and fish, and clink and motion. Now discarded fruit littered empty stalls and a handful of men lingered outside the drinking houses. Nuriya had never walked the street except accompanied by an old and respected healer and despite her frayed nerves, she felt the thrill of rare freedom.

Torches burned in front of open establishments and at intervals down to the docks. As she passed the first torch, the men loitering outside the tavern suspended their conversation. There was laughter inside, and someone whistled. Nuriya's blood raced. All was quiet near the torch at the inn but approaching the third torch, she heard arguing. The men in the doorway divided their attention between her and the commotion inside. She picked up her pace. In a dozen more steps she would be on the road to the fishing village and the countryside beyond.

She heard voices coming from the direction of the docks but kept her eyes on the dark path ahead. Just before she reached the fork, two men stepped onto the street supporting a third between them, who slurred, "Where's the place to get a drink?" Nuriya kept up her pace, attempting to step around them.

The man on the right grabbed her bag and swung her backward.

"He's talking to ya," he bellowed. Nuriya felt the air suck out of her.

"Looky here, a pretty one," mocked the sailor on the other side. He was tall, and maybe less drunk than the other two, but she heard no kindness in him. "Who are you to be walking alone at night?"

"Let me go. I'm a free woman," she said, trying to sound indignant, for slaves were not allowed out at night.

"Ahha," the men laughed.

"Tha's cheap," announced the one who released her but now blocked her path. "Where's your father, pretty girl?" he asked, waggling his hips, his beard spattered disgustingly with bits of food.

Nuriya tried dodging, only to be caught by the tall man who sneered, "Where're your brothers?"

"Let me go." She hated the whine in her voice.

"No brothers, no husband? The pretty one needs an escort!" The sailor with the filthy beard took her by the waist and turned her in the direction of the docks, leaning his sweaty stink into her neck. "I'm gonna kiss me a free woman."

Nuriya yanked loose, bumping smack into the drunkest man. He was her height and thickly muscled, and he crushed her to his body as she struggled against him. "I like 'em wild," he simpered. Foreboding darkness began to rise around Nuriya. *Don't faint!* she berated herself. *Don't faint!* Her drunken captor turned her to face him. An ugly scar ran the length of his cheek, eclipsing any other feature save the bloodshot eyes. "You're a pretty night walker. How much for tha' kiss?"

"Don't hurt me."

"Jus' a kiss, honey. How much?"

"She's free!" his comrade reminded.

The drunk sailor held Nuriya's face and pushed his mouth onto hers, forcing his tongue between her teeth. Without forethought, Nuriya raised her knee with all her might. It grazed the man's thigh and met, with diluted force, his vulnerable flesh. "Cunt!" He slapped her hard and she fell backward into the low wall. His comrades laughed. "Shut up!" the man roared. Immediately they hushed. The sailor swayed on his feet a long moment then ordered, "Beat it."

"We're just playin', Toma. Let 'er be."

"Leave me be if ya know what's good."

"Don't hurt her."

"Nah." He leered over his shoulder. "Just a lesson in manners. Beat it!" His comrades turned and headed up to the tavern.

The loathsome man stood menacing over Nuriya. "Bitch, all I asked was a kiss." Nuriya was frozen—powerless. The sailor grunted to one knee and yanked her legs apart. A scream stuck in Nuriya's throat but she forced hands like claws toward bloodshot eyes. "Bitch," the man jeered and pinned her arms over her head. She writhed but he jabbed his other hand between her legs. Lecherous fingers pawed her, probed her, hurt her. "Ahhaa," the beast approved as the scream unstuck from Nuriya's throat.

In the midst of her scream, Nuriya's mind began to float away from her body. She demanded it, Go! Go! to a faraway place, where she could imagine a different ending to this story. In her desperate imagining, Nuriya heard the shouted command, "De-SIST!" The monster made a noise between a snarl and a sneer, and fumbled with his tunic, grinding his knee into her thigh, pinning her, readying her for worse. Nuriya prayed for the dreaming to take her, for the swirling blackness, for anything but this...and before she drew another breath, her dream took hold. The man flew off and smashed backward into the wall. He fell on top of her, and she had to fight for air. She saw him lift his head, turn, and smash again into the wall. She knew that her mind was shattering, for even in her dreaming nothing made sense. She didn't care. She pulled herself from under the monster's weight and curled tight, willing herself firmly, determinedly, into blackness.

4.

Ilobaal Of Tyre

❧

"**B**astard!" The drunk groped to his knees, reached for a foot and missed. He made to pursue his attacker but was yet unable to pull himself up.

"Away from the woman!"

"I will cut you, boy—when I'm standing."

"Cover yourself, man." A uniformed soldier was standing out of arm's reach with his sword drawn.

The drunk gained unsteady feet and pulled his disheveled tunic decent. The interloper was younger than the sailor, with a dark moustache and trimmed beard on an otherwise clean-shaven face and a serious but untested look about him. The sailor straightened himself, lifting his chest, then lurched to one side to catch his balance. He looked up the alley in the direction his comrades disappeared then down to the woman huddled against the wall. His hand began moving toward his crotch when his eye caught on the glint of the soldier's sword, focusing his attention.

"Malta Port is claimed by Tyre," the soldier was speaking in a clipped, military style, "and governed by the Magistrate Eshebaal. You have no right to defile..."

"Deflower more likely," the sailor guffawed.

The soldier glanced fleetingly toward the woman then shouted, "Get back to your ship and stay on it."

"No one commands me but my cap'n and the weapon's mate. Who are you to order me?"

"I am Ilobaal of Tyre, son of the Magistrate Eshebaal."

"Well, well," the sailor mocked. "The pretty boy with a sword and his daddy's ear. You got no right to command me, boy."

Ilobaal of Tyre had a good idea of who this sailor was as well. A ship had arrived from Carthage four days earlier with an urgent message for his father regarding the Libyan trade. Ilobaal was present when the captain delivered the official scroll. The crew had been given leave for the bad weather while they awaited return sail and had been drinking heavily ever since. "You have been trouble since you arrived. Our taverns are not meant for drunkards the likes of you."

"Is that so?" the sailor laughed. "Didn't know you had classes o' sots on your shitty little rock."

"You will go back to your ship, now."

"Piss off, pretty boy."

With a flick of his wrist, Ilobaal sliced the sailor's tunic hip to hem. "I'm not playing old man."

"He has a temper," the sailor announced with glee. Grasping the knife from his belt he drew it on his junior. "I don't play neither, boy." He sunk into a crouch, his long knife to Ilobaal's curved sword, and they began to circle. A dozen or so late drinking market workers, sailors and guard gathered, drawn by the commotion. Ilobaal's compatriots flanked him, unsheathing swords and knives. Companions of the sailor stepped forward, drawing their weapons as well.

"If he wasn't a pussy he'd draw his knife and fight man to man," the sailor taunted.

"I'm not here to fight old men. I'm here to send you to your ship."

"Toma, if it's over the girl, leave it be."

"I can fight him," Toma roared.

"And all of us?" a comrade of Ilobaal challenged. The sailor spat and continued his threatening dance.

"We sail tomorrow, Toma. You'll have your pick of all the whores in Carthage."

Toma ignored them but when a movement near the wall caught his eye, he shot a quick glance and witnessed Nuriya's body convulsing in the fit of a seizure. He bolted upright, made a quick sign to ward evil then sheathed his knife and lurched down the alley without a word, his comrades trailing after.

"Watch for the girl!" someone shouted but Ilobaal did not take his eyes from the retreating men nor lower his sword. "Demons," someone else hissed. Only when the Carthaginians were out of sight, did Ilobaal turn to see the woman's arm jerk and her body shudder.

While the rest of the crowd drew back, Ilobaal moved forward, his curiosity aroused. Before he joined his father in Malta, Ilobaal had taken an offering to the Temple Melquart in Tyre. It was well received and the Oracle Priest had gone into a trance, like this, his body shaking, and making sounds in the mysterious language of the Gods. Afterward, the Oracle gave to Ilobaal a prophesy, sacred words he carried in his heart every day of his life. Ilobaal knew of no priestess here but nonetheless, he felt the urge to shield this woman from judging eyes. He took off his night cloak and as he leaned in to cover her, Nuriya unconsciously rolled toward him. Ilobaal's breath stopped.

Before his breath could resume, Ilobaal knew he wanted her; by the fire in his head and the furnace in his loins, he knew. Her wide-spaced, almond eyes fluttered under delicate lids. Her bronze skin glistened in the faint torch light. Her lips were parted and moving, as in prayer or love frenzy. Even the saliva that slipped from the corners of her mouth, enchanted. Ilobaal had traveled far with his father of the wandering eye and knew this was a rare beauty. "Lady," he whispered. "Can you hear me?"

Nuriya was in a twilight state, her head rolling left and right. Ilobaal pulled her tunic down, his eyes tracing her form through the sweat-soaked cloth. The line from a love poem floated to his mind: "A sachet of myrrh is my head between your breasts."

Then he shook his head sharply. He had just saved this woman from being forced and now he was thinking of lying with her, even knowing she might be an acolyte or, Ba'al only knows, a priestess. The excitement of the fight must be disorienting him. He finished covering her and forced himself to call, "Does anyone know this woman?"

"She lives with the Healer Korba," someone yelled from a safe distance. Ilobaal searched his memory for the reference.

"She is also a healer," another shouted.

"What is her name?"

"Nuriya."

Ilobaal addressed the vendor who shouted her name. "Hector, fetch the Healer Korba."

"She lives at Mnajdra, my lord."

Now he remembered...Korba, the witch of Mnajdra. Why is one of our people living with a native witch? Is she undergoing special training? He brushed hair from the beauty's face, and Nuriya whimpered. Even in her distress she was so lovely. He caressed her cheek and, in a manner more gentle than he knew himself capable of, whispered, "Wake up, Lady. I will let no harm come to you." At just that moment, by some magic or whim of the Gods, the woman's eyes fluttered open in little peeks. At seeing him they went wide with dread then snapped shut as she turned away. "You're safe," Ilobaal soothed. "No one will hurt you." He babbled more comforting sounds, wanting that lovely face to turn back to him, wanting to feast on that exquisite countenance.

Eventually the vision of loveliness did turn back and focused on his face. "Father?" she asked confusedly.

"No, my lady," Ilobaal chuckled. "I am not your father. I am Ilobaal of Tyre." The woman's eyes closed. She seemed to doze before they again fluttered open. Ba'al, those eyes!

"Ilobaal of Tyre?" she whispered.

"Yes," he said, "whoever you are." The poem returned to his mind, "Thou hast ravished my heart, my sister, thou hast ravished my heart with one of thine eyes." A clattering of wheels and hooves turned Ilobaal's attention. "Adnan, why are you up so late?" Ilobaal sounded positively jovial in contrast to the worry on his cousin's face.

"Aboro woke me. He said bring the wagon. There was a fight."

"Help me." Ilobaal picked up the woman and laid her in the back of the wagon. "Can you sit now?" She looked at him as if she was drunk. Perhaps if he took her to his father's home and let a servant care for her... No. Ilobaal's emotions were tumbled but his thoughts were calculating. This was a delicate time— just this evening he and his father had supper with the steward who would precede them to Tyre to make ready for their arrival. He was on his way from that late meeting to check the night guard when he heard the scream. No, it was better that his cousin take her to be tended by the healer. "Adnan, I want you to take this woman to the Healer Korba at Mnajdra."

"Now?" At twelve, Adnan was eight years younger than his beloved cousin, and making every effort to become his trusted aide, but he sat now with only his night cloak over a sleeping shift.

"Yes, now." Ilobaal called to Hector. "Go with Adnan. Walk ahead with the torch if need be." He shook a purse from his sash and handed Hector two silver shekels. The vendor's eyes gleamed at the treasure. "As you say, Lord," Hector replied with a bow.

To Adnan Ilobaal said, "Tell the healer I will come myself, tomorrow. Tonight I must speak to father about this. Go carefully, Adnan. There is something precious in this wagon."

5.

Binding The Wound

⊚⊘

Korba had returned home shortly after dark. She had lain awake a long time, thinking about the children in Baqra and worrying about Nuri. It was a big step, attending a death unassisted. Korba wondered if it made it easier or harder for Nuri that it was a Phoenician family. As soon as she heard the rattle of wheels in the distance she was up again, lighting a lamp and trekking to the fork to mark the way. A man was leading by torchlight as a wagon lumbered past the Standing Stones. While Korba waited, she looked to the stars she had not seen for many nights. Her eyes sought the Wanderers as she had taught Nuri to do. In the sign of the Lion, the mighty, red Fire Star hugged close to the Golden Teacher. Korba did not know the meaning behind the movements of the Wanderers, for she was not a star-reader, but she became suddenly more aware of the chill of the night. Late or no, she was glad her Nuri was home.

When the wagon was close, a young male called out in Canaanite, "Healer, I have your daughter."

"Where is she?" Korba asked sharply as she hurried to find Nuri in the back of the wagon, blanketed in a purple cloak, her head resting on a wad of cloth. Her eyes were open but she did not acknowledge Korba. "What happened?"

"She was attacked, mistress. My cousin rescued her."

"My baby," Korba murmured, reaching to touch her face. Nuriya mumbled toward something only she could see. Korba checked her pupils, noting the puffy eye with the bruise forming underneath. "She was hit?"

"We didn't see, mistress."

The healer lifted the cloak, noting her muddy, crumpled tunic, and checked the pulse at her wrists. "She had...shaking?" Korba asked, stumbling to find the Canaanite word.

The boy looked at the torchbearer then at the ground. "I heard it said, mistress." Nuriya allowed herself to be propped to sitting and with support on either side was helped to stand, her head flopping forward. The boy and the man half-carried her to the dwelling and onto a pile of blankets.

"My cousin will come tomorrow," the boy said.

"Thank him. You, I thank, both." She began to rummage her spare dwelling for something other than herbs to repay them.

Adnan guessed her action. "Nothing for us, Healer. We brought her because my cousin asked."

"May I offer food?"

"No, thank you. We must go back."

Korba tended Nuriya somberly, brushing mud from her hair and washing her legs. She faltered, seeing the abrasion on Nuri's upper thigh. She applied salve, prepared a sedative, and pulled up a mat to keep vigil.

Nuriya roused from her stupor in the dim light before dawn. Panic flooded her senses. Freezing fire shot through her veins. No, oh no! Something terrible! A man towered over her; he had no mercy.

"I'm here, Nuri."

Nuriya's terror receded at the sound of her teacher's voice. "Stay with me, Korba."

"Of course. I'm right here."

She slept again.

As the morning became full, Korba moved about, tending the fire, preparing food and medicine. When Nuriya stirred, Korba came to the bedside. Nuriya allowed the healer to prop her to sitting and hold the mug of borage and carrot to her lips. After she drank, Korba asked, "What happened?" Nuriya shook her head, folded back into her blanket and faced the wall.

When Nuri slept again, Korba set out with determined steps to Mnajdra. The wind whipped round, as wild as her heart. The healer contained herself long enough to pick her requisite offering, pull a statue from the cupboard, and offer the flower, but as soon as that was done she let go without preamble. "Why did you let this happen? Mother! Where is Your protection? Where is Your power?" Korba squared off to the altar. "Why Nuri? Why now?" She took two steps to the fire ring and spit, wiping her mouth unapologetically. She went back to the altar and continued in a sadder tone, "She is a new woman and who does she have but me to protect her? I am old, Mother. I beg You, watch over her."

She sat on the stones of the fire ring, her hanging head to her chest, shaking it bitterly. "What to do, what to do?" Then, inspiration came. She stood with a new surge of energy and spread her arms wide, speaking heavenward, "I call on Nuri's true mother. Woman, you who gave birth to Nuri, I have not given your daughter much," Korba's eyes welled with tears, "but I give her all I can. You must help her now. You must watch over her and guide her to a good life. Please, I ask this of you, true mother of Nuri." At this Korba felt some kindling of hope. "Thank you," she said. "Thank you, true mother of Nuri."

She tended their chores and returned often to check on Nuri. Each time she found her dry-eyed and unmoved, the food untouched. With misgiving for leaving, she hurried medicine to Bon's for the children in Baqra but when she returned, Nuri still had scarcely moved. She decided to take a direct approach. "Nuri, I need to examine you." At the healer's touch, Nuriya rolled to her back but held her tunic tight to her legs.

"Please, leave me alone."

Korba was relieved to hear her speak, but she also wanted to see her walk. "I will leave you alone if you come outside for tea."

"I don't want tea."

"Either you walk outside, or I examine you," the healer declared.

Nuriya was determined that Korba would not be examining her. Her body ached like she fell from a cliff then ran all night long and between her legs, it burned, but the gravest wound was so much deeper than her body. She pushed to standing, and forced herself to walk into the day.

She sat gingerly, accepting the cup that Korba offered, but not drinking, staring out toward the horizon where the clouds competed and roiled. After a while Korba prodded her, "How do you feel?"

Nuriya contemplated her question. When she was young, Korba taught her about the soul, the breath of Great Mother that each person carried. It felt like the membrane that held her soul was torn, and would never again be whole. *Something is broken,* she heard inside. Her lip trembled and she pushed against it. Hardness came into her jaw.

"What happened, Nuri? Please, tell me." After a silence Korba tried again. "I was hurt by a man, many years ago."

Nuriya cut her eyes toward her teacher.

"My husband's brother..." Korba answered the unasked question, "after my husband died."

"Is that why you ran away?"

"Yes."

Nuriya pulled her mouth into a grim line and they sat again in silence. After a while Korba asked, "Will you come with me to the temple?"

"Don't ask me that! You think that fixes everything." Then Nuriya turned her head, made a squeaking sound, and disappeared inside the dwelling. Korba looked to see what had caused her to flee. On the path from the Standing Stones, sitting tall upon a horse, a stranger approached, his purple cloak flying behind him like the wing of a great bird.

There was only one horse on the island that Korba knew of and it belonged to the Magistrate. Anxiety tensed her shoulders. If this man meant harm she would bar him from the door with her own body. She straightened her spine, and stood to wait.

The stranger dismounted at the fork and tied his horse to the signal post. His hair was raven black, falling to his shoulders. He wore the sword and cape of a soldier's garb but his tunic was a fine weave linen. Engraved silver discs belted his waist and a gold buckle adorned his cape. He stopped before the crest where Korba stood motionless, bowing low. "I am Ilobaal of Tyre, son of Eshebaal, Magistrate of Malta." He spoke the Maltese words haltingly, thick with the flourish of his native accent.

"I am Healer Korba."

"My cousin brought the woman, Lady Nurija, here. I come to see her."

Korba's shoulders eased; she had forgotten to expect the rescuer. "You are welcome." She motioned toward the fire ring, trying to recall the name he had given.

She offered her bench, refilled her battered and blackened

pot and kindled the fire. She sat opposite him saying, "Thank you for helping my daughter."

"That should never have happened." The man on the bench seemed like a mirage, his posture formal to exaggeration, his sword and buckle glinting light around the humble setting. He leaned forward and asked urgently, "How is she?"

"Troubled."

"Yes."

"She did not tell me what happened."

"The Lady Nurija was attacked near the docks, by a drunk Carthaginian sailor."

His words, and all that was unsaid, pierced Korba's heart. Distracting herself to maintain composure, she pointed to the kopis slung at the soldier's side. "You are good with your sword then?"

"Yes." There was pride of skill but no smile on his face. "That man is trouble. If he was my man, he would be whipped. I forbid that he return to Malta."

Korba nodded; her mind and heart were struggling mightily. "Excuse me, please, to check on her."

She knelt by Nuriya's still form. "The Magistrate's son has come to inquire. Will you come outside?"

"Not like this," Nuriya whispered.

"Should I ask him to come again?" Nuriya turned to Korba with pleading in her eyes and nodded.

"She is not up to a visit, sir. Would you come another time?"

"You are a healer. Was she...harmed?"

Korba's chest squeezed. "She will heal," she managed.

The young man stood. "I will come back."

"The tea..." Korba lifted her pot from the fire.

"Thank you. I must go. My regret."

"Very well. You may visit again."

Korba watched the man to his horse and then turned to see her daughter watching also from the shadow of the doorway.

Nuriya stood until the soldier disappeared past the Standing Stones then without comment, she curled back into her mat.

Korba followed her inside. "Will you tell me what happened, Nuri? It's like pus in a wound if it stays inside." The healer waited in vain then went back to Mnajdra for further prayer and guidance.

◎◎

In the twilight of the evening Nuriya jolted awake at Korba's touch. "It's me. I made something for you."

Nuriya roused herself. Lying on her side all day had not helped the achiness and her mouth was dry. She sipped Korba's medicine, trying not to think what was in it.

"Let me work with you?" Korba asked. "A little massage? Just your head?" Pressure had been building behind Nuriya's eyes all day; maybe the massage would help. She lay down and Korba smoothed calloused thumbs across her forehead, making circles at the temples and drawing fingers up her cheeks. It wasn't long before Nuriya put a fist to her mouth to stifle a cry. "This deserves your tears," Korba told her, continuing the gentle, hypnotic motions.

"It was so terrible," Nuriya whispered.

"I know."

"I don't want to remember."

"I know, but let it come." Nuriya squeezed herself so tight that her sob came out like a grunt. "Let me sing for you, Nuri," Korba said and began a lullaby in her low, rumbling alto:

Earth Mother holding us in Her arms
Warm and safe
Warm and safe
Moon Mother loving us into dream
Calm and peace
Calm and peace

It was a familiar song and it worked to relax Nuriya's fight while the medicine worked to relax her fear. As she listened to Korba, Nuriya thought she heard other voices weaving into the song. Women's voices. She caught some words and jerked to cover her ears.

"Let it come," the healer urged.

Without willing or wanting it, an inner eye opened, and Nuriya found herself looking into the face of a woman she did not know, a frightened woman. "I, too, was harmed," the woman told her. Behind her someone screeched, "I was beaten!" and beside her, yet another woman whispered, "I, too, was badly used." Nuriya saw, and heard, all around her then, countless women, voicing their pain. It was too much! She recoiled and fell backward, falling for a long, long time. The voices grew distant, the occasional "me, too," reaching her in her descent. Finally, Nuriya landed with a splash. She was in a sea—but a sea that was all eyes. To her horror she saw that she, too, was becoming only eyes. Bone and skin sloughed, each part moving from the other. Her hips floated out, but she had no hands with which to grab them. One leg floated here and the other there and all she could do was watch, and grieve. It was too much to bear, but she bore it, she and the countless eyes. With nothing left, she floated in the sea that was heartbreak.

Then, she saw his eyes—the beast! the bastard!—frozen in a state of maniacal lust. Within them Nuriya saw brutality, and more brutality, generations of it. She ricocheted between outrage and fear. What good was rage when the man could crush her with one arm? But here in her mind's illusion, where no physicality could stop her, she let her fury fly. She clawed at the man's face until his skin ripped from bone. She gouged until his eye sockets were bare. She kicked until his balls were a bruised and bloodied pulp. She punched until nothing was left and she pummeled at dust. Yet her fury was unquenched. She kicked and clawed, feeling the power of it. She lashed at the memories in the minds of the grieving women, attacking every thought until she batted at nothingness, and all around her was quiet space. Wary, she peered into the quiet—but her mind conjured no further image to battle.

She lay then for a long time, barely breathing, conscious of nothing. When she became aware again, it was Korba's fervent prayer that she heard. She took a long, slow breath, and found a small bit of peace.

What remained to contend with was the place inside that burned with the memory of intrusion. Nuriya rolled to her back and did what she knew to do as the healer's apprentice. She thought of wholeness, and of beauty; she thought it in her mind, and in her heart, and took a deep breath to send it down to her woman wound—but her breath caught, and she couldn't regain her air until it came again as sobbing. She had wanted to send healing into her body, but her body was scattered to the four directions and all she could do was cry for her poor, poor, confused self. She rolled toward her teacher, her mentor, the only mother she knew, and buried her head into familiar worn wool. Korba held her and rocked her, until Nuriya told her all, how the man had scared and hurt her, and how broken she felt. Then finally, finally, she slept.

In the morning, before Nuriya was fully awake, Korba was beside her, dressed and holding altar flowers, saying, "Come."

They walked in the early light to Mnajdra. Korba had picked herb stalks in the pre-dawn hour and strewn them on the walkway to the central altar; the tender leaves emitted a spicy fragrance as they were crushed underfoot. On the altar were two Goddess statues and a large jug. Nuriya paused, taking it all in. "Korba," she said with effort to keep her voice steady, "I know you want to make a Great Mother ritual for me, but I don't..." She stopped, huffed out, began again. "Why would She

let..." her voice cracked. "That bastard!" She stood there, clenching and unclenching her fists. "All right," she said her voice low
and hard. "I'll do it for you." She pulled off her shift and uncer-
emoniously poured the entire contents of the jug over her head.
The water gave her a shock and she shivered as Korba, with
pain in her eyes, silently handed her the drying cloth.

Nuriya was determined not to think about the assault and gave
herself extra chores that day to keep her mind occupied. She
took all the floor and sleeping mats outside, beat them clean and
mended them. The blankets were shaken and aired in the wintry
sunlight. She swept every speck of dust from their packed earth
floor. She allowed herself only one subject of contemplation beyond the tasks at hand: Ilobaal of Tyre. If she focused on the
vague memory of waking in his arms, or the vision of his tall,
straight spine as he rode the path, or the thrill of being scooped
from the ground at the Autumn Festival, for those moments and
those moments alone, she felt safe. But if she let her mind drift,
she found herself floundering into dangerous waters. Each time
she forced her attention to her rescuer, Nuriya felt the rawness
inside patching over. She was patching a tear in her soul with the
image of a man who was gallant and brave, and who told her he
would let no harm come.

Late in the day Nuriya returned everything to the dwelling
with the sleeping mats in new arrangements, putting her own
farther back and hanging the length of pale green Sidonian lin-
en along the wall to beautify her space. She ate a little supper
and drank Korba's tea, but when the healer sat beside her at
bedtime and began to hum, Nuriya begged, "Please don't." She
was mending in her own way and did not want to unsettle her
tenuous peace. She studied the weave of the linen in the glow of
the fire light and hummed her own lullaby.

Nuriya spent the better part of the next morning foraging shoots
and greens, Korba checking on her often. Needing another task

after the midday meal, Nuriya took down the green linen and began to fashion herself a shift; even a simple tunic would be
beautiful in this fabric. As before, she kept her mind focused clearly on sewing or she forced it firmly toward the man with raven
black hair.

6.

Anat

ᘓᘔ

y the time the healer returned from her offering the next
morning, Nuriya was draping her finished shift over her
strong body. "How do I look?"

"Like spring," Korba answered with bittersweet sentiment.

"Can we go to the market today?"

Though puzzled by her choice, the healer made no argument
to deny her.

Nuriya walked into market that day with a sense of destiny
about her. Korba worried about revisiting so soon the site of her
assault, but Nuriya carried a single-minded focus that did not
acknowledge her trauma. Korba worried how the market workers
and others who knew would react, but it seemed that the crowd
parted before her daughter and approved of her bold action.

Midway up the street, Nuriya stopped to examine fruit, and
sure enough the vendor's son tripped over himself to impress
her. She graciously visited Kepi and practiced phrases of Egyptian. The spice vendor caught Korba's eye, but the healer shook
her head and continued following her daughter. The younger
woman tarried at the cloth merchant's table, admiring a length
of purple wool and the fabric next to it dyed with lapis lazuli.

She continued down the street, examining vegetables she would not be buying, even greeting the gruff-mannered fish seller. Korba recognized the moment that her lingering was rewarded, the moment she spotted the Magistrate's son. He was walking in their direction, speaking with another soldier. The two men stopped in front of the caged birds, the other soldier making a shallow bow and turning back the way he had come.

Ilobaal noticed Nuriya with a jerk of his head. A smile swept his face and Nuriya answered in kind. He wove his way through groupings of people and stood before her. "Lady Nurija," he said, rolling her name on his tongue in accented Maltese, "I am pleased to see you."

Nuriya looked breathless with excitement, but she responded in perfect Canaanite, "Thank you, sir, Ilobaal of Tyre."

The young man's smile broadened and he switched to his native tongue. "I am honored to meet you under more calm circumstances, Lady." He bowed low then courteously returned to Maltese to say, "Greetings, Healer Korba," and again bowed low.

"Greetings," Korba replied with reserve.

"May I buy for you a treat?" Ilobaal asked brightly. "We celebrate this meeting by chance." He guided them into an alley off the main street where an elder woman sat fanning an assortment of pastries. "Gorli, three of your most delicious sweetcakes."

Nuriya's eyes lit up when she took a bite. "So good," she cooed.

"My mother makes sesame cakes for festival days, but no one makes them as sweet as Gorli's."

Korba cleared her throat. She had trouble following Canaanite, and no wish to make the effort.

"Excuse me, Healer," Ilobaal said in Maltese. "I tell Nurija that mother of mine," he touched his chest, "also make sesame sweetcakes." He pointed to the vendor's pile.

Korba nodded, feeling uncharitably annoyed at his childish gesturing.

"I hope you enjoy." He tactfully kept his attention on the older woman until she finished eating then turned to the vendor. "Wrap two for the ladies." He handed the cakes to Korba and asked, "May I visit your home tomorrow?"

Korba glanced toward her swooning daughter. "You may," she said, without enthusiasm. "The flag is up if we are home." Mother, help us, Korba said to herself.

"That is well. I will see you tomorrow, Gods willing." He bowed to Korba then turned and bowed to Nuriya, lingering on her lovely, adoring features.

The next morning Nuriya awoke feeling her heart as light as the clouds soaring in the lapis sky. She put on a pot of mushrooms and dried meat, and when it simmered went to forage for greens. She was working in the garden when Ilobaal crested the hill at the Standing Stones. "Ilobaal is here!" she called to Korba and ran to wait by the fire ring. She stood there, beaming, as Ilobaal tied his horse and walked up the path. He walked slowly, seeming to fill his eyes with her. Nuriya felt her cheeks flush and her chest rise in the quick rhythm of her breath.

"Welcome, young man. Come sit with this old woman," Korba boldly called as she settled onto her customary seat.

"Thank you, Healer Korba," Ilobaal said graciously. "I brought you more treat."

Korba accepted the sweetcakes, handing one to each of the young people and taking one herself. They ate without speaking, Ilobaal poised as though he were conducting a critical summit, Nuriya forcing herself to swallow, so fluttery she felt inside, and Korba cutting her discerning eyes at their guest.

After finishing his cake, Ilobaal brushed off his hands and flung them wide, encompassing Mnajdra, the Standing Stones and the sea beyond. "Beautiful kingdom you live in," he said grandly, initiating the conversation.

"Queendom," Korba corrected dryly. "These are temples to the Great Mother after all."

"Excuse me, please. I am unfamiliar." Korba moved to pour tea and Ilobaal accepted the mug with formality.

"Have you seen Ta' Silġ, the temple above port?" Nuriya asked shyly.

"In fact, my father is rebuilding it."

"Oh?" the women chorused.

"He is using the old temple to build a shrine to Goddess Asherah." Concern flashed across his elegant features. "Is this disrespectful?"

The young people looked to Korba who, after a considering pause, replied, "I believe the Mother is pleased whenever Her temple is used as holy sanctuary."

Nuriya turned a relieved smile to her rescuer. "Good," he said, holding her gaze. Before the moment became awkward, he asked, "Do you know the Goddess Asherah, Lady Nurija?"

"I do not," she confessed.

"I raised Nuri here," Korba interceded. "I taught her the Goddess I honor. She is the Great Mother, Who gave birth to all things."

"Then She is like Goddess Asherah," Ilobaal announced.

"Tell us of Asherah," Korba suggested.

"Asherah is the wife of God King El-Al, King of all the Gods," he said with enthusiasm. "Asherah is 'She who Treads Upon the Waters.' She is the Mother of seventy Gods. Therefore, She is like your Goddess, Great Mother."

"I would not say They are the same," Korba drawled. It was her opinion that the naming of Gods—Father God, Mother God and Children Gods—was simply a way for men to divide power among themselves and led to no good thing. But with this particular example she had a different objection. "I believe if that Asherah wants something accomplished, She must first ask Her Husband."

Nuriya's jaw dropped, but Ilobaal responded as if debating native witches was an everyday occurrence. "Goddess Asherah can strongly influence King El-Al, Healer Korba."

"That is helpful I am sure, but it is El-Al Who decides to reward or punish, and not because He is wisest, but because He is the King. Is this not so?"

Nuriya gasped.

"The Gods fight El-Al if They do not like His decision," Ilobaal countered. "But Madame Korba," he raised a hand to halt her further response, "we Phoenicians do not force our religion. The warriors are here only to protect the trade route."

Korba seemed shocked that the young man had matched her bluntness. While she composed herself, Ilobaal tactfully looked away. Nuriya met his gaze, instantly feeling a pressure in her chest like a smile grown so large it couldn't be contained. Only when Korba cleared her throat, deliberate and loud, did Nuriya avert her eyes.

Ilobaal turned back to the healer and spoke with excessive courtesy, "Kind Mother, forgive me any rudeness. I would be most interested to see your Great Mother Temples."

"That can be arranged," Korba said crisply. Then after a long-drawn silence, she changed the subject entirely. "It is seldom we have a visitor from port. Tell me news from Phoenicia while I take my tea." She picked up her mug and sipped with exaggerated slowness.

Ilobaal composed himself to directly face the healer. "The news is as usual, Madame. Assyria fights like a beast. Tilgath-Pilner," he spat out the name of the Assyrian king, "obliterates every alliance we forge but we shall see if the dolphin or the beast wins this game. Assyria takes our land, but Tyre is a dolphin. Every year we build colonies farther west. Today we build on Malta, next year on Sicily, then Sardinia, and so on."

"I was in Sicily once," Korba said, her demeanor transforming with the sweet memory. Sicily was the first stop on a long-ago summer's journey, the first time she made love to her husband.

"How came you to travel there?"

"I was the cook on a Phoenician merchant galley."

"Do you speak Canaanite?" Ilobaal asked in his native tongue.

"I manage," the healer replied, but continued in the local dialect, commenting, "you speak Maltese well."

"Erdu is my tutor. I study well to learn." Then his expression became serious and Ilobaal spoke in a confidential tone, "I will tell you the problem with Sicily. Do you know the people Greek?"

"I have heard of them. They come from the east and bring with them many Gods."

"And many warriors. They built a colony on the east coast of Sicily, very large and very fast. Our trade route is along the west coast of Sicily, but there will be trouble with them, I think."

Korba withheld the reply on the tip of her tongue—about men vying over what was not theirs to begin with—and into that lull in conversation Nuriya blurted, "Korba-ma, may I take Ilobaal to see Mnajdra now?"

The healer took her time in replying. She considered that this brash young man was the answer to her temple prayers, for he clearly had the power to protect Nuri in ways she could not. But wasn't this—courtship, if that's where this was heading—too soon? True mother of Nuri, Korba silently pleaded, help me to understand your plan. Then she surrendered to unseen forces at work. "You may show Ilobaal our temple. I will gather my things and follow down." As they got up to go, she touched Ilobaal's arm. "Young man, treat my daughter with respect."

"Yes, mother," he replied with automatic acquiescence.

Nuriya moved barefoot with confident light steps over the path she had walked nearly every day of her life. She felt like she was swimming, so fluid her motion, a silver quick fish followed by a great sword fish. She felt her hips against the cloth of her shift and wondered what Ilobaal saw. She wanted to dance for him, prance for him, to be admired in his gaze. She picked up her pace, hopping over stones then turned to let him catch up. His physical presence startled; her thighs flushed and a shiver moved through her body. She hurried on to Mnajdra, rounding the boundary wall and waited in the courtyard, her nerves twanging with aliveness. When Ilobaal came to stand next to her, the part of her body near him felt deliciously like it was melting. Neither spoke as they waited for the tap-thwack of Korba's descent. When the healer rounded the wall, Ilobaal asked, "Will you join for the tour?"

"I want to do some cleaning. I will leave the tour to Nuri." Korba began sweeping the bricked courtyard; she could allow the young people time to themselves and still be within hearing range.

They went to the lower temple, Ilobaal stepping inside first. "Magnificent!" he exclaimed, sounding truly surprised. While the outer walls of the temple were an array of interestingly eroded megaliths and rubblestone ramparts, the inner walls were smooth and finely quarried limestone. Tall blocks formed the circumference of circular rooms. Horizontal blocks were laid across the uprights, each successive ring of blocks laid narrower than the last to form a corballed roofline. The right front room was halfway domed over but the left was mostly open to the sky, with a number of ceiling slabs strewn on the ground. "There was earthquake," Ilobaal declared.

"Earthquake?"

Remembering he could speak in his native tongue, he went on to explain, "This is how the Temple Astarte looked after the Great Earthquake. The stone blocks were thrown to the ground by the shaking of the earth." He turned in a circle. "Altars everywhere. Is there an eternal flame?"

"There are fire rings..."

"Those openings," he interrupted, pointing to square holes carved into vertical blocks at waist height. "Do they lead to a room beyond?" Nuriya nodded slowly as Ilobaal peered into a nearby doorway. She willed him not to step inside, in case she had left something that might embarrass her; the small room had been her private playroom when she was young, the openings being perfect spy holes.

"An Oracle chamber!" he exclaimed. "Fantastic!"

"Oracle chamber?"

Ilobaal turned to her, as if struck with inspiration. "Lady... Are you an Oracle?"

"Oracle?" she puzzled.

"Do you speak to the Gods? Foretell the future?" He stepped close, excitement in his dark eyes. "The night I met you, you were in a trance, like an Oracle."

Nuriya broke from his gaze, not wanting to think of that night. She composed herself and looked up, to find him studying her.

After a moment, he smiled cryptically, saying, "We need not speak of it yet." Then he turned and strode diagonally across the hall toward another stone doorway, this decorated with thousands of carved pits, creating an illusion of shimmering as one approached. "Profound," he said and indicated the room beyond. "Is any ritual required in order to enter?"

"I...don't think so".

He stepped over the threshold. "This temple is in much better condition than Ta' Silġ," he said looking around. "Do any ritual objects remain?"

Nuriya stepped over the threshold to join him. "Korba found six Goddess statues and a few bowls." She was astonished to discover that she and he now stood very close inside a very private space. She forced herself to keep talking. "Anything that was not hidden..." Ilobaal stepped toward her, "...was smashed." The end of her sentence was the breath of a whisper. She was staring at the dark, curling hairs in the neckline of his tunic. She could ruffle them with her breath.

"Lady, I was worried about you."

"You were?" She felt utterly dazed and didn't remember, nor care, to what he referred.

"That should never have happened. I don't want anything like that to ever happen again." She was self-conscious to the extreme to be standing so close to Ilobaal! The handsome, the brave! "Do you understand what I am saying?" he asked her.

"I guess so," she stammered.

Ilobaal cupped her chin and tilted it up. She shuddered at his touch. His brows were creased over his serious, handsome eyes. "I care for you," he said. He leaned and with the lightest touch, pressed his lips to hers. It dazzled Nuriya—the intensity of his masculinity, gentling itself, for her. She closed her eyes to memorize the sensation spreading through her face, her throat, her breasts, her sex. Not knowing what else to do, she turned then and stepped out of the chamber.

The rest of the tour was a blur. Nuriya described altars in a chatter bird voice though all she wanted to do was swoon.

Whenever she turned back, Ilobaal was looking her, not at the altars she described, which made her more flustered. When Korba stuck her head inside to call, "What do you think of our temple?" both of them jumped.

"Magnificent!" Ilobaal said loudly then recovered his poise and amended more calmly, "This is a beautiful temple, Healer Korba."

"Do you want to see the other building?" Nuriya chirped.

"Of course, but now I must return to port."

"Won't you stay? I made a meal."

He smiled to show that he was charmed. "I will stay and eat with you."

☙☙

Ilobaal paced himself up the hill with Korba, stopping often so she could point out to him how the shape of the temples matched the shape of the Goddess statues. After enjoying the tasty soup, he thanked them profusely and asked if he could call again.

"You may call on us," Korba answered authoritatively, making the granting of visits her prerogative.

"I will come on market day."

"Maybe we can come to market to see you," Nuriya suggested brightly.

"Oh, no. I will bring anything you need. Tell, and I will bring it."

"The walk is good for us," Korba said, wondering at the edge in Ilobaal's response.

"I insist. Wait here." Ilobaal used a commanding tone and as he hurried to his horse, Korba bristled, while Nuriya was simply awed.

When he returned carrying a leather knapsack, Korba asked tightly, "Are you insisting that we wait here for your visit?"

"Dear mother, I make the journey and back in less time than you walk one way. Here, let me show you." Without delay he removed from the knapsack a flat wooden box. He opened the hinge to reveal two surfaces of wax, one smooth, the other marked with etchings. Korba was immediately drawn to the object, never having seen a diptych up close.

"You can write?" Nuriya squealed.

"Of course. Not pretty like the scribe, but well enough." He circled his wrist, flourishing the stylus. "I will bring for you bread." He pressed the tool into wax, making symbols right to left. "And wine." He made more shapes then touched the stylus to his chin in a pose of thought. "What more may I bring for you, Mother?"

Korba patted Ilobaal's arm, charmed, annoyed, and baffled how to respond. "That will be fine. If we are not called out we will see you here market day."

Ilobaal closed the box and tucked it under his arm. "Good bye, Lady," he said bowing, and kissed them each on the back of the hand.

❦❧

That evening Nuriya asked Korba to braid her hair; it had been more than a year since she'd been willing to sit for it. The elder began the process of taming the unruly, freshly washed mane, and Nuriya relaxed into the firm and rhythmic tugging. "Ilobaal seems to be quite interested in you," the healer ventured.

Nuriya dreamily agreed.

"I wonder how boys in his culture..."

"Men. In my culture." Nuriya turned around. "Can't you see how happy I am, Korba?"

"I do see, and I'm glad, but we should know the proper way to go about things."

"You left home when you were my age and you didn't bother with the proper way."

"And it was a problem for us that Davi did not consult his brother."

"Will you stop fussing and braid my hair?" She turned the back of her head to the healer and whispered, "Just let me be happy." Korba resumed braiding. The next time she saw Kepi she would ask her about Phoenician marriage customs.

Suddenly Nuriya hunched over her knees, hair flying from Korba's grip. "My head!" Korba immediately began to massage her neck and encouraged her to breathe deeply. She gave her water, then spoonfuls of honey, and then willow to chew. "Not tonight," Nuriya groaned, and she accepted Korba's every offering, even going to bed early with a sip of sleeping draught.

The next morning Nuriya awoke refreshed and without a hint of pain. Korba finished braiding her hair by the time Bon arrived to take them to see the family in Baqra.

When they arrived at the compound, several women ran up to Korba and helped her from the cart. When Nuriya stepped down, however, a red-faced young man blocked her way. "What's she doing here?" he asked, scowling as if she was abhorrent to him.

"This is my assistant," Korba said loudly, turning back to take in the scene. Bon was already stepping from the cart. A girl ran up to the scowling man and held his arm, repeating, "This is the healer's assistant."

"I don't want her here," he said.

"Essa..." the girl whined. Bon now stood next to Nuriya, his broad chest lifted and his fists clenched.

"Essa!" came a booming command from somewhere out of sight. "Leave the women and come to the fields." The scowling young man shook the girl off his arm, pierced Nuriya with a hateful glare, and strode out of the compound, looking neither right nor left.

"He says the scribe cheated us," a young woman said. "Father doesn't let him go to port anymore because he makes trouble. Are you all right?"

Nuriya nodded, releasing the tension that had gripped her chest. She thanked Bon then began to marvel that she really was all right. Usually when something like this happened she would feel both scared and mortified, and would lament for days afterward at the unfairness of her life—no place for her at port and ever the alien in the countryside. But right now Nuriya felt exceptionally proud of who she was—she was beautiful in Ilobaal's eyes and certain she had a future bigger than anything Essa would ever know.

Korba kept Nuriya near, splitting her attention between the clan and her apprentice, asking her numerous times if she was all right. Nuriya allowed the healer her worry, and even chided herself that she was being too glib about what happened, but all she had to do was remember how Ilobaal spoke her name to feel instantly strong.

The children were doing well but the mother who tended them had succumbed to illness. Korba set about brewing herbs, airing the hut and ordering a chicken slaughtered to make a rich broth while Bon waited close by, and the three left before the men returned from the fields.

Up at the cistern the next morning, as Nuriya bent to hoist a full water jug, she saw Hawk coming round the path. She set down her jug for she hadn't seen Hawk since he offered his gift.

"I was wondering if you want to come visit Blaki," said Hawk.

"I can't just now. I have to get back."

"She's getting big." Hawk grinned, rounding out his arms to shape an enormous belly.

"I'll come soon," she promised.

Hawk looked disappointed then asked hopefully, "Do you want me to carry that?"

"No, thanks. I've got it." She hoisted the jug.

"Come visit," Hawk called after her as Nuriya hurried home.

Just before midday Ilobaal rode up, tied his horse at the fork and headed directly to Korba. "Greetings, Mother. You look in beautiful health." He kissed the healer's cheek and she indulged his flattery. "Hello, Lady Nurija," he said and Nuriya blushed. From a sack Ilobaal produced cheese, wine and bread then pulled out three sweetcakes. He went back to the saddlebags for more supplies and returned with, "A bag of chick peas, and," he gestured to Korba grandly, "cinnamon from the Egyptian seller."

"This is more than we need. I must repay you."

Ilobaal waved his hand. "Nothing of it." He lifted the wineskin. "I am celebrating my pleasure to spend time with you." He emptied dregs from three mugs and began to pour.

Barely had Korba accepted her mug before she commenced, "Tell me, Ilobaal, does your mother live on Malta? I would like to meet her."

Ilobaal continued pouring, a look of concentration, or was it irritation, tightening his brow. "Mother has remained in Tyre with my two sisters. I soon will see her."

"Oh?"

He handed a mug to Nuriya. "Father and I will be in Tyre for the Garland Festival."

"You're going to Tyre?!" Nuriya asked, her eyes popping wide and Ilobaal indulged a moment in those heavenly spheres.

"You will return to Malta?" Korba asked regaining his attention.

"Of course. We will be back before summer."

A thick silence followed. Ilobaal wanted to fill it before more questions came. "I toast my hosts," he said energetically, holding his mug high.

Korba raised her mug but Nuriya did not. "You risk your life to travel before the season," she accused.

"Do not fear, Lady. Do you not know we are the best sailors in all the Mediterranean? We have safe harbor every day if the weather is poor but if by the Gods' luck we sail by day and night by star, we arrive at Tyre in fifteen days."

"I don't believe it," Korba objected.

"We have a very fast ship and the very best crew. Of course, return is twice slow against the current. Please, Lady, join for the toast?" Reluctantly Nuriya raised her mug and they all sipped.

Ilobaal was determined to lead the discussion this day. "Do the ladies know the story of the God Ba'al, Rider of the Clouds?"

Nuriya shook her head, trying not to cough on the undiluted wine.

"Tell us," Korba encouraged settling into her mug; grape wine was a treat.

Ilobaal pulled his mug to his chest. "Ilobaal means 'chosen of Ba'al.'" He swept his free arm to the horizon where towers of cumulus massed on the horizon, saying, "Now is reign of Ba'al time. But soon," he made a cutting motion, "the God Mot will capture Ba'al, and hold Him in death."

"Who is Mot?" asked Korba.

"Mot is God of Death. When Mot has power the land is parched and the dry Sirocco blows. The Goddess Anat will rescue Ba'al from Death, to save the people and the land."

"Tell us of the Goddess Anat," Korba encouraged, leaning to refill her mug.

"Anat is the strongest warrior of all the Goddesses," Ilobaal declared. He recited lines from an ancient text, quoting in Canaanite and then translating for Korba:

Anat slaughters the people of the Western Shore
She destroys the men of the Eastern Sunrise
She hangs heads on Her back
She binds hands to Her belt
Her innards fill with laughter
The liver of Anat with triumph.

By this time he had set down his mug and was using both hands to punctuate his telling. As a boy, he had entertained his mother this way, reciting the texts and acting out the stories of the Gods. His father thought the ancient Gods not appropriate to the age they lived in but his mother had instilled in him a love of traditional religion. Ilobaal's favorite stories were those of the Gods Ba'al and Anat and as a youth he imagined the ingénue Goddess to be his secret lover. As he continued the storytelling, Ilobaal found the Maltese words more and more easily. "Anat pleads with Mot for the life of Ba'al, but Mot is unmoved. From the day to the moon, Anat yearns for Ba'al; like the heart of the ewe to the lamb is Her love for Him." He quoted a text to describe how Anat fights the God of Death:

With a blade She does cleave Him
With a fire She does burn Him
With a mill stone She grinds Him
In a field She scatters the remnants of Mot
To be devoured by birds.

Translating for Korba, Ilobaal summarized, "Anat kills Mot very much." He paused a moment, savoring the women's rapt attention, then continued his telling, "After a long, dry time, King El-Al dreams that Ba'al is alive and sends the Sun Goddess Sapash to find Him. Ba'al battles Mot again but this time El-Al declares Ba'al's victory. Ba'al rides on the clouds. His voice is the thunder! Boom! Kaboom! Lightning is His weapon. And rain returns to the land."

The women sat, stunned in the aftermath, until Korba huffed, "I would never have thought a Goddess could be such a savage."

"Anat is also the Goddess of Love, Healer Korba. She kills because She loves Ba'al very dear. If Ba'al says, 'Put war into the heart of the earth,' Anat will do it. If He says, 'Put loaves of peace into the earth,' this also Anat will do." As he spoke, a notion turned Ilobaal's gaze toward Nuriya and he realized with amazement that she was twin to his Anat, the wild-haired Goddess of his dreams! Oh, Gods, he thought, why do you love me so to bring me such a woman as this?

Korba was shaking her head doubtfully. "A Goddess of Love who kills armies of men?"

"You say the Mother is both life and death," Nuriya countered.

"The Mother welcomes the dying into Her heart but She doesn't revel in their death. This Goddess delights in death."

Nuriya set down her barely touched wine. "I would like to finish showing Mnajdra to Ilobaal."

Korba sighed. She looked like she was ready for a nap but she smiled weakly and nodded that she would follow them down.

"Come," Nuriya said and immediately dashed off. She turned to see Ilobaal following at a walk but she ran on, ducking into the front of the central temple. There she leaned against the north panel, the stone which reflected the first light of the breaking sun on winter solstice, and waited.

Ilobaal rounded the wall like a prince, quite pleased with himself. Nurija was the incarnation of his dream Anat. Why had he not seen it before? Even with her hair tamed back her wildness was apparent, and her complexion against that yellow-gold stone was sublime. He stepped toward her, placing one hand on her waist, and saw ardor in her eyes. Gods, you are too good to me. He leaned forward and kissed her. Her lips relaxed and Ilobaal eased his tongue between them with the same, deliberate, relentless momentum that had propelled him since the moment they met.

Nuriya jerked and ducked her head. Ilobaal waited for her to lift her face. He recognized her shyness and naiveté. You are eager, he reminded himself, but there is no hurry. Besides, he did not know what was acceptable to Korba's God; an unfamiliar temple was not the best place to explore new love. "I would like to see the perimeter," he said stepping back from her and extending his arm. Nuriya took it, smiling timidly and gratefully. They stepped over the threshold and he bowed to her with courtly manners. They could just hear the thwack of Korba's walking stick. "Lady Healer, please join," Ilobaal trumpeted as the healer rounded the wall.

The three strolled around the perimeter. Korba asked questions about sailing and Ilobaal answered politely, all the while plotting how to create time with Nurija away from the temples before he left for Tyre. She was his fate, of that he was certain. Why else would the Gods present him with a woman in the form of Anat? Could she be the ally predicted by the Oracle of Melquart? The prophesy had decreed, "When the Star of the Warrior and the Star of Gold ride with the Lion through the long night, you will meet an Ally." The time of the star alignment was now. Ilobaal had assumed that his ally would be male, but what greater ally was there than Anat? When the Goddess stood before El-Al to petition on Ba'al's behalf, did not El-Al say to Her, "I know, Daughter, that You are like men. There exists not among the Gods contempt like Yours. What do You desire, oh Maiden Anat?" No, one could not imagine a more perfect ally. In what way, he wondered, would she help him? Nuriya bent to pick a buttercup just then and the curve of her hip required his immediate attention. Oh, yes, Nurija. You, the Gods have sent to me.

Already Ilobaal felt he should be back at the docks. If he wanted a private moment with Nurija before he sailed, he must move quickly. He cleared his throat. "I must journey to Jaws Harbor in two days' time. Would the Ladies join for the excursion?" Nuriya turned to her guardian, and the old healer hesitated. It annoyed Ilobaal, she was not the girl's father. With excessive courtesy he pressed her. "I must survey the area for future development. It would please me to have your Ladies' company."

"Korba-ma, let's go. We need to check on Caron." Nuriya touched Ilobaal's arm, all flushed with eagerness, her earlier shyness forgotten. "Do you know Tarxien, Ilobaal? It's on the way to the Jaws."

"I will take you, yes."

"Ilobaal will take us, Korba. Please."

Laggardly, the healer yielded. "We will join you if there is no call for our healing," she said, making her reluctance known.

With the abundant rain followed by days of cool sunshine, the rocky hillside was blanketed with new growth and the women spent the next day harvesting storksbill, mustard and fennel shoots. Nuriya took a basket of greens over to Bon's, some they packed into jugs with vinegared mead and then they enjoyed a delicious salad for supper.

Nuriya hummed that evening as she massaged rosemary oil into Korba's legs. She worked strong fingers between the bones of Korba's feet, musing dreamily, "I know Ilobaal will take me to Tyre someday..."

"Dear child, go slow with your heart."

Nuriya dropped her hands to her lap. "I'm not a child anymore, Korba."

"No," the healer said wistfully, "not a child anymore." Then she reminded Nuriya of a recent conversation she'd had with Rena after she gave birth to her fifth child. Nuriya groaned but resumed her massage and did not interrupt Korba's retelling of how to prevent pregnancy using the seeds of wild carrot. Afterward, Nuriya went back to humming. It was not babies she was thinking about. She could hardly believe her fortune to have met Ilobaal, the fulfillment of a thousand secret dreams. He was handsome, and brave, and mannered, and if she were to become Ilobaal's wife, she would never again be the outcast. She would live in port, in a home with real walls, and have a real family, and maybe her father would come back to live with them.

Ilobaal arrived in an ornate wagon belonging to his father, pulled by two oxen. The day was delightfully warm. Clouds like tufts of fresh-pulled wool soared in the brilliant midwinter sky. Ilobaal waited while the healers finished preparing herbs for a patient and when they turned their attention to him, he presented two parcels. The first he gave to Korba. She opened it to find a fine linen shawl. When she looked up to thank him, his attention had already turned. He was shaking out a length of butter yellow silk. Nuriya's hands flew to cover her mouth. Never, never, never had she seen such beautiful fabric. "Let me put it over your shoulders," Ilobaal said but Nuriya could not move. "Don't be afraid. Come." She obeyed then, and felt the queen as he draped the shawl around her.

"It's beautiful. Thank you so much."

"Not nearly as beautiful as the woman wearing it," he murmured so only she could hear.

They left the packet of herbs in the basket at the fork reserved for pick up, and climbed aboard the wagon. Korba arranged herself in the middle and resumed her interrogations.

Ilobaal relaxed into managing the oxen and answering the healer's queries. "My father came here to make successful the Malta colony. He was sent in service to King Hiram of Tyre, like the father of Nurija."

Nuriya lunged across Korba's body. "Do you know my father?"

"I do not know, but I hear he was assistant to Emershell, Overseer of the Dock."

"Oh." Her disappointment was evident. "Could you—when you're in Tyre—if you hear anything..."

"You are wanting of news. Yes. I will see."

"Thank you." Nuriya sank back to her seat, fervently hopeful that after all these years she would hear real news. She imagined Ilobaal introducing himself to her father, and asking for her hand in marriage, and her father being very pleased.

Korba commented that there had been other attempts to build up the port but only when Ilobaal's father came did things quickly develop.

Ilobaal laughed. "My father could make a good business selling rags." He told them how his father had enticed craftsmen to Malta to create a reputation for ship repair and was constructing the cothon, an artificial harbor, to further that reputation, although there was ample sandy shoreline. Building taverns had also been important, but Ilobaal kept to himself his opinion that a brothel was needed if they were to entice more ships to over-winter.

"Will your mother move to Malta?" Korba wanted to know.

"My father will build a house at Motya port on Sicily. Maybe she will come then." More likely, his father would install his mistress in the palatial dwelling he was planning for Sicily. As for her part, why would his mother want to live the frontier life when she was used to the luxuries of Tyre?

"Your father will leave Malta?"

"He prefers Sicily. He prepares me to be Magistrate of Malta."
He puffed up his chest as he said this and Nuriya put her head
to her lap to hide the extent of her open-mouthed grin.

"Tell me," Korba said, "what is the responsibility of magistrate?"

"Number one is to be leader of the council."

"I've wanted to know about the council. As far as I know, no
locals attend."

"No locals except Erdu. The council meets every market day
to decide what will be done for the colony, what to pay for
grain, what tribute for Tyre, things like this."

"Do any women attend?"

"Women?" he asked.

"Women do live here. More families come all the time. On
Lipari we had a council of men and a council of women. In difficult matters it was the women who had final say."

"Were they priests? In Tyre, priests have final say over important decisions because they consult the Gods."

"There are no priests on Lipari," Korba chuckled. "But we do
say that women know more clearly the will of the Mother."

By this time they were skirting the hill of Tarxien and Korba
directed him to Borg's land. Children followed from the fields,
laughing and jumping in the back of the wagon. Ilobaal tolerat-
ed them good-naturedly. By the time he and the women in their
fancy shawls dismounted, the entire clan had assembled. Children ran their hands over the carvings of horse and warrior
along the sides of the wagon and looked into the wrapped food
bundles, all the while their mothers called them to manners.
Even Grof came to welcome them and for the first time Korba
saw him smile. Traveling with celebrity had its perks.

Ilobaal was introduced to Borg and he in turn introduced all
his family, beginning with his wife. Borg took the honored guest
by the arm and showed him the compound while the women

administered to Caron. After a brief refreshment of barley beer and bread they got back on their way.

Ilobaal drove them north to the deep double harbor that locals called Sharpjaws and Littlejaw. Sharpjaws was a long channel, edged on one side by a series of peninsulas like the teeth of a long-nosed beast. Littlejaw was a smaller mouth of water protecting the small island called North Rock. A rocky palisade separated the two harbors. Ilobaal drove the cart around the area, skirting and crossing the creeks that emptied into the bays. The expedition eventually dismounted near North Rock and set up a picnic. Ilobaal served bread and cheese, and having noted Korba's enjoyment on his previous visit, another skin of wine. While they ate, Ilobaal spoke of his vision for the Jaws. He would put a "royal city" on North Rock, with a Temple to Anat and a dwelling for its priestess. He looked significantly at Nuriya when he said this, though she could not decipher his meaning. Along the shore he would locate a "city of the people," and, he pointed to the mount that divided the harbors, there he would build temples to Melquart and Astarte. He pontificated about Tyre needing a western fleet and why the Jaws was the perfect harbor for that fleet, located at the midpoint between Iberia and Tyre, Africa and the Etruscan coastline. "Many pirates are on the sea, the Greeks covet our silver, and who is to say what our relations with Carthage will be? Bad blood is between the descendants of Elissa and the family of Hiram."

Nuriya hung on Ilobaal's every word, while Korba listened as to a story teller, enjoying the telling, knowing all the while that Malta was too small to support the future he envisioned. The wine was good and the day was fair; who was she to inject a note of reality?

Two fishermen came ashore and after speaking with them, Ilobaal informed the ladies that the men would row them across the moat of open water to North Rock. Korba declined and without too much deliberation allowed Nuriya to go. "I'll watch from here," she said pointedly. Ilobaal solicitously set her up with more wine and sweetcake before helping Nuriya into the boat.

Nuriya was beside herself, with the sea breeze on her face, the thrill of being on the water for the first time in her life, and the feeling of being a very important person fanned by the curious glances of the fishermen who set their sturdy backs to the oars. They tethered the boat to a rocky mooring on the far shore within eyesight of the healer. Ilobaal helped Nuriya out and gave the men each a copper shekel, promising a second for their wait.

As they walked the shoreline, Ilobaal spoke freely, boasting how he would attempt to speak at King's council while in Tyre. He wanted approval to build something at the Jaws before the inland construction began in the fall.

"What inland construction?"

"We will establish a proper road to mid-island and build an estate there for one of our merchants." He turned to point out the area but the slope obscured his view. He waved in the general direction. "Near the old village."

On the crest of one of the mid-island hills, commanding a view of island and sea in all directions, was a cluster of ancient rubble huts and a crumbling stone wall. The clans who farmed that region rebuilt some of the huts to use as storerooms and put newer farmhouses nearby. "That land is already farmed," Nuriya said.

"Erdu has a contact who is negotiating the arrangement."

Farmers who resented the Phoenician presence at Marsaxlokk would not look kindly on their spread inland, and yet Nuriya had heard no rumor of this news. "Do the neighbors know?"

Ilobaal turned up his palms with a shrug.

"You can't do something like that without consulting the neighboring clans," she challenged with a smile. "How will you know who opposes it? How will you understand their water rights?"

"It is the decree of Tyre that we establish an inland base. The natives will be compensated for any loss."

"But you can't..." she began with stronger emphasis.

"Nurija," Ilobaal interrupted her. "You are sounding like Lady Korba. This is not women's business. We'll speak of it no more." While she sought a proper retort Ilobaal reached for her hand, and then Nuriya quite lost her thread of thought. She became conscious only of the manliness communicating through his palm and five fingers. Ilobaal confirmed that they had passed out of Korba's line of sight and turned to her, brushing back a coil of hair that had loosed from her braid. "You are so beautiful." He lifted her chin. "I want you. Do you know that?"

Nuriya was flooded with a pure and effervescent joy. They were standing on a rock ledge, the sea lapping at their feet. Ilobaal led her to a flat boulder and there she sat, her legs dangling, her nerves twanging with aliveness.

"I need to tell you something, Nurija. I want you to listen, and not to worry." As she wondered up into his serious, elegant face, Ilobaal leaned close and whispered, "It won't change a thing about how I feel." Then instead of telling her, he kissed her full on the mouth. Her breath caught, but she had promised herself a hundred times that if he kissed her again, she would kiss him back. She did—and it was wonderful. Ilobaal put a hand on her breast and a thrill like lightning shot throughout her body. His kiss grew stronger, and a magical feeling awakened inside her, like melting and smiling and screaming all at the same time and she wanted it to fill every part of her. But all of a sudden her body lurched like she lost her footing. Dark gravity pulled and she couldn't get breath. She felt cold, and deep, like at the bottom of a cistern. Ilobaal stopped caressing and was calling her name, "Nurija." She wanted to go to him. "Nurija!" He shook her and she felt herself rise, emerge finally, into light, his face, her hero.

"What happened?" his tone was sharp.

"I'm fine, I just…"

"Just what?" he snapped. "You fainted." His hands were hard on her shoulders. "Should I get Korba?"

"No. Please. I'm sorry…" She was lying on her back where Ilobaal had lowered her. She felt strange—hysterical—and Ilobaal was staring at her, looking angry. She pushed up to sitting and hid her face in her hands, breathing hard, trying not to cry. Ilobaal wrapped his arm around her, saying, "Don't cry," which then made her cry in earnest.

"I'm sorry," she hiccupped.

With his arm about her shoulders, Ilobaal began telling her a story. It was a story of the Goddess Anat fighting the God of the Sea and drinking Him down like beer. He made it more and more ludicrous until finally she laughed out loud. "That's better," he said, sounding pleased. "I should get you back now. I would not want to incur the wrath of mother Korba."

"No, you would not want that," Nuriya said, implying fearsome consequences.

Ilobaal held her hand as they strolled back around the rocky point. He seemed at ease, his displeasure with her passed and Nuriya marveled once again at her good fortune.

When the boat landed on the shore, they packed up and headed home. Korba resumed the role of inquisitor. "When do you sail for Tyre?"

"As soon as the portent is good. Likely in three days or four." That launched a lively discussion of sheep liver augury that kept Korba's interest for most of the ride.

They dismounted at the fork, all tired and fairly relaxed. "Thank you, dear mother, for your company. I bid you have a good night," Ilobaal said to Korba. To Nuriya he spoke in a low tone, "Tomorrow I will be occupied, but the next evening, I promise I will come to you. I must see you before I go." He kissed her hand, murmuring, "My beautiful Anat." She watched him disappear past the Standing Stones, feeling glorious and strange that he had called her by the name of the Goddess.

She retied the welcome flag and noticed in the basket a wedge of Sema's cheese topped with a bunch of yellow and white flowers...from Hawk, surely. She was in such a grand, good mood that she didn't begrudge Hawk's gesture. She inhaled the broom and sweet alyssum then called out loud, "Ilobaal-wants-me," and on the last word, tossed the stalks to the wind.

The next day, as Nuriya struggled to focus on weaving, with her anticipation of Ilobaal's visit making her crazy with distraction, a message was sent from their neighbor, Cassia, asking Korba to look in on her aging mother. Nuriya went with her.

"Hello, dears," said Coral in a frail, high voice as she tugged her blankets tighter round her neck. She coughed weakly then added, "Cassia needn't have bothered you."

"It's no bother for an old friend," Korba said. "Let's have a look. Stoke up the fire, Nuri." Korba clucked over Coral's swollen glands then cajoled her to her side so she could listen to her rattling lungs.

Coral lay back and told her healer, "I'm not much longer for this world, I think. But I'd like to see my next great-grandbaby born before I go."

Suddenly Nuriya felt a sharp jabbing behind her right eye. "I'll be back," she said and stepped out into the cloudy afternoon. She walked briskly, her hand to her head, saying, "No, no, no," to the pain, and to herself: "Coral is old. She will die and it's all right. It's the way of things." She pulled willow from her bag and stuffed it into her mouth. She chewed bark, massaged her temples and wondered why the headaches were coming back. When the pain lessened, she went back inside. Medicine was already cooking and the two old women were chatting amiably about Coral's clan. Nuriya tended to the fire, resuming her role.

After supper her headache dissipated completely and Nuriya returned her thoughts to anticipating her magnificent future with Ilobaal of Tyre.

The next morning, as soon as Nuriya awoke, she asked Korba, "Can we go to market today?" Korba thought it a fine idea.

The healer had always imagined that Nuri would bond with a Maltese man of the land and, as distasteful as the idea was to a woman from Lipari, she intended to do as Maltese fathers did, that is, "negotiate" with the father of her suitor. But with Nuri daydreaming about marrying the man from Tyre, Korba needed to learn about Phoenician customs and learn quickly. She even had the bold thought she might be introduced to the formidable father before they sailed.

They packed snacks, shawls, and walking stick and set out as soon as the chores were done. It had rained in the night, brief but hard. Now the sun danced through multi-hued clouds and the air was fresh with the scent of wet green earth.

When they got close to port they saw that there was more than market day going on. Dozens of purple pennants flew aloft two galleys and an unusual amount of traffic moved up and down the alleyway. The crowd parted and Ilobaal's father strode toward the Astarte shrine. Kepi was among a crowd of locals hanging back by the fork. She caught Korba's eye and motioned her over while Nuriya edged closer to the action.

Nuriya was delighted with their timing. Ilobaal had told them there would be the reading of the liver of a sacrificed lamb but had discouraged them from coming to watch because his father wished it a private affair. It hardly looked private with soldiers and sailors and market workers crowded round. There was Ilobaal, next to the shrine, in a fine long robe with a wreath on his head. His father's voice boomed an announcement that Nuriya was unable to make out.

A procession from the shrine led to the gaily decorated ships. Uniformed men paraded the deck, placed incense in the sterns, and descended to parade up the alley with the crowd surging behind. As Ilobaal passed abreast where Nuriya stood, he spotted her. A strange expression crossed his face. He spoke to his father and a sharp word was returned. He nodded to Nuriya and moved on. She would have liked him to stop but understood that he was involved in an important ceremony. She considered whether or not to follow the crowd when Korba came bounding toward her like a fury.

"We have to go."

"Did you see him?"

Korba grabbed her hand. "Yes. We have to leave. Now."

"What's wrong?"

The healer's gaze swept the line of dark clouds on the horizon. "There's an emergency," she said ominously.

She dragged her charge almost to the village before Nuriya finally said, "Let go now. I'll walk. But you have to tell me what's wrong."

"I will." But Korba didn't, not until much later, when they were within sight of home. "Did Ilobaal tell you why he's sailing to Tyre?"

"For the festival. To see his mother."

"Did he say anything else?"

"No." The small word reverberated inside Nuriya's mouth, containing worlds of uncertainty. Before she fainted, he wanted to tell her something, something that might upset her.

"He's going to Tyre to be married."

The words cut like a knife, entering below the ribs and tracing a crescent through the gut. Nuriya doubled over. Then she lifted her eyes and glared at the pain in her teacher's expression. "I don't believe you," she said and then she ran.

Nuriya sat on the bench facing the path, cinching her thoughts and feelings tighter and tighter. There, pinched in all her being, she waited.

When the elder healer arrived she sat nearby, watching ominous clouds drift landward, reflecting on her conversation with Kepi: "The Magistrate's son is going to Tyre to marry a princess."

"The Magistrate's son?"

"Um hmm. 'Ilobaal of Tyre' he calls himself. No Garland Festival for us this year. Everyone who is anyone is going to Tyre. They need to prove loyalty to a king who has the nerve to ask them to sail this early. You wouldn't catch me on the sea before the longest day."

"Ilobaal of Tyre is courting Nuri."

"Hmph. He may be courting her, but not to be his wife."

A clatter of hooves announced Ilobaal's arrival in the thickening dusk. "Greeting healers," he called, forcing his voice gay.

Nuriya stood and pushed past him. Turning from Korba's accusing glare, Ilobaal followed her down the path to Mnajdra. When he stepped into the lower temple, Nuriya turned on him. "What did your fine augury predict?" she demanded.

"If it rains tonight and is clear on the morrow, it will be Astarte's blessing," Ilobaal said, his voice even and his expression blank. "We're ready to leave at first light."

"Did Astarte also bless your wedding?" Nuriya hissed.

A nervous smile played about his lips. "That is what I wanted to tell you, Nurija. I am to marry the grand niece of King Elulaios, daughter of Zacardon and Eliah. But dear, it needn't change anything between us."

A strangled grunt emitted from Nuriya's throat. "Does the princess know how you entertain yourself on the side?"

"She is not a princess..."

"I am a fool!"

"You are not a fool. I love you." He spoke this declaration carefully, as if marveling at his own words.

"Don't say it!" She raised a hand to cut off his speech... Because I will believe you, she told herself. I will believe you and you will leave me.

"I will have a marriage in name, but I have the right to love whom I please."

"And what right do I have?" she shouted. "Do you think I dream of a future here?" She waved toward her hillside home.

"I am going to build a beautiful home for you on North Rock. You will see."

Nuriya clenched her fists, growling her pain.

"I met the daughter of Zacardon once, at the agreement negotiation, before ever I knew you, Nurija. The king wanted ties to his colonies and it was done." He did not tell her what a coup this was, marrying into the royal extended family, or that the warship he brought to Malta last spring was his condition for the bargain. "I promise you, Nurija, we can go on as before. My father keeps a household in Carthage for his mistress..."

"You think I want to be your mistress? Did you not consider my dreams? To be your wife—to have a family?" She choked on the words.

"You wouldn't want to be a magistrate's wife," Ilobaal chided as to a petulant child. "Your life would be full of duties. You don't know the festivals."

"Now you insult my upbringing! At least I was raised to think for myself!"

"Nurija, I want nothing more than to spend time with you. You are my destiny. Ba'al and Anat were not husband and wife, but theirs was the greatest love story of all time..."

"I-am-not-Anat," she seethed, covering her ears. But the image of the warrior goddess wearing a belt of severed hands appeared, unbidden before her eyes. *Go away!* she commanded the image in her mind, but the menacing Goddess stayed, growing clearer and larger until wild, savage Anat filled every part of her. Anat's fierceness steadied Nuriya somehow, and brought her an unexpected calm. She did not know if it was a good thing, or a bad thing, but a conviction rose within that strange calm: I will claim something for myself. That conviction became like a solid thing, a shield to protect her shattering heart. She dropped her hands saying, "Make love to me."

"What?"

"You want to." She hardly recognized her voice. She reached for Ilobaal's hand and placed it on her breast. Fear ripped through her. *Anat, stay with me!* she begged. She placed Ilobaal's other hand atop her thigh. Lightning flickered in a distant cloud. The rain would come. She wanted to weep but filled her mouth with him instead. She would not lose him before ever she had him. She would drink him in as the Goddess Anat drank down the God of the Sea. Her dream of being his wife was crushed, and the taste was bitter, but she would be fierce, now, in her decision to experience this man as a woman.

Nuriya stood naked as the first cold drops began to fall. After a long and deep throated kiss in which she did not faint, and she did not falter, Ilobaal drew her back under the overhang, lay down his cloak and peeled off his tunic.

"Nurija" He gazed at her, a starving man before his desired feast. He kissed her breast, then her throat, then her mouth. He closed his eyes as if reciting a prayer and then pushed into her.

Nuriya stifled a cry as pain shocked inside her, whether tearing or memory she did not know. *You want this!* she screamed inside her mind. *Anat, be with me,* she prayed, over and over, until she moved beyond fear and pain, and a new mystery overtook. Space she did not know existed opened within to embrace this man; a new territory of her being watched, awed, as he moved inside, saying her name into her hair, into her shoulder, into the night.

The moment for Nuriya was an indefinable thing, and not altogether wholesome. It was magic and amazement—but also anger and defiance. Still, she told herself: remember this, before she moved beyond thought.

She felt Ilobaal's release more in the air than inside her body. It felt as if lightning had struck very near and then he sagged into her, his weight bringing her back into thought. Her heart clutched and she squeezed him tight.

Ilobaal opened one eye. "I love you," he said.

Do not believe him, she told herself. Do not feel his words. She had to draw herself away as quickly as she had drawn him in. She had to prepare for the next day, and the next, and all the days when she would be here, and he, with another. She would not say: I love you more than Anat loved Ba'al, but said instead,

"You got what you wanted." It was bitter to say for all the chaos of pain and longing inside her.

"Don't say that."

She saw hurt in his eyes. Good. It was she who was hurt beyond measure. She pushed to standing and pulled on her tunic. She bit her tongue until she tasted blood, and listened to the slowing patter of the rain. "Please, leave now."

Ilobaal propped onto his elbow. "I don't want to leave you like this."

Like what? Cold and wet? Ravaged by your lust? Brokenhearted? She would not fall apart in front of him. "I will be fine. I want to think."

"We will have a life together, Nurija, you will see."

The swell of his chest as he tied his tunic wrenched from her another surge of longing. When he slung his sword and bent to situate it, he looked happy—and why not? He had all he desired: tonight, "Nurija," tomorrow, his new wife. He kissed her cheek, saying, "I will think of you constantly."

She stared into the wet darkness that swallowed his form, wiping her cheek as if removing a smudge of charcoal. Then she screamed into the night, even knowing he would not hear, "If you marry, do not return to me, Ilobaal of Tyre!"

She did not go home. When the rain stopped she sank to the ground and there remained until Korba came looking.

The healer set down her lamp and draped a blanket over Nuriya's shoulders saying, "I'm sorry, dear." She kissed the top of her head. "I'll be back."

Nuriya pulled the blanket around her. The ground felt like it was spinning yet she was completely without anxiety for it. "Take me," she said to the spinning void. "Come and get me."

But no visions came, no trance, no blessed darkness. She felt wretched. She was a fool to imagine she could have a happy life—a normal life—that she would be favored by a man like

Ilobaal. Now her heart would be broken along with her tattered soul. And she was ashamed for throwing herself at him, knowing how desperate she would feel afterward. She pushed breath through clenched teeth saying, "I hate you, Father!" for leaving her on this forsaken isle; he could have raised her in Tyre, but instead she was here, on the rocky floor of a ruined building, abandoned by yet another man. She tore at her shift, at her throat, rubbed silt into her hair and crawled from the doorway, banging into an altar, the jolt fraying her nerves so that pitiful wails spilled out, "I don't want to be me. I don't want to be me." Again it started to rain.

Korba returned as the second, brief shower abated, carrying a bundle of firemakings, a mug of borage and her traveling bag. She built a small fire, prodded Nuri out of her blanket and into a dry one then sat with her a long while, her every overture at consolation denied. Finally Korba fished her pipe from her bag, "If you want to talk, Nuri, I'll be here," and she went to the outer courtyard to puff and ponder just what Nuri's true mother had in mind when she sent this young man, and to beseech her and Great Mother, all over again, to watch over her beloved child.

By morning the rain clouds had moved on. Korba, achy from dozing outside, found Nuri sleeping by the cold fire ring. She went up to their dwelling and brought down a barley loaf but Nuri did not rouse for it. Korba sighed and went about their chores. Bon came to fetch medicine for his wife's family; he would be traveling to Gozo to visit them the next day. Korba sent him with an assortment of remedies and again checked on Nuri. She still wanted to be left alone. By midafternoon Korba managed to get her to take tea, but then she only sat glumly, staring into her empty mug. Korba issued a tired reprimand, "Enough. Come home." Nuriya shook her head and Korba muttered that she would know where to find her.

The flatness of the healer's tone stirred Nuriya. "Korba?" The healer's face was gray and weary. Nuriya roused herself to standing, a stiff knee making to give out. She shook her blanket and wrapped it around Korba's shoulders, noting the damp and heat of her skin. How did I not see this coming? she wondered. But she knew how, and her heart seized at the memory. She pushed it aside; Korba needed her. She took the healer's arm and they walked up the path, both of them weak, and Nuriya filled with shame; she was not even a worthy daughter.

She helped Korba change her shift and piled her with blankets. She brought in stones and coals and made a small fire indoors. By then Korba was pushing off blankets, her skin trailing sweat. Nuriya built up the outdoor fire and set a pot on the cook-stones, slicing in rose hips and elderflowers, and found her way to the garden for thyme. When the brew was ready, she made Korba drink then lie back and allow her body to fight its battle.

Throughout the night and next morning Korba alternated between heat and chills with Nuriya making her endless mugs of tea. By late afternoon Korba's temperature had stabilized but she coughed with a hack.

When Nuriya went outside to look for horehound, her emotion nearly overwhelmed her, but she squelched it at the throat; her neck was already sore from all her "not-crying." She picked fennel greens as she passed, remembering she hadn't eaten— two sick healers would help no one. She brought in the pot of grains Korba had prepared the day before.

Nuriya sat with her long into the night. She couldn't remember Korba succumbing to an illness like this, but if she hadn't kept vigil outside Mnajdra she never would have. When Korba's coughing abated enough for her to sleep, Nuriya dozed beside her.

When Nuriya awoke the next morning, the first picture that entered her mind was princely Ilobaal in purple silk. The second image was Ilobaal embracing a beautiful bride. Nuriya slipped into the crisp outside air, her tears blurring the stars in the predawn sky. She went to the garden and dropped to her knees, putting her head to the earth, and pounding, a moan breaking through her clenched jaws. When the intensity ebbed, Nuriya lifted her eyes to see the horizon rimmed with gold. She dusted off her hands and shift, smoothed her hair, and went back to the dwelling.

When Korba awoke later, she announced that she was feeling better. Nuriya bundled her up to sit in the sun. A smile was on the old healer's face, but Nuriya's guilt was not assuaged; it jumbled together with her grief, all of it, a mess.

7.

Ulma

❧

The elder healer was the first to notice the girl waiting next to the Standing Stones. Nuriya waved the cloth and the girl spotted her. She had come from mid-island to seek the healer but it would be Nuriya who would go.

"Bon's away. Get Tul to take you," Korba said.

"We can walk." Nuriya didn't want to run into Hawk. Korba pursed her lips and cut her eyes pointedly toward the young girl who had probably been running since daybreak. Nuriya took in her ragged appearance and amended, "Of course I'll go to Tul's." She was ashamed for thinking of herself first, again. She put grain and greens in a pot for Korba and gathered her supplies. "I wish I could be here to cook for you."

"If you get a ride perhaps you will, but I am perfectly capable of feeding myself." As they were leaving, Korba said sternly, "Get a ride back or spend the night. Do you promise?"

"I promise."

The girl, Leni, had indeed run since daybreak. As they trotted to Tul's, Nuriya learned that her toddler-age brother had been stung by a scorpion the evening before. Her mother had lanced it and sucked the poison, but today, as soon as her husband was off to the fields, she sent Leni for more help.

As luck would have it Hawk was the only one available at Tul's and they couldn't very well wait for someone else. Nuriya visited Blaki while Hawk haltered another ox. She felt awkward and unworthy of Blaki's calf.

When they got underway she tried asking Leni about her brother, but the girl wouldn't talk in front of Hawk. They rode in silence until Hawk commented, "I heard Korba's sick."

"She's better this morning." What else had he heard? It was a long ride out to mid-island.

Leni directed them to a meager compound of several small huts. Nuriya jumped down and went directly to the woman huddled over her swaddled child. The mother lifted a distressed face and uncovered her son's arm. It was swollen and purple beyond a tight bandage. The boy fussed feebly as Nuriya unwrapped the bandage, finding pus at the lancing and discoloration of the skin. She checked the pulse of his other arm, it was too fast, then found that his pupils were of different sizes. Something else was amiss, too... The boy's forehead was abraded and there was dried blood in his hair. "What happened here?"

The woman spoke rapidly in a foreign dialect that Nuriya was unable to follow. Leni stepped forward. "What happened to your brother?" Nuriya asked her.

"He got stung."

"Why is there a cut on his head?"

"Jaron kicked him."

Nuriya forced all emotion out of her voice. "Who is Jaron?"

"My brother."

Nuriya looked toward the mother but her eyes were averted. Another young child crouched behind her. "Why did Jaron do that?"

"Jesi was crying," Leni said. "And Jaron's mean." Her mother spoke again. "Better hurry," Leni told Nuriya. "You should leave before my father gets home."

"Does he know I'm here?"

"No, please," the mother urged.

Nuriya looked to Hawk, wishing he was Korba. "How can I help?" he asked. His voice was steady and reassuring. She could do this. Nuriya told the mother to give her baby dips of honey while Hawk kindled a fire. She crumpled rosemary and rue into steaming water, and as the water took on color, she dipped in a cloth. The mother extended her son's arm and Nuriya dripped the herbed water over the site, wiping away pus. She pressed one end of a short reed to the lancing and blew into the other. More pus erupted. She cleaned the site several times.

With Hawk's help she examined the boy's head, backside and legs. Hawk shared her alarm at the old bruises they found, while the mother stared away, across the field. Nuriya directed Hawk to apply salve to the bruises while she prepared a poultice and pounded rue into honey and flour to form pellets. The baby would take rue pellets morning and night.

As she was showing the mother how to change the poultice, they heard the distinct clatter of an oxcart. The woman clutched her son as if she might flee. Hawk stepped protectively before them while the other children looked on with mild curiosity.

A woman drove into the yard. "Jila," she called, "It's Bete. Is everything okay?"

"Jesi was stung by a scorpion." Though unusually accented, Jila's Maltese was quite proper.

Bete jumped down. "Is he all right?"

The woman loosened her grip on her son and smiled bleakly. "He will be all right."

"I'm glad to hear that." Bete stood over them with her forehead creased. "You can always come to us if you need help. Do you remember where we live?"

Jila looked down. "Yes," she said in a whisper. "I remember."

Bete nodded to Hawk then said, "You must be Nuri."

"I am Nuriya."

"My neighbor saw you turn in here. I'm Ulma's granddaughter, Bete," she said with the expectation that Nuriya would recognize the name. "Ulma fell. Can you see her as soon as you're done here or should I go on to fetch Korba?"

"I'll come. Korba isn't well."

Nuriya finished giving instructions, telling Jila that her son needed to stay in a dark room all day and be monitored throughout the night. She looked up to the position of the sun then indicated Bete with a nod. "I'll stay with this woman tonight. If you have any concern, send one of your children right away. I'll check Jesi again tomorrow."

"When will you come?"

"When should I come?"

"My husband goes to the field at daybreak and comes home midday.

"I'll come midmorning then."

Hawk promised to tell Korba the situation and see to her needs. Nuriya was grateful to him, and watched him go before climbing into Bete's cart. "Do you know Jaron?" she asked as soon as Bete rolled out of the yard.

"I do."

"Jesi has bruises on his head and back. Leni says that Jaron kicks him."

Bete muttered an oath under her breath. "He takes after his father then. I found Jila by the road once. Jaro hurt her pretty bad."

"That's terrible."

"We sent our men over but Jaro won't talk to them. He hardly speaks to his own family anymore. His clan's up there," she pointed to the hilltop where new farmhouses stood alongside ancient huts. "Jaro works his share, but stays down here mostly." Bete glanced sideways at Nuriya. "You don't remember me do you?"

She didn't look familiar. She had a round, earnest face, dark hair and brows so thick they met across her forehead. "Should I?"

"Korba used to bring you to visit when you first lived with her."

"Will your grandmother be upset that I'm coming instead of Korba?"

Bete's eyes reddened. "She doesn't even know me right now."

"I'm sorry."

Bete shook her head and smiled tightly. "No one will be disappointed to see you. You have a good reputation."

Nuriya felt pride at Bete's words and immediately thought of Ilobaal—she wanted him to know that people thought well of her. Then she remembered it didn't matter what he thought. She pushed against the pain and hardened her jaw, forcing herself to focus on her surroundings. They had traversed from Jaro's farm on the lower slope of one hill and were winding their way up the next. Rubblestone huts were scattered amongst terraced fields of tilled soil, vegetables and barley. Nuriya could see down to Jaro's farm on one side and nearly to port town on the other, the sea shining in all directions as far as the eye could see. No wonder Tyre wanted an inland base. "The people from port are going to build up here," she said.

Bete gave her a sharp look. "What are you talking about?"

Maybe she shouldn't have said anything, but why shouldn't Bete know? "They're going to build an estate, over there, I think," she pointed to the hill Jaro's clan shared with others.

"Who told you?"

Nuriya's throat clenched. "Someone from port," she managed.

Bete turned onto a stone-lined path and hurried the ox. "We're here. We'll talk later." She pulled the cart into a semicircle of buildings wrapping a large hearth and well. A man and a woman stood awaiting them. Bete explained about Korba and introduced Nuriya.

The woman held her hands palm up. "Welcome, Nuriya. I am Sky, clan leader."

Nuriya rested her hands on the woman's palms. "Greetings, Sky."

Sky led her to one of the dwellings as a girl came out through the door flap. She was younger than Nuriya, with a thick braid of dark hair and a strong, thin body. Her worried expression lightened when she saw their guest. "I'm so glad you're here. I'm Lili." Bete had explained that her grandmother, Ulma, and Lili, her cousin, were the healers in the family, spending most of their time together.

"I'm Nuriya. How is your grandmother?"

Lili pulled her away from the door. "Not good," she said.

"Tell me what happened."

"Nanna was on a step stringing up nettles. She said something that sounded garbled, and then she just fell." Lili's voice trailed into tears as she said, "It didn't look like she even tried to stop herself." She tightened her jaw and continued in measured tones, "I'm afraid she broke her leg and I think she hit her head. I put a poultice on the hip but I didn't know what else to do."

Nuriya put a hand on the girl's shoulder. "She's lucky to have you, Lili. Let's go in."

The dwelling was pungent with herbs, at first delighting, then reminding Nuriya unhappily of Korba's absence. Ulma lay on the floor, her head, crowned with pure white hair, resting on a roll of blankets. Her eyes were half lidded with no pupils showing.

"Nan," Lili called brightly before she lost her smile and chewed on her lip.

"Grandmother, I'm Nuriya. Can you hear me?" No response. "Squeeze my hands?" No response. Nuriya checked the woman's wrist, pushing away anxiousness as she sought the faint pulse. When she reached to Ulma's temples it felt like something repelled her so she decided to examine the leg and come back to the head. "I'm going to check your leg, Ulma." It felt awkward, but Korba always spoke to her patients even if they weren't able to respond. Nuriya peeled back the blanket and lifted Ulma's shift, made of fine wool with embroidery along the hem. A dark bruise spread across the top of the right thigh beyond the poultice. "May I remove this?" Lili nodded and Nuriya lifted off the pounded leaves. The skin underneath was intact but the area was hot and the color, a deep purple red. "This may hurt," Nuriya said. "I have to check." She felt the bone above and below the line of bruising, on either side, and behind. It was well aligned and she was relieved she would not have to set it.

She sat back on her heels and silently recited the invocation. She hadn't used it for a long time, but she needed to calm herself before this daunting task. In the quiet of the moment, Nuriya could sense the peacefulness of her surroundings. "Your grandmother is well loved," she said aloud.

Lili spoke with her eyes squeezed to slits in her effort not to cry, "What's happening to her? Why doesn't she talk or move?"

The look on Ulma's face was something that Nuriya had seen before. Korba was called to help a man named Peter at the fishing village. Like Ulma, Peter was not dead but neither was he alive. Korba told Peter's daughter that his spirit was on a journey, and like a journey out to sea, there was no telling if or when his spirit would return. His spirit did return but Peter was never the same. He didn't walk and could hardly speak; he lived for some days with his daughter caring for his every need. "I see how much she means to you, Lili. I'll do everything I can."

She looked around to survey what supplies were available, and as she did a small point of pain snuck behind Nuriya's right eye. She determined to ignore it, but it reminded her that she hadn't checked for injury to Ulma's skull. She moved to Ulma's head, and began walking delicate fingertips through her hair.

"It bled there," Lili offered.

Just then the point behind Nuriya's eye sharpened to the level of a screech. Remembering Rdum, when pain left her unable to function, she gathered her will to silently declare, "I am here to help Ulma. I will not let this overtake me." She squeezed her eyes tight, and took slow breaths. She became acutely aware of noises from outside the hut: the scrape of grinding stones, concerned conversations, the sound of wind. She hadn't noticed the wind before, but it obviously was picking up. Suddenly and without warning the wind roared as if the full force of a gale had been unleashed inside the room. She opened her eyes. The room had been plunged into darkness.

Within the fury of wind, a sound caught Nuriya's attention. Someone called. Someone needed her help. Nuriya leaned into the wind, toward the sound, ignoring her own head that pounded like someone hacked it with an axe. Nothing made sense, but there was something she had to do. It mattered...it mattered... There it was—the call. She strained toward it though all around her was chaos and darkness. In the next instant everything changed. As if she had been at the bottom of a churning sea and broke through to the surface, everything became light, and bright, and spacious.

"I am here, Nuriya."

The voice came not from one direction but from all directions. "Ulma, is it you?"

"It is I."

"Where are you?"

"Here. With you."

Nuriya's own head pain was completely gone. It came to her to ask, "Are you in pain, Ulma?"

"No, child. I am at peace."

Ulma's presence surrounded Nuriya. She felt cocooned in peace. She did not question the strangeness of it—all was as it should be. The presence that was Ulma spoke, "My grand-daughter wants me to return."

"Yes."

"You can help me."

"I want to help," she said, though at this moment, Nuriya felt no yearning at all.

"You can heal me."

"How?"

"Look into my eyes."

Nuriya became aware of two ancient eyes gazing into hers. An indescribable feeling of being known filled her. The eyes saw her through and through, witnessed her pain, and her shame, and accepted her without judgment, verily with unconditional love. How badly she needed this.

Then behind the eyes, she saw that something was broken. A place was spilling blood, damaging like a mudslide killing a wheat field, and it had something to do with making Ulma's spirit leave. Alarm rang inside—danger!—shocking Nuriya to her task. There was too much pressure from the blood. It would kill if it continued to grow, and kill quickly.

"I don't know what to do, I don't know what to do," she whined inside, even as she followed her body's impulse to place her hands on either side of Ulma's head. She had to lessen the pressure. She leaned forward, and without knowing why, put her lips to Ulma's forehead. An image came to her of the pressure inside being sucked into her mouth. She sucked then lifted her head and blew. She repeated the motion, lips to forehead, sucking, blowing, and again.

She thought of the wholeness she had felt cocooned in Ulma's peace. She wanted that same wholeness to be here, inside her head, behind her eyes, and she held that thought for as long as she could. Then she waited to know what to do next.

Something compelled her to move to the woman's feet,

though even as she did she fretted inside, "I don't know what I'm doing. I don't know what to do." She held the pressure points on Ulma's feet and found that she was "seeing" with strange sight. It was not flesh and blood feet she looked at, but images like dreams, in the forms of feet. On Ulma's left side she saw busyness, like port town on market day. On her right side she saw a still, barren landscape. She followed the stillness up Ulma's right leg to see how far it went. Through the knee all was quiet, but when she got to the upper thigh there was an explosion of activity. Nuriya was drawn into an image of molten fire oozing from a crack in the bone near the top of the leg. Her strange sight magnified the action and it mesmerized her, the red and the heat mirroring the turmoil in her own heart. She, too, wanted to break bones. She, too, wanted to burn like fire. For the first time since she entered Ulma's dwelling she thought of Ilobaal and imagined him before her, he and his wife, burning in the oozing fire. Her heart grew dark. She forgot what she was there to do.

A garbled sound came from Ulma. Nuriya shot out of her dark vision, appalled at herself. The old woman's eyes were twitching behind closed lids. Nuriya started to hum—it's what Korba would have done. She hummed until a melody and rhythm emerged and Lili's voice joined hers. Ulma's twitching calmed, but then her breath became too slow and Nuriya worried anew—perhaps she wouldn't come back—but she must! Another voice joined their chant from the doorway and three voices put fervent desire into wordless prayer. Tears streamed down Nuriya's face, her longing for Ulma to live, her frustration at not knowing what more to do.

When Lili's voice dropped out Nuriya was afraid to open her eyes. She continued to chant until she heard Lili's tentative plea, "Nanna?" Only then did she dare look. She witnessed Ulma open her eyes and focus on her granddaughter.

"Nan!" Lili shrieked.

Ulma gazed at her granddaughter a long while. "Li-li," she said, a labored breath between each syllable.

"Oh, Nanna." Lili laid her head on her grandmother's chest, and sobbed.

Ulma's coming to consciousness drained away the intensity of Nuriya's focus and she felt suddenly unmoored. Lili turned to her, joy beaming through her tears, and said, "Grandmother, this is Nuriya."

"Nu...a," Ulma said as if trying a foreign tongue.

"Are you feeling pain?" Nuriya asked, ignoring her own disorientation.

Ulma mumbled confusedly then closed her eyes. Nuriya showed Lili points to hold above each eye, while she refreshed the poultice on Ulma's leg. By the time she was finished, the old woman was dozing peacefully, a lopsided smile upon her face, looking like she indulged in a pleasant dream. Sky came forward and sat by her mother's side, resting one hand on Ulma's chest, the other lightly brushing her mother's cheek. Sky caught Nuriya's eye. "Bless you. Thank you."

Nuriya tried to focus on the clan leader's face but her vision still wasn't right. "I think I need air," she whispered. Sky nodded, kissed her mother and rose to lead the healer outside.

Nuriya blinked into bright sunlight and a sea of unfamiliar faces. Sky acknowledged the gathered throng but led Nuriya apart. "Are you all right?" she asked.

Nuriya nodded.

"I don't understand it, but I know you brought her back. Will she...recover?"

Nuriya could see that Sky was hurting from worry and it steadied her to know what to focus on. "Your mother is going to need a lot of help. She has a crack in the bone of her leg and she might not be able to use one side of her body."

A battle of emotions played across Sky's face but she asked, simply, "May the family go in to see her?"

"It would be better to wait."

Seeing Nuriya sway on her feet, Sky put a hand on her arm and called, "Grebe, fetch water." A young girl ran to the well, dipped a mug in a bucket and ran back.

Nuriya put the mug to her lips and drank. The water felt like a miracle in her throat. She closed her eyes and welcomed the silver glow gliding inside. The movement of air in her lungs felt exquisite, and the warmth of the setting sun on her closed lids was almost euphoric. Nuriya felt immersed in a blissful experience of water, air and sun in the same way she was immersed in Ulma's peace in that other place. She smiled...and something within these things smiled back.

When she opened her eyes Sky was looking at her curiously. "Would you like to rest inside?" she asked.

"Yes. Thank you." Sky led her into one of the dwellings. It was neat and spare. On a low table sat a stone lamp and a water jug. Along the back wall hung tools, satchels, and clothes. Sky unrolled a sleeping mat and told Nuriya to call Grebe if she needed anything.

The beautiful experience that Nuriya felt outside was with her still, enveloping her like a cloud, comforting her bruised heart and her tattered soul. Then it streamed through her like a current, and she let it flow, drifting her gently, peacefully into sleep.

Someone tapped on the door covering. Grebe, a pigtailed, bright-eyed, miniature Bete, bore a lit lamp for it had turned dark while Nuriya slept. "Lili wants to know if Ulma can eat." Nuriya rose, feeling quite refreshed and followed Grebe around the cook hearth, the smell of roast meat enticing them. Sky stepped forward. "We sacrificed a goat to celebrate mother's recovery and make broth for her healing. You would honor us to be first at the feast."

"Thank you," said Nuriya, not sure what the honor would entail. "I'm on my way to check her now."

Ulma acknowledged her entrance into the room with the lift of a hand. "How are you feeling?" Nuriya asked.

"A-live," Ulma croaked.

"I'd like to check your hands and feet. May I?" Ulma dropped her head in an abrupt nod. Nuriya held one hand above each foot. "Move your toes?" There was no response so the young healer flicked a fingernail up the left foot and smiled as the toes curled in reaction. She flicked the right foot also but it remained inert. She grasped Ulma's hands and gave each a squeeze. There was responding pressure from Ulma's left, but nothing from the right. "How's that leg?"

"Hh-urts."

"Lily, is that willow?"

"Yes. I just gave her some."

"Give her more." Ulma made a face. "Then you will get a few sips of a delicious broth."

"Lu-cky-me," Ulma managed.

Nuriya pulled out the poppy cake from her bag. "In case she needs it later," she said to Lili. "But I hope not."

Lili nodded. "You should go now. They're waiting."

"Gather!" Josep called to his kin as Nuriya joined Sky next to the hearth. She waited nervously while the clan assembled. Then Sky picked up a bowl containing blood from the goat and spoke in a loud, clear voice, "We thank the earth for our sustenance and goat for our food. We pray for the health of our dear mother Ulma." Sounds of affirmation rippled throughout. Sky placed the bowl into Nuriya's hands and she received it solemnly, not knowing what to do with it. The leader motioned her toward Grebe, who waved her to follow. The girl led the way into a stone walled garden. There, between the borage and the baby cabbages, was a freshly dug hole. "Pour there," Grebe urged. Nuriya knelt and poured out the contents. Grebe sprinkled dirt over blood and they returned to the waiting clan. Sky took the empty bowl, thanked Nuriya and turned to her family, "We eat!"

Women, men and children sprang into action, cutting, stirring, carrying and clearing, handing out bowls and lining little ones in front of the great hearth. Even though the children were served, no one took a bite until Sky watched Nuriya taste her food then told them, "Now you can eat."

Nuriya was seated with Sky and Josep on one side and Bete on the other. Many of the clan introduced themselves during the meal. One older woman took Nuriya's hands in hers. "You have grown into a beautiful woman. We are so grateful you came to help us." She found all the attention daunting.

After the meal Bete leaned over and told Sky that Nuriya knew of a plan to build a Phoenician estate nearby. Sky's eyebrows shot up. "Would you tell me what you know?" Nuriya nodded but before she could begin Sky asked others to join them. Nuriya had to call up her courage when she saw the number of people listening in. As she told what little she knew, angry comments began bouncing around:

"Who decided this?"

"This is our land."

"They have trained warriors."

At that, Sky interjected, "We have no intention of this coming to a fight, but we need to be included in the discussion. Who else knows about this?"

Nuriya hesitated. Was she being disloyal to Ilobaal—who had no loyalty to her? This clan was treating her with respect—unlike that other person. They deserved to know about decisions that would affect them. "Someone negotiates with them through Erdu," she said.

"Who would do that and not tell us?"

"Erdu brings Jaro wine," someone said. "Is that negotiating?"

"Could we speak to you about this after we see what our neighbors know?" Sky asked.

"Yes. And I think I should check Ulma now." She was ready to be done with the unfamiliar group experience. "Thank you for the delicious food," she remembered to say.

Ulma was asleep and Nuriya sent Lili out to eat. They would take turns watching through the night.

When morning sun filtered through the window covering, Nuriya awoke to find Lili dozing at her grandmother's side. With hand motions, she cajoled the girl to lie down on the sleeping mat and went to take her turn. She studied the lines of Ulma's face, wondering what actually happened the day before.

After a time one of Ulma's eyes blinked open. She turned slightly and met Nuriya with a piercing, single-eyed gaze. "Thank you for what you did." Nuriya was astounded to hear her speech, slow and a bit clumsy, but clear.

"I don't know what I did," Nuriya said honestly.

"You met me in another place, and brought me home. You have a gift, dear." Ulma must have noticed the shadow that crossed Nuriya's face for she asked, "What's wrong?"

"Korba said I had a gift. I told her I didn't want it and I prayed for it to go away."

"But why?"

"Because—I can't control it."

"Who can control a mystery?"

"And the pain..." Then she waved her hand to wipe away that concern; it was selfish and trivial next to what Ulma faced.

"I don't know about the pain, but dear, if you refused your gift, I—would—be—dead." She spoke with certainty, her gaze hard on Nuriya's. "Why are you so sad, child?"

Nuriya shook her head.

"Heartache?"

She nodded.

"Ahh."

They were quiet for a time as Nuriya fought with her emotion. When she could hold her voice steady, she asked, "Why don't you and Korba visit anymore?"

"Your Korba and I had a difference of opinion."

"About what?"

"If she never told you, I don't think it's my place. I will say, your Korba can hold a grudge."

The plain-spoken statement surprised Nuriya, but she knew it was true. "Bete says that you're teaching the herbs to Lili. Did Korba teach you?"

Ulma moved her head in a jerk to the left. "All women from Lipari know plants."

"You come from Lipari?"

"My mother did."

"I wondered about Sky being clan leader."

Ulma crooked a smile. "My husband inherited this land through me. He agreed to share decisions, but it wasn't in him." She raised one hand in a gesture of futility then licked her lips. Nuriya poured water and held it for her. Ulma sipped, stretching her neck to aid the swallowing. "When my husband died, I gave leadership to Sky, and I'm here—" her throat caught, "to—overrule." She went into a spasm of coughing. Nuriya massaged her back and chest and Ulma received her ministrations with gratitude then asked Nuriya about herself.

To avoid talking about her heartache, Nuriya tried to put words to the experience of the day before, the presence and the blissful energy.

"Ahh. The Goddess revealed Herself," Ulma said reverently. "She revealed Herself to me, too."

Goosebumps shivered on Nuriya's skin. "What do you mean?"

"When I was in the place where you found me, the Great

Mother showed me Her radiance." Ulma's good eye glistened, and Nuriya longed to be sucked back into its crystalline gaze. "But She told me I needed to come back here and I needed your help for that."

A tumble of questions rose inside Nuriya but she found no words.

"I'm going to make an altar," Ulma announced. "Do you keep one?"

"Korba keeps the altar at Mnajdra."

"Let me tell you something you are not to repeat. My mother used to say, if you pray to a 'fat lady' on an altar, you might forget the Goddess is everywhere." Nuriya's eyes popped at Ulma's irreverence but the old woman continued on, "Mother made us sit in the field and she'd say, 'Do you feel Her, your true Mother? She's all around you.' We pretended she was..." Ulma waggled a finger at her head, "but she taught true." She touched her throat and Nuriya lifted the mug to her lips. She drank more easily this time then lay back, closing her eyes. "Here I've been, all these children, this blessing of land, and I forget to thank Her. That's one thing your Korba does well." Without opening her eyes, she told Nuriya that she must develop her relationship with the Goddess, now that they were "better acquainted." "It will bring you the comfort you need, dear." Ulma drifted gently toward sleep then suddenly bellowed that her leg felt like it was crushed under a rock. Just as suddenly, she faded again. As Nuriya rummaged through her bag for the poppy-heads, Ulma spoke once more, "Tell Korba she's welcome, with or without a peace offering."

When the matriarch was sleeping soundly, Nuriya discussed her care with Lili and promised to return soon. Then Bete took her to see Jila's boy.

Although she had appreciated Hawk's presence the day before, Nuriya was annoyed to find him waiting at the crossroads.

"This is for Ulma," he said before she could comment, and handed Bete a jug of Korba's wine and a fresh made salve. "And Jaro's home."

"I still have to check the boy."

"I know. That's why I'm here."

Hawk's wagon and Bete's cart rolled one after another into the drab courtyard, the contrast with Sky's tidy homestead now glaring. Jaro stood beside his wife, wiry and tense. "Bete," he acknowledged stiffly, then to Nuriya, "Are you the witch?"

"She's the healer," Hawk corrected as he dismounted.

"I already told you, boy, to mind your own business."

Hawk spoke slowly, as if Jaro might be dim, "A friend is my business."

"Well, I don't want your 'friend' messing with my family." He picked up the bowl of rue pellets and threw it across the yard. It smashed into a pile of empty amphoras, the soft pellets splattering everywhere. "Leaves is fine. We always got along fine with just leaves for scorpions. I don't know why she sent for you anyway." Jaro glared at his cowered family and his silent neighbor and spat. "Go ahead, check 'im. But no fancy medicines."

Nuriya's hands were shaking as Hawk helped her from the cart. Jila held her son on her lap. His pupils were more even, and that was the biggest relief. The skin at the lancing was closing without further pus and the amount of redness looked normal. "You did good," Nuriya said.

Jila smiled until her husband cleared his throat to remark, "I don't have all day for this."

Nuriya had wanted Jesi to continue the rue pellets and hoped he got enough the day before. "He needs to be watched carefully," she said.

"He'll be fine."

"I should check him in a few days."

"We won't be needing that. Now what do I owe you?"

"Payment is up to you."

"I don't want to be owing you. What is it?"

Hawk pointed to a half sack of grain next to the amphora pile. "That'll be fine."

"We're done then. Get on now."

Bete wrapped Jila in a hug and reminded her that she was welcome any time. Hawk and Nuriya got into the wagon and left.

"If you go back there, make sure you take me, Nuriya. You can't trust that man. Did he scare you? Are you all right?" Hawk was too upset for his usual awkwardness.

"Yes. I'm glad you were here."

"I knew I had to come when you said you were going to check Jesi. I didn't like how they were all afraid of their father. Did you see all those wine jugs? And Leni doesn't seem right to me. I'm worried about her, too."

Nuriya was comforted riding alongside Hawk as he worried aloud and in earnest. But despite his concern and despite everything that happened at Ulma's the day before, her shame rose to torment her. What would Hawk think if he knew about Ilobaal?

Hawk interrupted the downward spiral of her thinking when he informed her, "Your calf's going to be born soon."

She forced herself to say, "It's all right if you change your mind, Hawk."

"I won't change my mind," he said emphatically. "I won't ever forget what you did." Then, his tongue unstuck, Hawk went on to report about Blaki's health and who else was giving birth, and Nuriya sank back into her own private pain.

8.

The Spiral Altar

⊙⊘

Korba listened intently as Nuriya described Ulma's situation. "I'm sorry to hear it," Korba said.

"Ulma welcomes you to her home."

Korba nodded, but said only that she wanted to harvest chickweed. Nuriya bundled her warmly and walked her to an abundant patch outside the garden wall before excusing herself. Ulma's words bubbled inside her, "Your Korba is a good woman, but she is sometimes too serious."

Nuriya wanted to get some rest, but after staring unpeacefully at the roof thatching, she decided to follow Ulma's advice and find a place for her personal altar. She clung to the promise: "It will bring you the comfort you need." Ulma said that her altar could be anywhere that helped her remember her relationship with the Goddess. Nuriya didn't care about *relationship* just now, but she desperately needed that promised comfort.

She wandered downhill, away from the garden, and found a rock to sit on that gave an expansive view of sky and sea. She closed her eyes and filled her lungs as best she could, the chill air hiccupping over the knot that remained in her throat. It wasn't long before a sob broke through her best effort at calm. She had a good cry, and afterward, she felt better. She marked the place with three stacked rocks and wandered on.

She headed up toward the Standing Stones temple. With their dwelling overlooking Mnajdra, the healers rarely used the Standing Stones other than as a landmark by which people located them. Walking up from below, the four megaliths at the south boundary looked like giant, shrouded beings nodding toward the sea. The entrance trilithion was itself impressively bold and Nuriya paused before it, remembering the temple's true name that Korba had taught her: "Ħaġar Qim." She stepped inside.

At some time in the ancient history of the temple the central altar had been removed to create a long hallway front to back. Nuriya's legs gave a buzzy sensation as she walked the passage. Twenty paces beyond the back doorway was another small building, and beyond that a stand of oaks. Nuriya turned back inside. The alcove on her left was the most perfectly formed of all the rooms; the upright slabs were smooth with red ocher clinging to bits of plaster between the stones. The corbelled ceiling formed a partial dome here, whereas the rest of the temple was almost completely open to the sky. Her legs felt funny, but nothing registered in her heart to say, this was the place.

The alcove on the sea side had been reshaped into a cluster of rooms, each with its own altar and adornments. From where she stood in the hallway, Nuriya could look through one of the rooms and out its window to a perfectly framed Filfla. It cheered her to think that a long ago temple builder enjoyed gazing at Filfla as much as she did. She moved toward the front. There was the grain altar on her right, its pedestal engraved with leaves and stems. Stepping past it, she poked her head through a carved doorway and into yet another chamber.

There was an immediate sensation on the back of her neck, like her skin was being tickled by delicate fingers. She turned slowly, wonderingly. Her gaze fell to a stone slab resting atop a pit marked altar. Carved into the face of the slab were two descending spirals. Her eyes traced the spirals, one turn, two turns, three, four, and before she completed the last, she was catapulted into an otherworldly place. The spirals were like Ulma's eyes peering into her, seeing to the core of her. A dissolving sensation spread from her legs throughout her entire body and Nuriya sank to the ground.

A presence conveyed itself through the spirals, a presence that poured unconditional love into the slash across her heart. Nuriya was filled—and then she was overflowing, weeping at the goodness of it, the improbable healing of it, here before a stone slab, touched by the hand of an unknown, ancient artist. Was this what Ulma meant by Goddess?

Nuriya didn't care what anyone called this—this was what she craved.

She sat a long while before she returned to the garden and found Korba still absorbed in her private thoughts. She walked her teacher back to their dwelling, set aside greens for their midday meal, and spread the rest on loose mats to dry. She added onion and cabbage to their bowls and the two ate a quiet meal.

Afterward, Korba went to nap and Nuriya to harvest, but before she filled her first basket she was reliving the humiliation of Ilobaal's betrayal. Without stopping to think, she ran to Ħaġar Qim and sat before the stone slab, feeling small and hard. She waited until she could bear to look into the spirals, until she could bear to hope. When finally she did look up, a wave of love rolled out and over her, filling her, amazingly and profoundly. This can't be, her mind protested, but the greater portion of her simply and gratefully, received.

Nuriya continued to harvest all that day and the next. Korba liked a huge amount of greens dried to use during the hot months when the plants stood like straw ghosts, returning themselves to the earth. As Nuriya gathered, she found she couldn't keep her mind calm for long. Like a tongue worrying a sick tooth, her mind sought again and again to review the details of her humiliation, cataloguing every facet of her unlovability. Every time she was overcome with anger or longing or despair she would trudge up to Ħaġar Qim, and every time she came away soothed. She sat however long it took, until a shift came, until she received the mysterious offering, and then she returned to the work of harvest.

Korba scarcely spoke for two full days. She sat hours in the sun, recovering her strength and mulling her private thoughts. When Hawk brought cheese from his mother on the third morning, Korba asked if he would take them to mid-island. He said he would pick them up at noon.

As soon as they set out in the wagon, Hawk brought up the subject of Jaro and was surprised that Korba didn't know the details. He filled her in and then, though he could have followed a different route, he drove right past Jaro's compound. At the crossroads, there he was, slouched against Erdu's cart, smoking his pipe. "Greetings, Jaro," Hawk offered. Jaro only glared.

"Greetings, Erdu," Korba called.

"Greetings, Healer Korba, Nuriya," Erdu replied.

When Hawk turned back to the women, his eyes were wide. "Did you see all the wine in Erdu's cart? If that's all for Jaro, better watch out."

Korba was welcomed warmly by Sky and immediately ushered into Ulma's hut. Lili took Hawk and Nuriya to meet the rest of the clan. The children wanted Nuriya to join their games, the elders spoke to her respectfully, and the boys flirted with her wildly. Hawk soon excused himself. The children were teaching Nuriya a catching game when she was summoned.

Ulma sat regally on a strange-looking bench—a tall board and two legs were fastened to the back and cart wheels were attached to the sides—with her right leg resting on a stool. Korba stood beside her. The women's features were remarkably similar and their relationship seemed written in the arrangement of their bodies: Ulma as elder sister, and Korba, the younger. It was disconcerting, for Nuriya had never seen her teacher subordinate to anyone. "Do you want to know about it?" Ulma asked, with only a slight slur to her words. Nuriya nodded. "I didn't think she was fit to raise you, and I told her so. Being eccentric is fine, but raising a child alone when you've never raised one and you're old enough to be a grandmother, is another thing. Of course, she never told me the whole story." Ulma pursed her lips and her mouth pulled to one side. "My husband was kin to Korba's husband. He insisted that Korba's brother-in-law should decide about raising you and she insisted not. We didn't see her after that."

Nuriya's mind was racing: I could have known Ulma, I could have known Lili, I could have had friends.

"Do you have anything to add, Korba?" Ulma asked.

Korba's face displayed rare uncertainty. "I hope I did well to raise you as I did, Nuri. I never regretted that your father left you with me." Nuriya offered a weak smile but remained speechless.

"Let us speak again, Korba, after I've napped. Now, I would like some time alone with Nuri." Korba nodded, touched Nuriya's arm and went out.

"Your life seems to have a most unusual design," Ulma said to her. "I am glad our paths crossed again."

"Me, too," Nuriya croaked. Of this one thing at least, she could be certain.

"I want to thank you again for coming to my rescue. Do you see all the lovely attention I'm getting because of my illness?" Indeed, Ulma was getting along amazingly well, with men and boys vying to push the clever chair and Lili coaxing her every day to work at regaining use of her arm and leg. "Is that the young man you're having trouble with?" Ulma asked, eyeing Hawk out the door.

"That's not—the young man," Nuriya mumbled.

The matriarch studied Hawk. "No," she decided. "He seems more a mender than a breaker to me."

Sky invited the visitors to a dinner of porridge and greens and poured mugs of Korba's honey wine. After her nap, Ulma was brought outside and the mood was light-hearted...for the most part. Korba tried to appear interested in conversation but Nuriya knew she waited for a response from her. Nuriya added water to her wine and took it to the garden to ponder her reaction. Korba had sacrificed this wonderful clan to raise her without interference from her dead husband's family, which left Nuriya without any family at all. Of course, it was her father who left her without a true family and Korba who mothered her in all ways but one. She was grateful, but resentful, too, and she mulled a long while before going back to the hearth. Korba's eyes met hers as she approached. Nuriya kissed Korba on the cheek, still looking for words that were true in both her mind and heart.

"I love you, daughter," Korba said.

Just then a boy raced up and plopped a leather ball into Nuriya's unsuspecting hands. "You're it!" he shouted and ran off to hide.

"Go on. Have fun," Korba encouraged. And relieved of having to say more, Nuriya kissed her again. Then, feigning nonchalance, she hid the ball behind her and wandered back into the throng.

Before they left, Sky told Nuriya that she had talked to the neighbors about the Phoenician construction. Jaro was the only one who knew anything but he was either extremely vague on details or willfully evasive and his brothers were angry to hear of it. Who officially, Sky wanted to know, could they talk to?

"The council decides these things," Nuriya said carefully.

"Does the person who told you have any connection to the council?" Nuriya nodded, swallowing her anxiety and fighting the urge to flee. "Could you make an introduction?"

You don't know what you're asking! Nuriya's heart screeched, but she answered as steadily as she could, "Everyone on the council has gone to Tyre. Maybe when they're back." She excused herself, saying she had left something in Ulma's hut.

Even though it was late, Korba asked Hawk to take them to see Caron on their way home. Caron's baby had settled low and she was having light contractions. Yes, she was taking yellow dock and nettles, and yes, she was feeling well.

Borg walked Korba a little apart to speak to her privately. "My sisters want to attend the birth."

"Of course. All the women should come."

Borg's jocularity was completely absent. "They don't want you here, Korba."

"Ah."

"I want you here."

"If you want me, Borg, I'll be here."

"Caron wants to be accepted by them." He was clearly troubled by what he was saying.

Korba stood very still, seeming to look straight through Borg. Finally she announced, "Caron is healthy and I trust her to her sisters. If you have concern, send for me. I will come immediately."

"Thank you, Korba-ma. I'm sorry."

Korba made a bed in the back of the wagon for the trip home. Nuriya knew how disappointed she was, after all she'd done to bring Caron back to health and to still be distrusted. Nuriya wished she'd been able to show her more appreciation earlier; maybe it would have softened this blow. She was thinking what to say when Hawk interrupted her thoughts. "It's almost time, you know."

"For what?"

"For your calf."

Nuriya hadn't let herself think about the calf that might be hers. "I haven't told Korba yet," she said quietly.

"I'll leave that to you."

Hawk was so nice to her, and all because of something that she couldn't really take credit for. Maybe she could learn from him about gratitude, and how to be more generous with hers. "Thanks for everything, Hawk."

"You're welcome," he said with sincerity.

Four days later Borg arrived with three cousins, all singing at the top of their lungs. He raced up to their dwelling with an armload of fresh picked wildflowers for Korba and requested her presence that very morning to the naming of her newest patient. "She's perfect and Caron is well. I can't thank you enough."

"It is my pleasure to serve," Korba replied.

"You know I'll make it up to you, Korba."

"I know you will." The women climbed into the cart with a bag of thistle seed for Caron's milk and Borg led them in song all the way to Tarxien.

It was a busy season of herb gathering, medicine making, and late winter illnesses, and the healers were often busy past dark. Nuriya visited her altar every day, however, even if it meant walking to Ħaġar Qim with lamp in hand. Each time she brought whatever pain or regret had crept into her heart since her last visit, and each time she came away soothed by the mysterious communion that awaited.

The full moon of the spring equinox called Nuriya one night from her sleeping mat. She went outside and found a place to sit among the rustling, shimmering grasses. Nearby sprawling castor bean plants offered up quivering palmfuls of moonlight. Nuriya offered her own palms to the moon then turned them over to trace shadows in the dirt. Tonight was Ilobaal's wedding night. She sat a long while, watching the moonglow on her feet, trying to ignore that inevitable fact. Then she lay back, splaying her arms and legs wide, and asked the same moon which shone over his wedding bed to read her heart. She felt the moon received her missive, demonstrating its capacity to shine alike on joy and pain, love and sorrow. After a while, Nuriya rose and went to the temple to make her own attempt at equanimity.

Not long after the equinox Nuriya woke before dawn to a child's voice calling excitedly, "Hawk says to come!" With a brief word to Korba, Nuriya followed Bell's short, quick legs over the ridge.

Blaki was on her side, waves of contraction rippling under her skin. Hawk flashed a grin as Nuriya entered the enclosure.

"It's time!" Zac shouted as two encapsulated hoofs descended into the world. Hawk punctured the sac before another contraction pushed the hooves farther out. "Grab a hoof, Zac. Don't let her slip." Hawk studied Blaki to time his actions. They leaned back and out popped the head. On the next contractions they leaned again. Then in a great gush it was out, all slime and blood and baby calf. Hawk wiped its face clean, cleared the nostrils and pulled the calf to its mother's head. Blaki lick-licked every place she could reach, her strong tongue revealing fur from slime. "Girl," Hawk proudly announced.

Before long they were treated to a most endearing performance. The baby cinched her hind legs up then splayed them wide; cinched them up then toppled to the right; legs up and elbows, too, then plopped back down. On the seventh try, the baby stood on shaky, spindly legs. Blaki had lumbered up and was licking her wobbly calf until she managed three steps forward to latch a bulging udder. A cheer roared and Nuriya looked around, amazed to see how many of the clan had gathered. Sema brought out bread and clabbered milk and the atmosphere was of celebration.

"What are you going to name her?" Zac asked.

"Ghoga. That's how we say calf." Nuriya wished she could swallow back the words as soon as they left her mouth for reminding everyone of her foreignness, but Sema came up and gave her a big hug, saying, "That's a beautiful name." Nuriya had worried that Sema would resent Hawk's gift and she received her hug with special relief.

Three days later as the healers were drinking morning tea, Nuriya looked to the crest of the hill to see Hawk walking the calf in their direction. She went to meet them.

"Look what we have here," Korba drawled as the young people arrived with Ghoga.

"I promise I'll still give rides whenever you need," Hawk told her.

The calf nudged into Korba's skirt and Nuriya handed her a bowl of grains. "See if she'll eat from your fingers." Korba dipped, and Ghoga sucked and the old healer actually giggled. "Smitten already, Mother?"

"I didn't say that," she replied dryly.

Nuriya walked Hawk and Ghoga up to the cistern. She bent to her calf, nuzzling her fur and breathing in her musky, mild scent. Her heart felt full. She smiled up at Hawk; he blushed.

Life found an even busier pace: working the garden, gathering medicine, sitting before her altar and visiting Ghoga. Nuriya found that she gradually thought about Ilobaal less and less, and amazingly, some of those thoughts didn't make her want to cry.

She was sorting rush bundles for a new storage basket one fine spring morning, when an old man leading a boy on a donkey appeared at the fork. Korba came out from the storeroom and the two watched the boy limp the path after his elder.

The old man had brought his grandson so the healers could "fix 'im." "He's only good for woman's work now," the grandfather complained.

"Was he born like so?" Korba asked, pointing to his misshapen ankle.

"Last year he was fine and could work like any boy."

"Was he sick in any other way?"

"Nothing I would note, except that he moves like an old man now." The grandfather hunched his shoulders to imitate an even older man.

"What's your name?" Korba asked.

"Rom."

"Does your ankle hurt?"

The boy shrugged then nodded. "And the knee?" It, too, was misshapen, as if the bones were growing without guide or pattern. Again, the shrug and nod.

Korba sat him down and conducted the exam. She found he had a low fever and swollen glands in the groin; the ankle was hot and had lost quite a lot of movement. "Nuri, work with the ankle while I prepare a poultice." They had dug mallow plants the day before and she headed to the storeroom to fetch them.

The grandfather faced toward port while Nuriya laid the mat on the opposite side of the fire ring. Before Rom reclined, he pointed to one of her reed bundles. "How did you get them so dark?"

"I mix charcoal with mud and bury them."

"We use willow to dye."

"I used willow with this." Nuriya picked up a dark brown bundle and Rom pinched brows as he compared the colors. "I'll show you how to dye black after we work on your ankle," she offered.

Rom gave a happy smile and then lay down.

With his eyes closed, the boy looked like he was waiting for a happy surprise and already Nuriya's heart was stirred by him. How could this have happened in less than a year? Something was crippling this sweet boy, rapidly dooming his future. Nuriya felt agitated. To calm herself, she closed her eyes and imagined sitting before her altar. Then she touched Rom's ankle. The sensation was wild, like a turbulent energy was trapped inside his bones. It brought to mind a wadi that someone had filled with old stumps and debris. When the rains came the water backed up behind the debris, eddying and creating a tumult, the banks eroding until the blockage was broken through. What kind of block could be in Rom's ankle, and could she dismantle it so that energy flowed instead of damaging? Nuriya rested her hands on either side of the ankle and imagined removing debris, dirt wad by dirt wad and twig by twig. After a time, something eased under her hands. But still the ankle was too hot. "He should eat only green," she said out loud. "Nothing to make heat for a few days."

Korba looked up from where she sat by the fire ring. She nodded and said, "I'll brew elderflowers, too. 'Cool like the moon,' my auntie used to say." The healer had poured steaming water over whole mallow plants and was letting them steep. Now she poured off the liquid and gave it to Rom. He thanked her politely and drank. When the healer touched the ankle, her brows rose and a smile touched her face. "Check the knee, too, daughter."

Nuriya did; she worked with the knee as she had with the ankle and then went through his whole body looking for other unseen blocks. Where the collar bone met the sternum was a spot, and at the joint of the jaw, another. Nuriya felt glorious as she worked, sweeping through Rom's body, looking for obstacles, remembering the feeling of the spirals, and encouraging that feeling to flow here. She wished she could always feel like this: useful and connected to a mysterious healing power.

Korba brought a bowl with the warm mass of mallow leaves and pounded root over to the mat. Nuriya smeared plant material over Rom's ankle and knee then wrapped them with cloth. "He should stay with us I suppose," said Korba.

"Yes," Nuriya agreed.

The healer made arrangements with the grandfather. For the next two days she had Rom rest in the sun stripped to his loin cloth, feeding him nettles and mallow and medicinal tea, and teaching him every plant she used. She set times for Nuriya to lay on hands, insightfully sending her to sit before her altar before each session. Rom's joints cooled and by the third day he could walk without pain. Korba took him to the hillside to gather their meal of salad greens, and the smile on Rom's face when he returned with his basket carried all the enthusiasm of a devotee. Over supper, Korba impressed upon Rom that only he would know when activity had passed the point of usefulness, into destructiveness. Heat would be his guide but, she admonished, "The plants are allies, not magicians."

They sent Rom home with enough elderflower and rosemary to last a year and the secret to obsidian black reeds. His grandfather was guarded in his reception, but his offering of a wool blanket, a sack of barley and a plump laying hen, conveyed the high value he placed on their ministrations.

"How did you feel working with Rom?" Korba asked after they left.

"I felt good," Nuriya replied noncommittally when in fact she had felt amazing! It was the first time healing power had moved through her without any head pain at all. But she knew to guard against wanting it too much; she could not forget her ignorance. She wasn't going to seek healing power, only to have it go out of control again.

After Rom's healing, if a call wasn't urgent, Korba always made it a point to encourage Nuriya to visit her altar before they headed out.

Bon dropped off pots one afternoon and told the women of the merry mood at port. "You'd think their king was here with all that commotion. The Magistrate's back and word is, his son got married to a princess. A royal person living on Malta, imagine that." Nuriya's heart grew dark and she stayed long in Ħaġar Qim that evening.

The next day, Nuriya heard hoof beats as she sat outside weaving. She did not turn from her work to watch the gold-trimmed cape swirl around Ilobaal as he dismounted and bounded up the hill. He bowed formally before her and he waited a good long time before she deigned to acknowledge him. Then he straightened and gushed, "You are the most beautiful, Lady Nurija. How good it is to behold your face after these long days."

"Are you married?" she asked flatly.

Ilobaal dropped to one knee. "I promise you, it will never change how I..."

"We have nothing to say to each other," she cut him off with a bravado she did not feel.

"Nurija," Ilobaal pouted, then he said brightly, "Let me show you what I brought for you."

"I don't want it." She stood, stepped around him, and went inside, closing the door. She pressed her forehead into the rock until it cut. She wanted him... She hated him.

Ilobaal knocked on the door. "Nurija, come talk to me." He pounded and said more sharply, "Come out. Please!" The door held no bolt and Nuriya feared he would barge in. Korba emerged from the storeroom and watched, her mouth pulled tight. Ilobaal spoke through the closed door. "I am married, yes. It is my duty as a son and citizen of Tyre. But I know you are meant to be by my side. I will not beg now because you are angry, but you will come to me, my love. As sure as my name, I know you will come." There was a taut silence before he whispered achingly, "I long for you, Nurija."

When she was sure he had gone, Nuriya went out. On the bench next to her unfinished basket lay a cloth-wrapped box. She stared at it then turned away and went to visit her altar.

The next morning Adnan arrived by donkey cart, bearing a length of linen, two sacks of barley, and a bag of sweetcakes. Nuriya took the sweetcakes for Korba and sent the unopened box back with the rest of the goods.

The next day Adnan arrived with two baskets of sweetcakes and the cloth-wrapped box. Nuriya waved him off but he approached lifting the lid to reveal an exquisite necklace of red coral set in silver. Nuriya felt longing but she could never accept it. She put a hand on the boy's shoulder. "Ilobaal is married and not to me. He must live with that as will I." Confusion muddled the boy's features but he continued to resolutely hold the box. "You must not come with gifts, Adnan. Do you understand? Go, and tell him." She turned and entered her dwelling.

Word got around that the Phoenician elite had returned and on their next visit to Ulma's, Sky took Nuriya aside to say that an audience was sought with the council. Would she make the introduction and translate if need be?

"What about Erdu?" Nuriya asked softly though her insides screamed, *Don't ask me this!*

"Erdu is not our friend."

"Women aren't allowed at council meetings."

"You only need make an introduction and state our claim. I would trust Erdu to translate once the claim is stated."

While Nuriya scrambled for another excuse, her mind slipped from dread to indignation. It wasn't right that the council made plans for mid-island without farmers present. Did they think the natives without opinion or power? Is that how Ilobaal saw her? A dumb islander? Good enough for mistress, but not good enough for wife? Her anger, finally, cleared her excuses. "I will do it."

Sky and Josep arrived early one gorgeous day. Clouds shaped like bird wings soared in the cobalt sky, yellow and lavender wildflowers covered the hillsides, but Nuriya saw none of it. When Sky told her how she convinced Jaro's brothers to let Josep represent them, Sky's words were a blue jay's chattering. It took all Nuriya's energy to keep her mind from anticipating the moment she would face Ilobaal.

They left the wagon at the fork and walked through market. Except for a brief nod to Kepi, Nuriya kept her eyes straight and her head low. Men loitered near the meeting house and a young guard stood at the entry, wearing a purple sash over a clean, white tunic. "What business have you here?" the guard asked.

Nuriya, standing at Josep's side, recited the words she'd been rehearsing, "I am here to introduce Josep who has come on behalf of the landholders of mid-island. He wishes for dialogue with the council."

There was a movement at the door. "It's the healer woman!" Adnan piped before disappearing inside. The guard craned his neck to peer after him. Presently Adnan re-emerged, followed by Ilobaal in a formal long robe. A smile quivered on his lips and his eyes were hopeful. "Good to see you, Lady Nurija," he said in Maltese. Nuriya did not reply. After a moment Ilobaal registered Josep's presence, and a few steps behind him, Sky. "I see you would like me to consult the farmers," Ilobaal said in Canaanite with a hint of sarcasm.

Nuriya's anger simmered. She repeated her recitation, "I am here to introduce Josep who has come on behalf of the land-holders of mid-island. He wishes for dialogue with the council."

Ilobaal returned to the local tongue. "I miss you, Nurija." He reached toward her.

"Don't," she said firmly, her hands fisting at her sides.

"I want—to talk to you."

"We have nothing to talk about."

"You are wrong."

"Don't do this. Let me speak for Josep, then let me go."

The loitering men were listening intently and more heads were poking out of the building. Ilobaal took in the crowd with a sweep of his eyes. "I will translate for Josep of mid-island," he announced with the formality of office and Nuriya passed the message.

Josep did his best with the awkward Canaanite word for "Thank you."

"I do this as a favor to the Lady Healer," Ilobaal said with a flagrant, lingering gaze. Then he motioned for Josep to follow and turned inside.

Sky and Nuriya moved to a shaded area to wait. "Your young man is quite handsome," Sky said.

"He is not my young man."

"He would like to be."

"He is married—to the niece of his king." A long silence followed.

"I am sorry. I did not know this was such a sacrifice for you."

"I wanted to do it," Nuriya said unconvincingly as she looked out past the ships in the harbor, trying to see beyond her broken dream of sailing to Tyre as Ilobaal's cherished wife.

Later, Josep appeared alone. "It is a beginning. I am to return next market day." He turned to Nuriya, "Ilobaal of Tyre begs you to wait. He will be out shortly."

Nuriya looked to Sky. "Can we leave now?"

"Do we have further business with these people today?" Sky asked her husband.

"No."

"Then we go." They piled into the wagon and were off without looking back.

Nuriya collapsed onto her bed, exhausted from the tension of the day. Korba made her borage tea which she gratefully drank, then she returned to her mat, too tired to even visit her altar.

◎◎

While Korba cleaned up from her own meal she heard the clip clop of horse and knew its rider. She stood alone to greet him. "I do not think she wishes to see you."

"I beg her speak to me."

"Perhaps it is me you should beg."

"I did not expect to love her but it is so. It was not possible to alter my marriage with agreements of trade and diplomacy depending upon it."

"You married for commerce," Korba stated dully.

"For duty, and for good relation, but I know love, madam."

"You evaded the truth."

"Do you blame me?"

"I blame you, sir," Korba said with contempt. "I will see if she wishes to speak to you." She went in and laid a hand on Nuriya's shoulder.

"I don't want to see him. I want to get on with my life. He made his decision and I've made mine."

Korba repeated Nuriya's words to Ilobaal.

"I do not accept," he said and moved to enter the dwelling. The old healer placed a hand on the young man's chest and Ilobaal was surprised by the force in her body and the fierceness in her eye. True to her name, the witch of Mnajdra, he reminded himself.

"This is my home. I will ask you to leave," Korba stated.

Ilobaal considered his options, then nodded and backed away. "I will leave you."

The next morning when Nuriya went to her altar, she waited a good long while for the voices inside to grow quiet. Then she lifted her eyes to her beloved spirals, and welcomed the blessing of their mysterious communion.

Afterward she walked down the hill, thinking how her pain about Ilobaal still felt as vast and present as the sky. Then she reminded herself firmly—the presence of the sky did not interfere with the tasks at hand, and, indeed, hardly warranted comment.

Nuriya tried to visit her growing calf often, bringing her grain mixed with honey or digging tasty roots as she walked the path. Ghoga would run to meet her and if Hawk was there he would imitate her bleats and Blaki's bellows. If Nuriya was unable to visit for too many days, Hawk would walk the calf over to Korba's, saying it was her training. Nuriya would accompany them back to the cistern, and the simple pleasure of leading her calf up the hill was like good medicine for her heart.

9.

The Oracle

☺☺

Nuriya knew that Hawk was going to kiss her for the first time before it happened. She was sitting before her altar one evening after a long day of work, watching the play of lamplight across the spirals. That cherished feeling of love had settled upon her and as sometimes happened, she had the sensation of her self extending out beyond the confines of her skin. The feeling expanded until it seemed that Nuriya's body included the terrain below and all the dark sky above. The ground seemed to spin and in the next instant Nuriya found herself soaring through wind and cloud. There was a momentary tumble and she braced for disaster, but then the sensation righted. Below her, from the vantage of high in the sky, Nuriya saw two ships sailing on a sparkling sea. She felt curious, and her vision drew closer to the ships. When she was near enough to spy the octopus sprawled across one ship's gray banner and see the faces of the men working the sails, Hawk suddenly appeared before her, his rosemary eyes smiling. He kissed her roundly, and Nuriya's eyes shot open. She found herself sitting still, before lamp-lit spirals, in the dark of the night, bewildered but smiling.

The next day Hawk arrived with Ghoga, bearing milk. Korba sent back a sample of her latest salve and Nuriya walked man and calf up the hill. When they arrived at the cistern, Hawk reached for her hand. His kiss, Nuriya found, was quite like his smile— slightly goofy and genuinely sweet. "Thank you," she was about to say when, moving past her vision of the night before, Hawk took her by the shoulders and pulled her close, melting his velvety soft lips onto hers. He lingered there shamelessly long, creating waves of euphoria inside her. Nuriya was as shocked by Hawk's daring as by her body's reaction to it. Gradually they moved apart, each of them mildly stunned and definitely delighted. Nuriya was looking forward to the next kiss, when her gaze slipped past Hawk to spy two ships idling near Filfla. Her breath caught. "Those ships! I saw them last night."

Hawk glanced to the ships and back to Nuriya's worried expression. "What's the matter?"

"I'm not sure," she said but her heart was pounding.

"What do you mean, 'you saw them last night?'"

She turned so she could gauge Hawk's reaction and told him about sitting before her altar and seeing the ships.

"Were there torches on the ships?"

"No, it was daytime. I mean, it was night when I was in the temple, but what I saw was daytime."

Hawk grinned, looking pleased to have figured out the puzzle. "Nuriya, you saw into *tomorrow*. Last night you saw into today."

She tried to tell if he was mocking, but saw only sincerity. Still, the idea did not ease her. She looked toward the ships with foreboding.

"Don't worry about it."

But she was worried. Why had she seen them and why did they frighten her?

"Are you all right?"

She pulled her gaze from the ships and gave him a weak smile. "Yes."

Hawk shifted his feet, awkward again. He tugged on Ghoga's rope. "I guess I'll be going then."

"Thanks for bringing her," Nuriya said as she turned toward Ħaġar Qim, the kiss vanishing from her mind.

"I'll come tomorrow if I can," Hawk called after her.

Nuriya was barely watching her step. Her eyes were on the ships and her mind on the spirals. She was determined to know why they frightened her. As she entered the back of the temple, a lone cloud was framed through the central passage. She sat before her altar and closed her eyes. In the next instant, she felt jerked upward, a series of images flashing before her:

night at dock's edge...
fire in a warehouse...
an axe blade cracking bone...
Ilobaal!...

With an exertion of will Nuriya forced her attention into her feet, her legs, and her breath. With a jolt, as if she'd jumped from the top of a very high wall, her eyes flew open. She was drenched in sweat. She looked out the entrance—the single cloud still floated lazily in the east. No hint of danger. But there was danger! She ran outside. The ships were moving east, toward Marsaxlokk, their sails billowing full. She ran to tell Korba, "I'm going to Hawk's. I need him to take me to port."

"What is it?"

"I'm not sure but there's a danger to Ilobaal. I need to warn him."

Korba kept her questions in check. "Be careful."

"I will."

Hawk was putting Ghoga in her pen when he saw Nuriya

running the path. "The ships—I saw them again," she puffed, out of breath. "Will you take me to town? I need to warn him."

Hawk searched her face. "Stay here. I'll bring a cart."

"I'll come. I need water."

"I'll bring it." He hastened away and Nuriya tried to calm herself and think...what was she going to say to Ilobaal?

Hawk brought the donkey cart and Sema came out with a half loaf of bread. "My son tells me you need to get to town for a healing. I thought you'd like something to eat on the way." Nuriya thanked her, casting a grateful nod to her son.

They set off at a fast clip. "What did you see?" Hawk asked.

A jumble of words tumbled out—ships, danger, fire, blood—the words rolling over themselves as the images had. Then they were silent a long while.

"Do you love him?"

Nuriya's heart clutched. Of course he knew! Probably the whole island knew. "No," she said sharply then amended more softly, "I don't know." She didn't have to look at Hawk to know the set of his jaw.

Before they turned up Wied Filfla, Nuriya spotted something. "Look there!" One of the ships was bobbing in the inlet to the grotto, the other was nowhere in sight. "We have to hurry."

As they reached the market fork, two soldiers in sweat-drenched tunics strode up from the docks. "Excuse me, where might we find Ilobaal of Tyre?"

"Who seeks him?"

"I am Nuriya."

The men conversed briefly. "You'll find him at the second warehouse."

Hawk turned the cart and they descended the slope. He was stopped halfway by the bustle of activity. Dockworkers moved about among rough sailors, foreign slaves, and Ilobaal's elegantly dressed guardsmen. Crates were being offloaded and pried open over loud barter negotiations. Ilobaal's father was holding council with a man in formal robes and Ilobaal, himself, was dividing his attention between two soldiers and a foreign captain. One of the mystery ships was beached past the far end of the wharf.

Nuriya stepped from the cart and fixed her gaze upon Ilobaal. All the bustle and shouting seemed to stop. Her heart lurched and the blood drained from her head. She forced one foot in front of the other into the unbearable tension. Ilobaal turned from the yellow-haired captain to face her. Nuriya continued forward, step by step, as Ilobaal bounded toward her, a gleam of triumph in his eyes. "My Lady..."

"I'm here to warn you."

Ilobaal took in the faces turned toward them. "Aboro, compile supplies for Greco. I will be back." He steered Nuriya into a passageway between two storehouses and through a door. Inside, mounds of grain and scores of amphoras were stacked ceiling high. Abruptly Ilobaal drew Nuriya to him, held her face and kissed her fiercely. Nuriya was stunned. Her world spun; her legs grew weak. "Darling," said Ilobaal, his voice low and husky.

Nuriya gasped for air and blurted, "The ship with the gray banner..."

"From Ibiza..." he murmured.

"...I saw fire, and blood. Tonight. I came to warn you."

"Warn me?"

"Yes."

"You had a vision?"

"Yes." The saying of it seemed to leach Nuriya's remaining strength. She backed away. She wanted to be gone from here, back to Hawk and his smiling eyes.

Ilobaal grabbed her arm, demanding, "What did you see?"

"Fighting. Your men. You." She looked down at her arm. "Let me go!" She pulled from him, and ran.

"Nurija!" Ilobaal shouted, but she did not stop. She ran from the building and up the passage toward the waiting cart, calls and whistles marking her passing.

Hawk lifted her to the seat. "Did he hurt you?"

"No!" Her hands flew to cover her eyes. "Take me home, please, now." They set off and did not look back.

Finally Nuriya turned to Hawk's angry profile. "I told him what I saw, that's all. He didn't hurt me."

"He's not good for you, Nuriya," Hawk said through clenched jaws. He dropped her at home and declined Korba's invitation for a meal.

Nuriya told Korba what she had done as she forced herself to eat. "You did what you had to," the healer stated, but her eyes showed worry. Nuriya went to bed before the sun was down.

The next morning a lone soldier rode the path past the Standing Stones. This was not the cocky young man of yesterday, but a sober-eyed warrior, his left arm bandaged and resting in a sling. He dismounted at the flag and moved haltingly up the path. He bent to one knee before Nuriya, reached for her hand and placed his forehead upon it. "I owe you my life," he murmured.

Nuriya pulled her hand away, but gently.

Ilobaal rose. Pain was in his eyes. He turned to Korba. "I greet you, Healer Korba," he said humbly. "Please, may I speak with Nurija?"

"It is not my choice."

Ilobaal turned again. "Nurija. Please."

Not knowing what she would do or say, Nuriya rose and moved toward the place that had become her sanctuary. As she walked up to Ħaġar Qim, her body burned like a flame. Fire to ashes, fire to ashes—the lyric from a children's song, repeated endlessly inside her.

Ilobaal sagged against the entrance stones before entering the temple. He had been up all night, first in wait, and then in battle. With Nuriya's warning, he had added a third man to the night guard, bid his rowing crew sleep lightly and ordered the weapon's unit to dress in battle readiness and hide among the cargo. Before midnight, four men from the Ibiza ship began to harass the guard at one end of the wharf while the second Ibiza ship rowed into harbor on muffled oars. When the ship pulled alongside the dock, twenty pirates leapt out into Ilobaal's counterattack. The melee was over before the rowing crew reinforcements poured in. Two of Ilobaal's men were dead, and eight of the pirates. The rest of the pirates were imprisoned in the hull of their ship.

"I cannot ask more than you have already given, but please, Lady, please, may I hold you?" Dirt and blood were caked on his slung arm; Nuriya wanted to check the wound. There was a bruise across his cheek, and his eyes showed shock from what he had seen in the night. "I need you," he pleaded.

She opened her arms to him. Ilobaal held her and spoke her name over and over like a prayer. He smelled of sweat and smoke and blood. Her aloofness began to evaporate. She was a fool to think that she could reject him, that she could accept a life that was not this—this breath, these arms. Ilobaal could have died! Her relief made her giddy. Need and desire surged inside her. Caring not at all for propriety, she reached for the cloth wrapped round his hips. Then in a frenzy they moved, fumbling to disrobe, and fumbling to the ground. Ilobaal made love to her like it was an affirmation of life, the triumph of living, and Nuriya was swept up into bliss; she wanted to float there forever.

Then she remembered how she had measured his spine, thinking she would never feel it again under her fingers, and a wave of sadness dropped her flat. It was the sadness of every moment that was not this. It pushed itself out until she was crying, deep throated and devastated.

"What's wrong? Are you hurt?"

"No—I'm happy—I'm sorry."

"You're not making sense."

"This—you—it cannot be."

"It can be, Nurija. It can be like this."

"You're married to someone else."

"Shhh." He put his fingers to her lips. "Just hold me. You scared me. Hold me now."

Nuriya held him while he dozed, and silently, she wept.

When Ilobaal woke, he immediately began to dress. He tied his tunic saying, "I must get back to my men. Are you all right now, Lady?"

That was it. Of course. Ilobaal had a life, a whole world, she would never be privileged to share. Once again disappointment and longing grasped the corners of her heart, and tore. Nuriya made herself stand. "Come," she said, her voice hollow. "I'll tend your arm."

Under the grim gaze of Korba who sat with an unfinished mat on her lap, Nuriya cleaned Ilobaal's sword wound. It had been soldier tended, that is, doused with wine and tightly wrapped. She coated the edges with honey, tied the flesh together, and held her hands with healing intent. She treated the cut on his skull that she found in their lovemaking and applied salve to his face. Then, without modesty or concern for Korba's appraisal, Ilobaal kissed her, flagrantly and passionately, before bidding the senior healer good day. He staggered to his horse, and was gone.

"Nuri?" Korba's expression was dismayed.

"I'll be all right," Nuriya said then she turned to seek refuge before her altar.

She sat, breathing as steadily as her body would allow, tormented by fresh hurt and reawakened desire. She did not know what to pray for except to not be stranded in this terrible tension. She had been hurt by Ilobaal, badly, yet she loved him—and wanted him. But—could she do this? Be his mistress? Still and always the outsider? Nuriya practiced all day, focusing on the spirals and on her breath, until finally she felt embraced, unanswered questions and all, by that cherished and blessed love.

When Hawk came at midday, Korba stood alone to greet him. "She's in the temple. I think it best to not disturb her."

Hawk stood a while working his mouth wordlessly. He did not want to pry, but now he was left to his imagination.

Korba pitied him. "There was an ambush. Two guards were killed and twenty pirates imprisoned. Maybe you could come tomorrow?" Hawk nodded and turned on his heel.

Nuriya sat in meditation until after dark, and early the next morning she went again to her altar, hoping to steady herself enough to resume her duties. When she exited the temple, Hawk was waiting for her. He looked like he hadn't slept. "Did he come see you?"

"Yes." The word fell heavily.

"Will you see him again?"

Nuriya answered honestly, "I don't know."

Hawk swayed as if he sustained a blow. He regained himself and stalked off. Nuriya went back inside, with Hawk's hurt, one more pain to bring before her altar.

Korba could not fathom what Nuri was up to but because she believed prayer to be the most important thing a troubled person could do, she was comforted to see Nuri spending large blocks of time at her altar. She decided to give her a few days of grappling on her own before insisting on a frank discussion. And so, the next day when Cassia sent a message asking the healer's help in easing her mother's pain, she decided to go alone, hoping no one would call while she was away, and that Nuri would have the time she needed to sort her mind and heart.

As fate would have it, Ilobaal found Nuriya sitting at her altar shortly after Korba left. He bounded into the temple, his energy bouncing off the megaliths. He extended his unbandaged arm and boomed, "Come let me hold you. I have missed you so."

Nuriya did not reach for Ilobaal's outstretched hand. She did not know what she wanted, and waited for her heart to tell her.

Ilobaal laughed. "Oh, my love, I have interrupted you at prayer. I am a sorry man. What do you expect when my thought is of you constantly?" She saw the hint of confusion in his eye and still, she waited.

Ilobaal hoisted her by the arm so that she stood facing him. She watched him sidestep confusion and throw himself into recreating the passion of their lovemaking. He took her face between his hands. "My love, how I want you." He nuzzled her neck, pressed his hips into hers and began lifting her tunic. Nuriya was appalled by his presumption, but even as she started to push him away, her body began to respond. He murmured her name and his voice was its own magic. Why was she resisting? Isn't this what she wanted? She tried to avoid her desire by meditating, but the wanting him was there, every moment. When he took her hand and pulled her to his cloak, she resisted no more.

As soon as Nuriya lay back and Ilobaal entered her, his sex

poured out of him like an avalanche. He exhaled thunderously and then fell to his side, pulling her close.

Nuriya lay, drenched by the passionate tide that had suddenly retreated, her senses quivering in bewilderment. What was this strange dance? And yet...and yet...Ilobaal held her so sweetly now... Yes, she said to this, too, and surrendered to the curve of his arm.

After a while Ilobaal stirred. "I have something for you, Nurija." He fished through a wad of cloth folded in his sash and pulled out a polished silver pendant on a copper chain. Nuriya shot bolt upright, pulling her tunic over her knees. Ilobaal held out the pendant like a supplicant. "It is thanks for your warning of the ambush." She shook her head warily. "A gift of thanks," he repeated. "Look here." He turned the pendant over on his palm. Etched into the back was a triangle with a perfect circle balanced on top. "It is the symbol of Goddess Tanit, for whom our ship is named. I offer this on behalf of those whose lives were spared and to honor our brothers who lost theirs. They would wish you to have it."

Nuriya bit her lip and hesitantly took the pendant, turning it in her hand, alternating between the precise etching on one side, the polished silver on the other, and wondering what to think.

"I am glad you like it," Ilobaal said. He stood to tie his sash and added, "I will ask something of you, Nurija, but you must keep this, regardless."

She dropped the necklace to her lap as if it scorched her. "What do you ask of me?"

"I need you to be my Oracle."

Nuriya's mouth popped open. She closed it, opened it again then said, "I'm not an oracle. I hardly know what that is."

"You have already proven that you are." He took both her hands, speaking excitedly, "Listen. Amangeel, envoy of King

Elulaios, is here on Malta. He has asked me to join his survey mission to Motya."

The island of Motya off the west coast of Sicily was one day's sail north of Malta. Although Phoenician traders had been stopping there for generations, it was now as Malta had been ten years before, without permanent establishment other than a few warehouses. Nuriya pulled her hands away. "Why do you need an oracle for that?"

"There has been trouble," Ilobaal said delicately.

"What trouble?"

While Ilobaal was in Tyre word reached King Elulaios that an encampment of Greeks had begun construction on a new colony at the mouth of the river Halycus, south of Motya. War ships patrolled the waters—as if they expected a fight. King Elulaios was enraged that Greeks were expanding into western Sicily and furious that Carthage, less than a day's sail east, had not dealt with the situation. He fumed that Carthage was too busy appropriating farmland in North Africa while being remiss in its responsibility to Tyre. The king needed to show both Carthage and the Greeks that his clout was not diminished by the Assyrian pressure. He ordered twenty ships from the Tyrian Navy to rout the Greeks and demanded that Carthage contribute another ten ships to the mission.

Ilobaal did his best to convince Amangeel that his warship should join the fleet but the envoy considered the Tanit, with its untested crew, unfit. "The Tanit is a peacock, not a fighting cock," Amangeel had quipped. Only under pressure from Ilobaal's new father-in-law did the envoy agree to pass through Malta to assess the Tanit's readiness. Every day since his return from the wedding, Ilobaal and his captain had strenuously worked their men, practicing endless drills and ramming maneuvers, and putting in long hours of sword practice.

The envoy arrived on Malta the evening after the pirate battle.

Prisoners locked in the hull of their own galley alongside accounts of Ilobaal's leadership persuaded him. He asked the Tanit's captain to join his ship to the Sicilian mission and Ilobaal to join the reconnaissance phase. Four ships would sail north in the guise of a survey mission, albeit with a crew of trained warriors. They would briefly survey Motya, while their main objective would be to evaluate the Greek defense. By the time the Tyrian fleet arrived in Carthage, Amangeel would be there to present his battle strategy, a demand for reparations would be sent, which the Greeks would surely ignore, a warning would follow, and a direct attack ensue.

Ilobaal withheld this information from Nuriya. "All I can tell you," he said, "is that it is a great honor to be asked to join Amangeel and the only reason is because of your vision. You must see for me again, Nurija; see if our way to Sicily and back is clear."

Nuriya set the necklace on the grain altar and smoothed her tunic over her hips. "I am a healer, not an oracle," she stated as if it was final.

"I know you are a healer." He pulled up his sleeve to reveal his wound mending cleanly. "But any witch can be a healer. Only a priestess can be a seer."

"Neither am I a priestess," she retorted, "as you can see."

"You would have been."

"What do you mean?"

"If you grew up in Tyre you would have been trained for the Temple. I am sure of it. You have all the signs."

"What signs?" Her voice cracked.

"Dear one," Ilobaal murmured. "I knew you were meant to be a priestess the night I met you. I have seen a divination trance before."

Nuriya's legs felt weak. "What are you saying?"

Ilobaal guided her to sit on the altar and pressed the necklace into her unresisting hands. "Before I left Tyre I took an offering to the Temple Melquart. It was well received and I was allowed to petition for a prophesy. The priest went into trance, like I saw you, and then he spoke these words: 'When the Star of the Warrior and the Star of Gold ride with the Lion through the long night, you will meet an ally. In the next turning of the season you will fly toward your ambition like a shooting star. And one day your son will return to Tyre, to live in the house of the King.'" Ilobaal's eyes glittered as he spoke. "My ally is you, Nurija. When we met, the stars of prophesy were moving together. I greeted every man who came into port, looking, but the ally was you! Ba'al was nothing without Anat and you are my Anat. I will lead a fleet in the western Mediterranean, that is my ambition, and you will be by my side, as my Oracle and my love."

Pressure was building inside Nuriya's head. She stood quickly, nearly fell over the altar. "No!" Her voice was sharp. "I am not Anat." She pushed from her mind the memory of the fierce Goddess streaming through her senses. "I don't know your Warrior Star. I want nothing to do with this." She held her head like it might break. Could it be true? Could she see *into tomorrow* at will? Could the priest in Tyre have been speaking of her?

"Nurija." Ilobaal's tone jarred her, but she did not lift her head. He placed a hand on her shoulder and softened his voice. "I need you to do this. My father is ready to give over magisterial duties now that I am..."

"Married?" she hissed.

"Yes—but the council has not agreed. This is an important opportunity to be seen favorably. It could be very good for me, for us."

She glared up at him and he stepped away. "You do not know this, but in Tyre, the Oracles have great power. All high ranking officials are advised by them. As Oracle you would have a place of honor among all our people, anywhere we traveled. I am asking you, Nurija, to be my Oracle."

She closed her eyes. Her mind was reeling. Hadn't she longed for a place inside Ilobaal's world—inside her father's world? Wouldn't it be better than sitting before her altar, sublimating her desires, waiting for Ilobaal to come to her? "I don't know if I can," she whispered.

"You will try?"

"What do you want to know?" Her voice sounded her defeat.

"Does the mission to Motya and back have the blessing of the Gods? That is all."

"I don't know your Gods."

"Great Mother then, I don't care. I just want you to look. Is there blessing or is there warning?"

Already a change was happening inside Nuriya's body, the subtle tingling, the expanding boundary of her skin. She rocked on her feet and Ilobaal fumbled to place the necklace around her neck. He helped her to sit and when she looked up, the eyes were waiting. "Motya, and Ilobaal's safety," she stated her silent intent.

All her concerns fell away. She was floating again, that beautiful, giddy sensation. She breathed deeply, fully. Her witnessing self merged with the space around her. She passed through wind and cloud, and over the sea, brightly shining below.

She moved north, toward Motya. Nearing the shoreline, her insides tumbled as if she was tossed in waves. The strangeness made her cry out before the sensation righted. Then she saw Phoenician ships beached in a sandy bay, men walking the land, marking out paces and diagramming on diptychs, Ilobaal and the envoy speaking together. There was another churning tumble and when it calmed, Nuriya saw more ships sailing into the bay. Colorful eyes of Osiris adorned the hulls, banners of purple with the crescent of white fluttered on the wind, horses paraded on decks and livestock bayed below. Men, women and children leaned over railings and the atmosphere was of a festival. There will be a large colony here, she thought.

Again the strange tumbling as if the sea was inside her. She fought to control her bowels. When the sensation ebbed, the images were more dreamlike. Ilobaal and the envoy were examining objects that appeared to be toy ships and toy people. They picked them up and put them down. They discussed how to arrange them, quietly, like they shared a secret. Then they were sailing again. Behind the ship something dragged, like kelp caught in a fishing net. Something was tangled into the kelp, rotting as it was dragged. Ilobaal and the envoy looked behind the ship, and laughed. Ilobaal moved to the prow and gazed straight into Nuriya's eyes. Go back, his eyes said.

I don't know how, Nuriya thought sadly. I will be forever in a world of dreams jumbled in time. She thought of the spirals and of the comfort they had been to her, and before she took another breath she was there, sitting before them, with Ilobaal at her side. She opened her eyes and turned toward him—too quickly. The sea rose up within her. She doubled over and vomited.

Ilobaal dabbed her chin with his sash. "Did you see, Nurija? I know you did. Tell me."

Nuriya felt wretched, but Ilobaal's enthusiasm buoyed her. She furrowed her brow, trying to remember something that would please him. "The colony at Motya will thrive." He bobbed his head encouragingly. "You and the envoy share a secret."

"That is as it should be," he said carefully.

"Something bad followed you."

His face tightened. "What was it?"

"Something dead, in a fishing net. You saw it, but you were happy." The words sounded mixed-up even as she spoke them.

"That is men's business. There is no need to concern yourself. You did as I asked and I am pleased. You saw me safe, yes?" She nodded.

Ilobaal helped her to stand, dropping his sash over the foul spot. Pulling her close he spoke into her hair, "You, beautiful one, will be honored as Oracle, here, and in Tyre, and all across the Mediterranean. This is only the beginning." He planted a kiss on her forehead. "I must get back. I leave tomorrow. My cousin will bring you gifts as befits a priestess. Do not turn him away. You will wear coriander and ambergris, the scent of Anat, and you will wear silk." He gathered his things and hurried to his waiting horse.

Nuriya watched him go, shaking from her the lingering image of the dead thing tangled in kelp. She remembered instead the approval in Ilobaal's eyes, feeling the goodness of it in the marrow of her bones.

Early the next morning Nuriya accepted gifts from Adnan, feeling she had done something of real value. He presented her with a jar of perfumed salve, a robe of wine-red silk, and a chemise of Sidonian blue. The ships had sailed, and were expected to return in four days, Gods willing. Nuriya hung the red silk above her sleeping place and tried on the blue.

When Korba arrived home from a day and a night of tending Coral through a gentle death, she was too fatigued to grasp Nuri's new vision of herself. Nuriya acknowledged her sorrow at Coral's passing then babbled that she had discovered how her gift was truly meant to be used. Korba made an effort to listen neutrally then told her to prepare for the honey harvest; they would place offerings before the sun went down. Korba was just trying to keep her occupied, Nuriya knew, but she graciously did as she was told.

The next day Nuriya magnanimously loved even the bees. As Korba gathered, Nuriya fingered the Tanit pendant, thinking that her life finally made sense. She was not destined to be a batty old seer like the woman on Lipari. She was destined, predicted even, to be Oracle to Ilobaal, the future Magistrate of

Malta. She had very little idea of what that meant but she knew the surety in Ilobaal's eye and her head swam with possibilities. She would travel to Tyre after all, not as Ilobaal's wife, but in a role of greater honor, as his Oracle. Her father would be astounded—and very proud. Later in the day Nuriya pulled the snake necklace out of hiding, thinking it appropriate to her new role, and unwadded the yellow scarf she had crammed in with it. She put the necklace on, resting it inside her chemise with the silver pendant facing out. She quelled all Korba's questions, saying, "Don't worry, Korba. This is different than Lipari. In my culture, Seers are advisors. They are respected." She did exaggerate her confidence but she desperately wanted it to be true.

Korba had recently delivered farmer Frer's fourth child and the next day he sought her to deliver his sister's first. It was expected to be an easy birth and Nuriya was eager to go along, wanting something more compelling to do than melt beeswax. As they came up to cliff road, Hawk stood waiting and Frer slowed his cart.

"He's not good for you," Hawk said flatly.

"It's none of your business," Nuriya replied tartly.

Hawk took in the blue dress and the silver pendant. "I wonder what service he pays for."

"Shut up. You don't know anything." Korba told Frer to proceed and Nuriya hunkered next to her.

"Ghoga misses you," Hawk called after the cart moved past.

"Will you be all right?" Korba asked her daughter.

Nuriya straightened. "I'm sorry, Frer. It won't affect my work."

"Lovers' spat," Korba opined. Nuriya did not correct her and Frer kept his comments to himself.

Several days later Nuriya was in the garden when two galleys flying the purple and white sailed east. She forced herself to finish her chores, though her mind sailed on with them to port. She washed carefully at the basin, shared a light supper with Korba, and as soon as the meal was finished she put on the wine-colored robe and went to sit in the temple in case Ilobaal would visit that evening. When it was full dark she climbed into bed without comment, and was up again at first light, setting out Korba's tea and returning to her vigil.

It was midmorning when hoof beats sounded. Nuriya's body was fluttery with anticipation but she remained seated, attempting to practice dignified decorum. When Ilobaal stepped into the temple she turned gracefully to greet him.

"I couldn't wait to see you," he gushed, helping her rise.

"How did the survey go?"

"Smooth as rabbit fur. Amangeel has taken me under his wing—a most excellent turn of events, thanks to you, my love." He pulled her close. "This is only the beginning," he breathed into her ear. "Let me look at you. So beautiful in that robe," he took a step back and she drank in his admiration. "But more beautiful without." He loosed her sash and slipped the robe from her shoulders. His eye caught a moment on the serpent dangling between her breasts then he slipped his hand between her thighs and put his tongue to her nipple. The thrill dazzled them both. He moved the mat to the alcove and invited her to it. He was patient this day, praising her beauty, nuzzling her and touching her until she begged for him. Nuriya took Ilobaal into her body, knowing full the wonder of it, marveling that this man, this warrior, honored by the envoy of the king, was here, loving her. She rode the rhythms of his pleasure, his enthusiasm pouring from him into her. Sparks of light twinkled all through her body at his peak, and she held him after, continuing to absorb into herself more of who he was, this growing power, this young prince.

After a while Ilobaal roused. Lazily, he traced her cheek. "Nurija, my love, I told my captain about you." She drew in a quick breath and he watched her absorb the news. "I told him that you are my Oracle." Nuriya felt ecstatic and giddy that she was no longer a secret! "His name is Rocannon," Ilobaal continued. "I will bring him to honor you. He will ask your blessing for the battle."

That last word felt like the sting of a bee. "What battle?" she asked, feeling that uncertain moment between the brief prick and the fiery pain to follow.

"I could not tell you before, love. The Tanit will join Tyre's mission to wipe the Greeks from western Sicily."

"What are you saying?"

Despite his undressed state, Ilobaal lapsed into oratory style: "Expansionists from Greece have defied us by sending colonists to the western shore. We will send the dogs back to their lair with their tails between their legs."

Nuriya felt dumped from lovely heights into a garbage midden. Her mind clouded over. The vision of a net dragging behind a galley came to her. She saw it clearly now—the rotting thing—was a dead man. Before her eyes the net grew large and many men dragged through a blood-dark sea. She sat up and tried to focus on the situation before her. "You said there was plenty of land on in Sicily."

Ilobaal seemed amused she should bring up this point. "There is land for farming, my love, but our concern is for shoreline. It would not do for the Greeks to have a site from which to harass our mining route."

"Why do you not council with them?" she challenged.

"We cannot negotiate with barbarians. Their warriors drink pig's blood to stir lust for battle. When they capture our people they make slaves of them. We cannot allow that kind to have a base near enough to threaten our colony of Motya."

"You've scarcely started that colony."

"Nurija, Nurija." His tone said she could not possibly understand the ways of men. "You said yourself that Motya will flourish. We are simply ensuring that western Sicily remains safe from the barbarous interlopers."

"Are your men so eager for battle as you?" she asked coldly.

"Of course. The soldiers complain they are only nursemaids to the dockworkers. Even the rowers are eager; all hope for plunder to supplement their wage." He saw her dismay and explained further, "We are reared to battle, my pet. I trained with my uncle since nine years of age. I was thirteen when he lost his life in Damascus and I regret to this day I was not there to avenge him. King Elulaios needs a champion of the western route and I will be that champion. The Greeks will leave western Sicily, or they will be annihilated."

Nuriya stood and planted her feet. "I want nothing to do with this. This is the opposite of healing."

"You are wrong, my Anat. A healer and a warrior are not so different. You battle with illness and with death."

"I don't think like that."

"Don't you?" He stood, and she turned from his nakedness. "Nurija, look at me." She turned back reluctantly, relieved to find him half dressed. "The Greeks are a tumor we must eliminate before it poisons the body of Sicily. We must act aggressively." He smiled at his eloquent comparison then pushed aside the folds of Nuriya's robe to fondle her breast.

She snapped her robe closed and paced away. "What does your wife say to this?" Her voice sounded shrill. Thus far she had not dared ask of her.

"Lady Johara will leave Tyre after the midsummer festival. She will know nothing of this. She is not my confidant, my Oracle is."

Nuriya's hands flew to her mouth. She could not forestall the flash of insight. "She carries your child."

Pleasure spread across Ilobaal's face. "Then it must be true. It is auspicious to birth an heir my first year." He realized too late that Nuriya did not share his enthusiasm; her back was turned again. He stepped close and spoke into her hair, "Do not think of it, Nurija. Know that you are the one I love. Come, my Oracle of Anat." He turned her around and said earnestly, "You are a Seer, and a Seer is beyond value. Only you can do this thing. One day I will command the western fleet and you will be at my side. You, my love, will be honored across all the Mediterranean. Remember this." He kissed her deeply. Then he finished dressing and fastened his sword belt. "I will be back with Rocannon in two days. Do not fret. He will love you." With seductive slowness he pulled the serpent from between her breasts and draped it over her robe. She also guards her secrets, Ilobaal mused, for only an initiate would wear such a talisman. He thanked his Gods that They allowed him to see through her guise. "My beautiful Anat," he whispered.

When he stepped from the temple, Adnan ran forward leading horse and donkey. Nuriya pulled her robe tight, abashed that the boy had been outside. Neither rider looked back however, as they mounted and rode toward port.

The next morning Korba tried once again to understand what Nuri was getting herself into, and once again Nuri insisted that she was being guided, that she was doing what she was meant to do; she did not mention the talk of battle or how it frightened her.

At midday, Bon came to fetch the women for a healing. En route Nuriya resumed a long forgotten habit of biting her nails, for it was an unwieldy burden she carried: her body reliving the magic of flesh upon flesh, her concern for what the captain would think, and her not-knowing of what Ilobaal would ask of her next.

Bon took them to a poor farm, a clan he knew from his childhood days. A boy came in from the fields, leaning heavily on his cane. Despite the warmth of the day, his skin was ashen and the women smelled infection as he approached. He had taken an axe blow to the muscle of his lower leg; his brother had been chopping wood at the time but neither would say how it happened. The wound had been dressed and then neglected until the boy fainted at work. It was Bon who convinced the father that a healer was needed.

He lay down as bid by his mother and she fussed over him in appropriate ways, though she was obviously guilty of either ignorance or neglect. There was a distinct line of redness rising up from the wound and the bandage did not peel easily from his skin. Korba made a wash of rosemary and hedge nettle and soaked the bandage until it came free. The wound bled where scabs did not hold. It had been packed with cobwebs, which worked well enough if wound and web were clean and regularly tended, but such was not the case. Flesh and dirt and remnants of web were festering together. Korba washed and squeezed out the putrid material while the boy watched, his expression teetering between horror and bravado. The healer asked the boy to identify a bird in a nearby tree and used the moment to scrape the wound with her knife. When it was clean, and the boy recovered from his shock, she went to speak to Bon. "He cannot be back in the field for at least five days." Bon frowned and Korba asked him, "Would you rather he lost his leg?"

"I know you're right. I'll speak to his father."

The healer told her apprentice to work with the boy while she brewed medicine. The moment Nuriya put her hands over the boy's leg, a memory came to her: sparks of light twinkling inside as Ilobaal made love to her. She decided that nothing could be putrid if imbued with that exquisiteness and so she welcomed the memory and thought to include the boy in it. She felt dazed later, and a little disappointed, when Korba interrupted her. So, too, the boy, for he looked stricken that Nuriya left his side, and followed her every move with the doleful eyes of a baby goat, even as Korba bandaged his leg and counseled him on work restrictions.

The next morning Nuriya went early to the temple to prepare for Ilobaal's arrival. Not until the sun was half way to its zenith did hoof beats sound in the distance. As they drew near, it sounded like a herd approached and unable to contain her curiosity, Nuriya went to the entryway. Gathering at the Aleppo pine were four men and Adnan, two wagons, the donkeys and the horse.

Despite the onlookers, Nuriya felt Ilobaal's presence like a thunderbolt. "My Lady Seer," Ilobaal proclaimed. "We come to honor you and ask your blessing on our mission against the Greeks." He approached her and bowed low. "How lovely you look today," he murmured. Stepping back he raised his voice again, "Rocannon, Captain of the Tanit, come forward."

A large man knelt before Nuriya. "Lady Seer, Rocannon, Captain of the Tanit, has brought an offering. Adnan?"

The boy hurried forward with two sacks of grain, went back to the wagon, and came forth bearing a heavy amphora of oil. Nuriya was overwhelmed. Not even a wife would be honored in this way. Ilobaal nudged Rocannon. "Lady Seer, bless the Tanit, and all who sail upon her," the big man said, keeping his eyes to the ground.

Ilobaal continued as acolyte, thinking he would train Adnan for the role: "Thank you, Rocannon, The Oracle of Anat hears your petition." Rocannon stood, nodded to Ilobaal, and stepped down.

"The ship's mate, Hilobaal, wishes to honor you." Ilobaal motioned another man forward who also genuflected before Nuriya. "Bring Hilobaal's gifts." Adnan brought an amphora of wine and then Hilobaal, himself, raised up a glass vial of perfume.

"Hilobaal," Nuriya said, trying out her voice.

The man looked up, his eyes wide with excitement, saying, "I ask your blessing for the men and the ship."

"The Oracle accepts your gifts and hears your petition," Ilobaal announced, nodding to Adnan to retrieve the vial. The ship's mate retreated. Ilobaal did not call the other man who remained by the wagon.

"What is expected of me?" Nuriya asked quietly so the men would not hear her ignorance.

"All you need say is that you bless our mission."

"Only the Goddess can mete out blessings."

"A Seer is mouthpiece for the Gods. A blessing from you comes from your Goddess.

"I don't know that."

"It is what Phoenicians believe," he said, mildly reproaching.

Nuriya glanced toward the men. "Tell them what you wish."

Ilobaal walked to the edge of the courtyard and raised his voice as if speaking to an army rather than three men and a boy. "The Oracle decrees that Anat and the seventy Gods bless our mission to free western Sicily from the Greeks." The men responded with words of thanks.

"You are excused. Tell the men of Anat's blessing and prepare for our departure." Ilobaal motioned Nuriya into the temple and followed her inside. "That was a bit of show for my men," he confided. "It will give them courage. But I know your real skills, love. I need your prophesy for the battle."

"No, Ilobaal! I know nothing of battle."

He clasped her hands and looked deep into her eyes. "The lives of forty-four men will be my responsibility. I need you to look to the battle, and see how they will fare...how Tyre will fare."

"I don't know if I can do it," she whispered.

"I know you can, Nurija. Your seeing will protect our people and serve our King. I request this on behalf of Elulaios and the kingdom of Tyre." He searched her features a long while and when he spoke again it was as if he cast a spell, "As I rise in power so, too, you rise, Nurija. You were born for this, to be my Oracle."

She took a breath, and let it out slowly. "I will try."

"My darling," he said with feeling.

As he helped her to sit before the altar Nuriya felt the tingling on her skin that heralded a shift into altered vision. She stated silently before the spirals: Ilobaal's safety, the Tyrian fleet, the mission against the Greeks, then closed her eyes.

Instantly she knew that something was wrong. She felt no expansive awareness of space, no communion with earth and sky, no connection—with anything at all. She adjusted her seat and took another breath. Still, she felt nothing. It was as if all creation had pulled into itself—an indrawn breath—and was held in suspense.

Then something crashed over her. "You enter unity with the request for division! You come to love in the name of war!" The message roared in the accusing voice of Nuriya's innermost self, and the truth wrenched her heart.

Before she could rescind her request, Nuriya was flooded with images: flailing arms and burning fires, axes flying, bodies wrestling and struggling and dying, sounds of splitting wood and curses and screams. Into the place she came for healing flooded scenes of men fighting men, killing men, murdering men.

Nuriya recognized Ilobaal in the prow of the Tanit, a pointed helm atop his head, a battle axe in one hand and shield in the other. Rocannon shouted an order and the ship propelled forward. A thunderous collision shook the galley. More orders were shouted and the rowers furiously changed direction. Creaking and crashing, the hull of an enemy ship was torn by the ram. Ilobaal leapt onto the damaged ship with his warrior crew close behind. Swords and axes swung and war cries split the air. There was the clanking of bronze upon bronze, curses and groans, and the sickening thuds of blades meeting bone. A horn blew above the riot and Ilobaal's warriors jumped off the sinking ship, back to their own. Again the crew was in formation, Ilobaal in the prow, Rocannon at the stern. Nuriya tried but could not pull herself away. Again she heard the shouted orders, the thundering collision and the charge onto the enemy ship. This time ugly details came to the fore: the death struggle of men drowning under splintered wood and armored chest plates, jaws shattered by battle axe blades, warriors choking blood as they begged for mercy. Nuriya saw the eyes of men, whose hands slick with blood slipped from their swords, crying for their mothers, or their Gods. Again the horn sounded. Revulsion filled every crevice of Nuriya's body, yet a third time the grisly scene repeated. A Greek rower caught Nuriya's eye as muscle and flesh were ripped from his body. His hands held back coils of gut as he beseeched her, "Athena, save me!" Above, on deck, another called, and suddenly Nuriya was beside him, the soldier clinging to her hem though his shoulder was cleaved to the bone. "Atherot, be with me!" he cried. She turned away to see yet another crumple before her, blood spurting from his throat as a misty form rose from his body, reaching for her and calling, "Help me, help me, Asherah." Franticly Nuriya sought Ilobaal. He was standing in the prow a fourth time. "I cannot bear this!" she screamed. But Ilobaal found no more Greek ships in his path.

A blood-dark sea was littered with bodies and splintered wood. The Phoenician ships gathered before beaching for the pillage, their proud standards waving high. They were twenty-four. Ilobaal strode to the back of the Tanit, lighting resin before a small statue of the Goddess Anat astride a lion. Pungent smoke rose heavenward.

Nuriya willed herself into the rising smoke. "Goddess Anat, Mother by any name, help me!" She folded into the scented haze, hearing still the cries of men and feeling their arms reach for her. She rose up and away from the scene of death. At last, she smelled untainted sea air and felt cool stone beneath her. She threw open her eyes.

"What did you see?"

Nuriya turned to Ilobaal, remembering him as if from a bad dream.

"Tell me, Nurija! Was I successful?"

Successful? What kind of question? Death and dying clung to her like a putrid stench.

Ilobaal dropped to his knees, pleading, "What did you see, Nurija?"

She focused on his purple sash and knew what he wanted to hear. She drew a ragged breath to say, "I saw you wearing the coned helm. You fell three ships. In the end Tyre will be twenty-four and the Greeks will retreat."

"You saw me successful in Sicily!" Ilobaal jumped up. "Oh, my love, I knew you could do it. You are my Anat, my Beauty beyond compare. You saw me wearing the helmet of 'Ba'al, The Smiting One'. I told you, Lady, you were sent to me by the Gods!"

Nuriya leaned over her arms, panting down a wave of nausea.

"Do you need water?" Ilobaal went out, called for water, and yelled to the hills that the Oracle prophesized victory.

He came back and Nuriya took the skin. She drank deeply, even upon discovering that he had brought her wine. She forgot for a moment what she was doing, why Ilobaal had come. She stared at him blankly.

Ilobaal's eyes were sparkling. "My sword is prepared, now too, my heart is ready. We shall be victorious. I must leave right away. You will be proud of me, my Seer, my love." He growled low in his throat, and was gone.

All about the periphery of Nuriya's vision wavered scenes from the carnage. "Do not fear," she told herself. "You know the path to peace." She faced her altar and settled into her breath—in-out—a soldier's voice moaned from some place beyond this—in-out. She closed her eyes.

Splintered jaws exploded across her brain. Bleeding mouths screeched cacophonous. Nuriya shot to her feet and lunged from the altar. She paced away to view Filfla through the stone window. Testing herself there, she closed her eyes. "No! No! No!" she screamed against the phantoms that instantly leered.

She went back to the altar. "Please, help!" she begged, focusing on the spirals, eyes open, waiting...and waiting. No soothing love emanated to embrace her. "I need you," she begged with a pounding, doubting heart. Finally, finally, there was a response. Something rippled out from the spirals, and broke over her—a wave of terrible, flawed, unbearable sorrow. Unbearable! She raced from the temple, ghosts dragging behind her. Echoey voices groaned, "Athena, Atherot, Asherah." Maybe the wine was bad.

She saw Korba coming up the path and ran to meet her. "They reach for me, Korba. I cannot help them."

"Who? Who can you not help?"

She took the water bag and tried to drink, her hands uncontrollable. "I did as I was asked. I saw the battle. It is still with me."

Korba enfolded Nuriya into her arms. "Daughter," she whispered, holding her close. "Can you walk home?"

"Yes." They staggered to their dwelling. Hallucinations of death lined Nuriya's path. She mistook a twig for an outstretched arm and nearly fell. She fought to keep her awareness on what was real: the earth underfoot, her teacher's hand, but the intervening shadows did not abate.

When they got to the fire ring, Nuriya pleaded, "Give me something to make me sleep."

The sun was past its zenith but would be a long time in setting. "You should eat," Korba said, reaching to check the pulse at her temple.

Nuriya snatched her hand. "I can't eat. Give me something." She could barely contain her hysteria.

"Tell me what happened."

"No, Korba. Please, sedate me." A door had opened in the making of the vision and Nuriya had no idea how to close it back. Specters haunted her sight; it was the blackness of the sleeping draught she wanted now. In the end, Korba gave her what she asked.

"Stay with me until I sleep," Nuriya begged. She stared at the limestone wall, studying the variations of color across the planes of stone. Her eyes crossed with the effort to focus on what was real, all the while voices groaned, "Asherah, Athena." *Please, oh please, henbane, poppy, grant me your gift of peace.*

Nuriya woke once to a darkened room. There was enough light to find a few drops of draught in the bottom of her mug. She slept again, waking after the sun was up. As she rolled over to stand, she caught a flash of wine-colored silk at the corner of her eye and that was all it took to flood her mind with blood-soaked swords and a blood-dark sea. She snapped her eyes shut but as before that was worse. She pushed out the door and stoked the fire. Keep busy, keep active, keep alert, she told herself. When the food was warm and Korba back from her offering, she announced that she would take her meal in the garden.

"You need purification," Korba said gravely.

"No. Thank you. I'll be fine." She had no intention of entering a temple in this tortured state for she knew no comfort awaited her there. She had transgressed against her precious love, and she had no knowing of how to amend her error. Korba could not help her with this.

She bit into her food and chewed mechanically as she weeded the garden. Then she hauled water, keeping her attention on the effort of her arms and the pace of her breath. It felt like her mind would crack if she allowed it to drift. After morning chores, she decided to build a pen for Ghoga and set about hauling stones, blocking persistent images by hoisting heavier and heavier ones, refusing to hear the moaning calls by repeating aloud simple phrases: "I am picking up this heavy stone. I am building this pen for Ghoga." The distraction worked somewhat, and the specters became fainter as the day wore on.

A call came for them after midday to see about a child who might or might not have the pox. Nuriya sat in the back of the cart, keeping her focus on the sounds of the cart wheels and the clop, clop of the ox. Several times when they traveled up a slope she got out and walked alongside. Korba tried to catch her eye but Nuriya avoided it. She did not want to admit that the haunting lurked.

When they arrived at the farm, Nuriya kept her attention full on the healer as she observed pupils and arm pits and frowned over raised bumps on the abdomen and back. Korba asked Nuri to check the other children while she examined the adults. Nuriya was meticulous, observing each and every possible sign. One boy had a swollen gland in his groin and a low fever. They moved him and the sick girl into a separate hut along with one of their mothers. The three in the hut were to consume medicine four times before night and were given a green broth for their meal. The entire clan was dosed with elderberry and any who exhibited rash or swollen glands would join the three in the sickhut.

The women returned home in the long twilight of the season. Nuriya hummed a children's song as she prepared food for Korba and then went to haul heavy stones as the full moon arose from the sea. She could feel the phantoms waiting for her to let down her guard. When she was ready for bed, she went to the storeroom and pulled down the sleeping draught.

"Using draught every night is not good," Korba said.

"I need to sleep."

"It would be better to talk."

"I don't want to talk. I don't want to dream. I just want to sleep."

"Don't use that up. The poppies aren't ready for another batch."

"I'll make my own then!" Nuriya flared. She banged around for her traveling bag, heated honey wine and scraped a sliver from her cake of poppy resin. Then she scraped in more as Korba grimly watched. "Don't say anything," Nuriya warned, "I know what I'm doing."

She woke the next morning groggy, thirsty, and with circles under her eyes, but as soon as she was upright she went about her chores and then to work on the wall. When she had a sizable pile of stones and had begun to stack them, she spotted two men making their way to the fork. She went to the dwelling to wait with Korba.

It was Oriole from Borg's clan and another they did not know. "Is Cara all right?" Korba asked worriedly.

"Cara is fine," Oriole said. "This is Caron's cousin. His brother's child is very sick."

Korba suggested that Nuri stay home but she insisted on going and she tried not to fidget on the way out to Mosta hill.

A tense compound awaited them. An older woman was reprimanding a group of children whose play took them too near the sick house. A line of stained diaper cloths were drying by the hearth. An exhausted man took them inside to where his wife sat with their sick child.

Korba interviewed the father. For two days his daughter had fussed with pain. She had black diarrhea and then vomited. He thought that would make her better but she only got worse. They stopped making her drink because she couldn't keep it down and since yesterday she was like this, listless, and burning with fever. "Is she going to die?" he whispered hoarsely while his wife hid her face in her hands.

The child, Bela, was indeed gravely ill. Her stomach was distended and hard, her cherub features, sunken and flat. Her eyes were glazed and she did not register the healers' presence. Nuriya held her breath as Korba placed her hands with exquisite tenderness on Bela's abdomen. The girl moaned through her stupor. "Nuri, heat water. I'll be out soon." Nuriya was relieved she was only the assistant.

When Korba came outside she spoke quietly, "Bela is full of sickness. The pain must be very bad. Do you remember Gia's baby?"

Nuriya remembered him well. Korba, usually so trusting of the Great Mother's wisdom, had suffered with that one. Gia's baby had sickness and pain in the right lower abdomen that Korba treated with poultices but suddenly his situation became deadly. Korba said the place that should have held the sickness burst like a weak spot in a water skin and poured the sickness throughout his body. The boy was at the edge of death for days and Nuriya remembered Korba raging at her prayers. It took a moon for him to recover fully.

"Gia didn't wait this long to call me," Korba said, "and I fear for Bela. Nuri, I want you to *see* if there is something inside that you could heal."

Nuriya was stunned. Did Korba know what she was asking? The voices had been quiet today, but what would happen if she tried to see? She wanted to do only simple tasks until the after-effect of the trance wore off. Why was Korba asking this? Was it her need for approval from Borg? No. Bela was really, really sick. Nuriya thought of her sweet, angelic face. Maybe, if she could focus on Bela completely and on nothing else, it would be all right. She had to try. She braced herself and reentered the room. Bela's mother was crying openly. The premonition of death lurked and Nuriya was determined it would not be Bela's.

She moved to the child's side. Bela's body was radiating intense heat, burning away what was left of her tiny light. Nuriya composed her intentions: I want to see if anything is broken, to bring coolness, and restore health. She focused on Bela's hard belly and sought to know what was inside, under the skin. Her hearing became instantly more acute—she heard a woman outside shushing children, and the wind in the roof reeds. The sound of wind reminded her of something...but she kept her focus on one desire: to help this child. She deepened her breath, but dared not close her eyes.

For a few precious moments Nuriya felt the blessed peace she had been missing these last days. Then, as if out of a mist, odd shapes began to rise. She knew the shapes—they were the ghosts of the warrior dead. She clenched her jaw and focused all her being on Bela. She saw beneath the skin now. Loops of intestine were hot and swollen, blood and pus spilling from a sac that looked so sick it was rotten. Nuriya began to hear echoey calls, "Atherot, Athena," and she prayed that little Bela could not see what shared space with her delicate being. Angrily Nuriya lifted her eyes, commanding the mists, Go away! When she returned her focus to Bela, her heart lurched to see a beautiful, ethereal energy bubbling up from the girl's body. Don't go! Nuriya's insides screamed. She felt torn in ten directions but she ignored all directions save one. In the center of her vision, she saw only Bela. She imagined washing pus and sickness from her gut with a basin of clean, clear water. She imagined weaving a web of healing over the rotten, torn place. She imagined cool, wet cloths on her skin and calling that ethereal energy back into her body. It was all Nuriya could do, and she could barely do it. Her vision was getting dark. She couldn't keep focus much longer. If she fainted, the ghosts would have her. Tears streamed down Nuriya's face as she flung the thought, *We love you, Bela!* Then she dragged herself up and out of the room. She tripped just outside the door but still she controlled her vision, studying carefully the three ants crawling there. When she could lift her gaze, she focused on a beetle making its way through threshing litter. Then Korba's hand was on her back. "Pull yourself together!" the healer snarled as she went inside.

At the hearth Nuriya splashed water on her face, trying to regain her balance. When Korba came out, she was short with her. "Settle yourself, and steam another pot."

Korba came again to sprinkle knotweed into the water saying, "I'm sorry I had to ask. You're going home as soon as I can arrange it."

"I can still assist."

"No, you cannot. Besides, I don't think Bela's parents want to see you again. Keep out of the way."

Nuriya gave herself the task of rewashing diapers, keeping her focus on her hands and what she could see before her eyes. The phantoms lurked; she could not even risk a prayer for little Bela.

In the late afternoon Korba waved her over. "Bela's keeping the medicine in. I think what you did helped. I'm going to stay and you're going home. Bon will be by tomorrow to pick up for Rita and I haven't finished it. Can you handle that?"

"Yes."

"When I get back, we are going to do a purification ceremony. You need my help." Nuriya nodded, desperate now for any help. "I wish I could be in two places at once," Korba said.

"I'll be all right."

Korba narrowed her gaze. "Not too much poppy."

Nuriya neither agreed nor disagreed. Oriole took her home and by lamplight she prepared medicine for Rita. Then she took a heavy dose of poppy wine.

It was almost midday when Nuriya awoke hearing her name being called. She hummed a tune to drown out the sound and studied the wall before her. She began to plan the rest of the day. The voice persisted. "Nuri. I'm calling for Nuri."

Slowly she arose, a headache threatening, pulled on a shift and squinted into the bright daylight.

"Are you Nuri?" A thin, sullen boy was standing by the fire ring, his oxcart tethered below.

"I'm Nuriya," she said, lifting a hand to placate her temple.

The boy identified himself as the grandson of Marna. "She wants you," he said.

"Korba isn't here. She should be back later."

"She don't want Korba. She wants you."

"Oh. What is needed?"

"She's dying. She wants medicine."

Nuriya rinsed her queasy mouth, guzzled two mugs of water and gathered her things. She was dismayed to think she would be tending a deathbed but she didn't see any way around it. She sensed around her, sniffing for phantoms. They were at bay for the moment, but it was a long ride to where Marna lived and she'd have to spend the night. If she kept things simple and on the surface—and dosed herself enough to sleep without overly sedating...or maybe she'd just stay awake all night.

She put a small cabbage and a strip of dried rabbit into her bag since she hadn't soaked grain. She remembered the medicine packet for Rita and they went by way of Bon's farm to drop it and leave word.

The ride across the island felt interminable and the effort it took to guard the borders of her mind, exhausting. Nuriya studied her surroundings, tended her hangover, and pondered why Marna requested her instead of her sister-in-law, Korba.

10.

The Dreamer

Late in the afternoon they came to a farm nestled against the slope of low hills, facing Mellieħa bay in the north. This was Korba's first home on the island.

Men milled the courtyard in a gloomy cadence. One stepped forward and without introducing himself, led Nuriya to a small hut where women clustered like bees to a hive. "Let the girl pass," the man ordered, and the cluster parted way.

"I heard you were a darkie." The words came from the withered woman bundled in the center of the room as Nuriya stepped inside. Nuriya looked behind her to see unsmiling faces lining either side of the doorway. "Don't go now, you've come all this way," the withered woman mocked. "If she raised you, you must have some skill. Korli, heat water, and tell the rest to leave." Marna spoke loudly for such a feeble-looking character. "I won't die before you have a chance to say your goodbyes," she told the departing ladies.

When the last of them shuffled out, Marna said, "They tend carefully to this old woman but the wine doesn't dull the pain anymore. I've been lying here, feeling the knife saw through my bones, and thinking. Ease my pain, then I'll say what I have to."

Nuriya performed a brief exam though she knew already she would use poppy, now being familiar with dose.

When Korli came in with steaming water Nuriya asked for warmed wine. This gave Korli offense for some reason and after a few unpleasant comments, she stormed back out. "No willow," Marna growled as Nuriya laid out her supplies. Korli brought in the warmed wine and was dismissed. Nuriya wished it was hotter but not wanting to face Korli again, managed to dissolve enough poppy as would put herself to sleep. As she worked, Marna spoke, "Do you know how beautiful she was? Every man wanted to lie with her." Nuriya knew she was talking about Korba. "My husband made me hate her, you know. I don't suppose she deserved it." When the medicine was ready, Nuriya offered the cup, suppressing her distaste for the woman. Marna grabbed her wrist, nearly spilling the medicine. She pulled Nuriya close, inspecting her carefully through cloudy old eyes. "So this is her replacement daughter," Marna said. "Ha. You didn't know. Korba's baby was born dead and she found you to take her place." The woman made a sputtering noise that turned into a fit of coughing. She released Nuriya to beat her own chest. "That, too," she croaked between coughs. Nuriya waited for the spell to subside then held the cup to Marna's lips, suppressing hate this time, understanding why Korba sacrificed to keep her from this family. The old woman drank most of the medicine then sank back to her blankets. Nuriya went to her bag to look for thyme and pull herself together. She didn't know Korba lost a baby but this hag had no right to say it that way, trying to make her feel low and make Korba sound self-serving. She wanted to go home, but it was too far to walk and too late to start out even with a cart; she had this awful woman to care for and still the phantoms to worry about. "I couldn't stop thinking about the bundles," Marna was saying, her speech already slowing. Nuriya didn't want to hear anything more this hag had to say. "I don't know what she'll do with 'em but they're hers." Marna was waving toward the back of the room. "Small basket. Bring it here."

Nuriya was gripped with an irrational need to find what Marna asked for. She moved to the dusky back wall where a jumble of jugs, mats and baskets were piled haphazardly and lifted up a small basket.

"Behind that."

The basket she found was neatly designed, the sides round like a bowl and decorated with zigzags. A dusty cloth protruded from it like a wick. She brought it to the bedside. "Pull it out," Marna barked. Feeling strangely nervous, Nuriya pulled out two fraying bundles of wool. "Open."

Unwrapping the first bundle, Nuriya found the carved stone figure of a woman sleeping on a low couch. She had the round thighs of the Goddess, ample breasts, shoulder-length hair and wore a pleated skirt. Nuriya's head started to swim. Her eyes began to blur. Marna's bark, "The other one," snapped her back to her senses. Nuriya rewrapped the figure and opened the second bundle. Inside she found an unusual necklace of pierced shell and drilled stone. Tiny points of pain pricked along the skin of Nuriya's arms as if she'd plunged into ice-cold water. What was going on? This was not the time or place for mysterious sensations. She carefully rewrapped the necklace, set it with the bundled figure and focused on the woman before her.

Marna spoke now with the cadence of reverie, "My husband stole 'em. Said they shouldn't go to a foreigner." Her face distorted and she made a high squealing sound. "I'm sorry..." She rocked her head back and forth. "After she lost her baby..." Marna's mouth fell open. She squealed again.

Korli raced in. "Mother! What's going on?"

"I wish I done better," Marna cried.

"Don't talk like that!"

"Aiyeee..." the old woman squealed.

"Can't you see she needs something?" Korli screamed.

"So much goes wrong..." Marna wailed then she started coughing uncontrollably.

"Do something!"

There was poppy left in the mug. Nuriya massaged Marna's back as she offered it. The woman calmed enough to drink then slurred, "Go. I wanna to talk to Korli."

Nuriya took the basket out into the late afternoon. She slipped through the morose crowd and found a rise of land facing out to sea. No one stopped her, and no one approached. Nuriya sat, dumbly watching sea birds dive and surface. She did not want to contemplate the old woman's regrets nor think about her own night ahead. At least Marna would sleep now.

The sun warmed the back of her neck. Distractedly, Nuriya closed her eyes. With a jolt she recalled the danger. Her eyes flew open, her senses hyper alert. But no shadows pressed upon her vision, nothing threatened, and the absence was stark. She dared try again. She closed her eyes—and felt only sweet, buoyant relief!

Her attention was drawn to the basket in her hands. It seemed that an energy radiated from it. In a flash Nuriya realized—the objects were holding the shades at bay. She wanted to tear open the bundles that instant, but not knowing what direction they might take her, she simply clutched the basket to her chest, feeling so, so, abundantly grateful. For the first time since the battle vision she could take a deep breath, here, among these not so friendly strangers. She indulged a wary doze right there in the afternoon sun, the basket of objects cleaved to her breast.

Footsteps woke her. "She wants you," Korli said fighting tears.

"She's awake?"

"Sort of."

Korli offered her hand and Nuriya pulled herself to standing, slipping the basket into her medicine bag, and went inside.

The room was crowded again. Marna was making sounds like, "Num, num, num," then smacking her lips and again, "Num, num, num." Nuriya filled a mug with water, but the woman wouldn't drink. She wet a cloth and offered water drops. Marna licked them off her chin between, "Num, num, num," and "Num, num, num." Then she waved Nuriya close. "I wanna hear Korba's prayer," she whispered loudly.

Nuriya glanced at the solemn faces behind her, cleared her throat, and began to recite the invocation: "Great Mother, guide my hands and guide my heart..."

"No," Marna shouted, waving her hand as if wafting an offensive odor. "The one—aiyeee—for the babyiee—her dead babyieee."

Nuriya understood what Marna asked for. It was Korba's prayer for the dead and comfort for the grieving. She steadied herself, and began again,

Great Mother,
You who are fierce as the storm
And forgiving as new spring
We call on you.
Great Mother,
Your embrace is as wide as the sky
And as deep as the sea
We call on you.
Into your Mother's heart welcome this spirit.
With grieving hearts we honor you.

In the quiet that followed there was only the soft, whistling sob of Marna's daughter.

"Korli," Marna croaked, "remember that." Then with a drunken gnash she roared, "More medicine!" But when Nuriya lifted the mug to her lips, she was already asleep.

A bed was prepared for the healer in a well-used hut. By lamplight Nuriya taught Korli to make medicine for her mother, then she lay with the basket on her chest and did not wake until morn.

Marna had slept through the night. She said she liked the medicine fine and Nuriya knew she would use too much. She left most of what she had, figuring she could get to Kepi for more, for it would likely be days before Marna died. Nothing further was asked of her. While Marna slept a morning nap, someone materialized to offer two skins of wine and a sack of wheat grain.

Nuriya traveled back across the island with the same sullen boy. It felt as if they moved through deep water, currents pulling this way and that, the mysterious objects in her lap parting the currents like the prow of a ship through a turbulent sea. All the forces of this world, and of that other world that menaced, bowed before the force of their presence. If Nuriya closed her eyes she was aware of that other world, but there was no threat to her person. It was as when the Magistrate walked through the market—no one save his son dared touch his hem—and not even that thought of Ilobaal threatened to disturb her.

The smell of food met Nuriya before they got to the fork, reminding her she'd hardly eaten for days. She invited the boy for a meal but he declined, turning his cart and leaving without asking to meet his kinswoman.

"How's Bela?" Nuriya asked, first thing.

"She's keeping barley water in and took milk last night, bless the Mother. Oriole will fetch me in the morning. But how are you, dear?"

Nuriya set her bag on the bench. "I need to show you something." She pulled out the basket and the two wrapped bundles.

Somehow Korba knew what they were and she stood stock still but for the tears forming in the corners of her eyes. In that moment, picturing the beautiful and courageous woman her foster mother had been, Nuriya realized how truly grateful she was for all Korba had given her. She watched Korba pick up the smaller bundle like it was an exquisitely fragile butterfly and peel back the folds of tattered cloth. A whimper of recognition came from her teacher's throat. "My wedding gift," Korba said, holding the necklace to her cheek a long moment before setting it back in its swaddling rag.

"Da'ani stole it."

Korba nodded, unsurprised. "It disappeared before I arrived on Malta." She took up the other bundle and unwrapped the sleeping woman. "Beautiful dreamer," she cooed. She cradled it to her heart then held it out. "Do you see, Nuri? She dreams sweet dreams. That's what Davi told me."

Nuriya did see. She ached to clutch the statue to her breast and never let go.

"What's wrong?"

Nuriya shook her head, afraid to speak.

"Do you want to hold her?"

Nuriya nodded and solemnly accepted the figure.

"Tell me," Korba said.

"When I hold her the phantoms don't come."

"When you hold her..."

"Yes," Nuri whispered

"She dreams sweetly—and you fear to dream."

"Yes."

Mother and daughter gazed into each other's eyes, Nuriya desperate to be understood and Korba determined to understand. As it came clear, Korba nodded once. "You need to ask permission. My husband didn't know to ask before taking a sacred object from its resting place."

Nuriya lunged to hug her mother. "Thank you, Korba. I'll ask right away. Where did he find her?"

"The Cave of Bones."

"These are?" Nuriya couldn't finish her sentence for the bile welling in her throat.

"Not grave goods, Nuri. Davi showed me exactly where he found her, and this." She touched the necklace. "Do you remember the temple underneath the Cave?"

"You told me," Nuriya said, the tension back in her shoulders. Long ago Korba showed her the entrance to an ancient burial cave near Tarxien, called the Cave of Bones. Through a bramble thicket all Nuriya could make out was a cave opening filled with a cascade of rocks. Nearby stood a lone trilithion, two massive blocks of stone several feet apart, supporting a third horizontal slab, marking the vicinity as a sacred place and lending it an eerie ambience. Korba told her that deep within the earth, carved two and three stories underneath the cave, was a temple as grandly adorned as Mnajdra. It seemed a fanciful tale.

"She was in a dream chamber," Korba said, coaxing Nuriya's hands to loosen so they could both look at the statue. "Look at the folds in her skirt, and the pattern on the bench. She is a dream priestess, I think. So lovely she is." Together they gazed upon the statue, absorbed each with their own yearnings.

"How—how do I get permission?"

"You need to ask the spirits of the Cave."

Nuriya swallowed with effort. "When can we go?"

"I'll be with Bela tomorrow."

"I know," Nuri said, disheartened and ashamed for frightening Bela's parents. She remembered then, "Marna said you had a baby. I didn't know."

"Yes," Korba said fingering the necklace. "My daughter was stillborn. That was a long time ago." She allowed herself a moment of reflection then refocused on what was before them. "If Bela is doing well we can go the next day. We need someone to clear the entrance, though. Hawk would do it if you asked."

"I don't want to ask. I haven't been very nice to him."

Korba's mouth tightened over something she did not say. Instead, she held out her hand. "I'm going to Mnajdra. Come with me?"

"I'm not ready," Nuriya said, bravely placing the statue onto Korba's palm. "I want to visit the Cave first. Then I'll do any purification you want me to."

As before, the moans echoed if Nuriya let her mind drift and specters stalked if she dared to close her eyes. She worked all afternoon on the pen, meticulously stacking stones and thus contained her anxiety until Korba returned from Mnajdra and placed the dreaming woman back into her hands.

Nuriya sat with the figure through much of the night watching the fire-glow play across her surfaces. Then, curling around her under the open sky, she found a deep and nourishing sleep.

The next morning Borg arrived with Oriole, telling them how well Bela was doing and thanking Korba repeatedly.

"Good morning, Borg. Your news does my heart good. Nuri, pour tea while I gather my things."

Korba asked Oriole to take her bag to the cart, telling him they would be along shortly. When he was out of earshot she tapped Borg's knee. "I've a favor to ask. Do you know the Cave of Bones?

"Naturally."

"Can you get us in there?"

"Why would you want...?" but registering his healer's inscrutable expression he didn't finish the sentence. "It was sealed without mortar and there's a bramble thicket in front but I can do it. When do you want it cleared?"

"Tomorrow."

Borg nearly spit out his tea. When he regained his composure he said, "Korba, I owe you my life. I am indebted to you for the lives of my wife, my daughter and my niece. I will do anything for you, but I don't want my father to hear of it."

"Would he hear it from me?"

"Oh, right." Borg's expression was chagrined. "But do you know the stories, Korba? They say the dead steal children in the night. That's why it was sealed."

"Do you believe everything you hear, Borg?"

"Maybe they told us that so we wouldn't play there?"

"Could be."

"There's a story about a secret kingdom inside."

"Few are willing to walk past the bones to find out."

Borg bowed his head. "I'll leave that to you, Korba."

"Fine. If you clear a large enough opening we won't need torches."

"Will you need a ride?

"We'll get ourselves there." She extended her hand.

"Coming, Nuri?" Borg asked as he helped Korba up.

Nuriya was surprised that he'd asked...maybe nothing too bad had been gossiped about her. "I'm going to stay. I'll see you tomorrow."

Nuriya worked on the wall all morning with her precious bundle tucked in a bag slung over her shoulder, then she tended to her usual chores. In the afternoon she would ask Bon to take them to the Cave, though she wasn't sure how she would explain it. She was thinking about that as she hauled a bucket from the cistern and didn't hear footsteps.

"I'm sorry for what I said."

Nuriya jumped then turned. "I'm sorry for what I said, too." They looked at each other a long awkward moment. "I'm making a pen for Ghoga," Nuriya offered.

"I heard." Hawk cleared his throat. "Korba asked me to take you tomorrow."

"When did you see her?"

"This morning. They came on the way to Mosta."

"Oh."

"I wanted to talk to you first."

She forced a smile. "Iva."

There was another awkward pause.

"I'll see you tomorrow then." Hawk turned and Nuriya watched him go, knowing she had disappointed him yet again.

Oriole dropped Korba off before dark. After the healers discussed Bela's progress, Nuriya asked, "What did you say to Hawk?"

"That we are going to visit the Cave of Bones. He wasn't keen on seeing you either I should say, but he respectfully obliged me."

"Korba..." Nuriya whined.

The healer raised a hand to quiet her. "Borg will need help to clear the opening."

Although it was late when Nuriya got up the next morning, Korba was not yet back from her offering. Nuriya lingered over breakfast, both reluctant and impatient to get going. The sun felt heavy and hot upon her as she gazed toward the horizon, fearing the day, yet seeing no other option.

"Solstice today," Korba reminded when she returned from Mnajdra wearing the shell and stone necklace. Her eyes shone as they always did after a good ritual—this morning she'd have watched the rising sun strike the summer panel and made special offerings. "Come with me to bathe?" Nuriya shook her head, dismayed that so distracted she had been she hadn't noticed the passage of time. "Come on," Korba coaxed. "Hawk won't be here until midday."

Shortly after the women returned from their bath, Hawk and Blaki drove up. Hawk, in a sober mood, climbed the hill to see if they had anything to carry; they had only their medicine bags and waterskins.

Korba talked incessantly as they rode toward Tarxien, commenting on the heat, the view, and the plants, with Hawk grunting single word replies. When they got close, Korba told him, "You will help Borg open the Cave mouth then Nuri and I will go through to the temple below."

"Why would anyone build a temple under a burial cave?" he asked.

"Do you have a burial site for your clan, Hawk?" Nuriya was appalled that Korba would use this tense moment for teaching.

"Yes, ma'am," Hawk replied.

"Is it a special place for you?"

"More like a place we avoid. We leave that field fallow."

"The Temple Builders felt differently. Death is the Mother's greatest mystery, and under the bones of their ancestors they carved a holy place to gather."

Nuriya knew already what the healer believed about death and she thought it childish; for certain that the dead soldiers were not resting peacefully in the heart of the Mother. In fact, despite the bundle she held in her lap, Nuriya felt them pressing close again. What if they attacked when she walked into the Cave, the domain of the dead? She was about to scream for Korba to shut up when she realized that her teacher's chatter was probably purposeful distraction, and for her benefit.

"You'll see for yourself, Hawk," Korba said.

"I don't think I'll be seeing, ma'am. I'll be waiting outside."

"As you choose."

"Yes, ma'am."

The sun was on its descent when they arrived but the day, still brutally hot. Borg had hacked away at brambles all morning and was now laboring to remove boulders and the smaller rocks. He was grateful for the refreshment Hawk brought, and for his help.

While the women sat in the shade of an oak, Korba pondered the irony of this moment. When she fled her husband's family so many years before, she camped near this spot. She came to the cave to grieve her husband and her stillborn daughter. The boy, Grof, had spied her going inside and when she emerged, he threw stones at her screaming, "Witch! Witch!" To make him leave Korba went back in and made enough wild noise to scare him good. Then she went out and broke camp, knowing she would need a new place to sleep. As she headed to find a more remote spot, Grof returned with his father and brothers. From a hiding place, Korba witnessed Grof's father whip him for playing where he should not, ordering his sons to seal the Cave, and planting those very brambles his grandson just spent the morning clearing.

When the entrance was open to Korba's satisfaction, Borg bid them good day. He did not want to engender questions as to what he had been doing, and the women had Hawk to watch for them. "Wait near," Korba told Hawk. "There's light from the sun now but we may be back for torches."

Hawk patted his smoke horn and assured her, "I'll be right here."

Before they went inside, the healer removed the necklace and placed it into Nuriya's palm. "I never intended to keep the necklace for myself. You may ask about keeping it, if you choose."

Nuriya stepped inside the Cave first. As her eyes adjusted to the dim light, she took in the cool stillness of the air and the not unpleasant smell of must and bone. The entrance walk was a steep ramp downward. She moved several steps forward before she heard the sound—was it the thrumming of bat wings? The buzzing of bees? No—it was a thousand voices quietly humming! Nuriya froze and waited for the inevitable, but the inevitable did not happen. No spirits blocked her passage. No one threatened, nor beseeched, nor taunted. Though her legs felt like animal fat melting over fire, she forced herself on, keeping her eyes on a spot of brightness in the distance, an archway lit by the sun filtering through the cave mouth behind her. Along each side of the passage a myriad of rounded out burial chambers were cut into the walls and floor of the cave. Nuriya did not investigate the piles of bones at the back of each chamber, nor the curled skeletons dusted with ocher near the front. She kept her sight forward, always forward, fixed on the dimly lit archway. The humming ebbed and flowed as she moved, with Korba close behind her.

She paused when she reached the end of the descending walk. The archway was a rounded opening cut into the back wall of the cave. Below and before her, visible through the archway, was a cavernous chamber. No natural cave was this; even in the dim light, Nuriya could make out trilithion marked doorways, pitted altars, columns painted red and circular windows opening into yet other spaces. The chamber was so improbable here under the earth, and so beautiful, it made her weep.

Korba stepped to Nuriya's side, blocking the light, then moved behind her daughter to look over her shoulder. "What do you think?"

"It is as you said," Nuriya marveled.

"Let me show you where Davi found those."

Korba lead a curving path down and through several archways until they stood on the floor of the central chamber. It was a roughly circular space, large enough to hold thirty people, with a layer of earth overlaying smooth rock. All the features, the pillars, the corbelling, and the archways, had been carved into living stone, mirroring the features of the temples above. The effect was breathtaking.

In the wall opposite the arched overlook was a massive doorway, the base of which was waist high. Its stone door had been moved to one side revealing another elaborate chamber within, and barely visible from Nuriya's vantage, a still smaller chamber within that. "The Holy of Holies," Korba said, pointing. The inner chambers had been carved directly in line with the arched window and the cave mouth so that, even though they were two stories underground, dim sunlight filtered into the space. To the left of the great door were openings to two egg-shaped hollows large enough for a person to sit or lie down in, with a stone bench next to each. Above were four similar openings. "The dream chambers," Korba said. "She was in one of those and the necklace was on a bench." Nuriya knelt by the bench farthest from the entrance and laid the necklace upon it. She unwrapped the small statue, and solemnly placed it in the chamber next to it.

Nuriya was here to ask if she could keep the dreaming figure. Korba had explained that this kind of asking was done in the heart, that she needed to connect with the spirits of this place and ask if she could keep the holy objects Davi found here. Nuriya knew already the spirits of this place, they were the thousand voices humming above. They seemed benevolent—respectful even—but connecting to them was a risk she was not ready to take.

"I thought you might want to sit in a dream chamber," Korba whispered.

"No!" Nuriya stood quickly. The harshness of her voice echoed off the chamber walls. When the echoes died she said softly, "I'm not ready."

"All right."

"Can I see the rest of the temple?"

"We'll need the torches."

They went out and Hawk lit a torch for each of them. The sun was dropping in the sky and he warned them not to take much longer.

Korba led the way back in. Nuriya kept her eyes on her silver hair, ignoring the hums that beckoned on either side. Korba stepped through several passages into a rectangular room, and holding her torch high, revealed the painted spirals that covered the ceiling and walls. Nuriya used her torch to study the ceiling, then jumped at the eerie drone that reverberated in her ear. "Just me, Nuri." Korba pointed out a hollow cut into the wall that had magnified her voice. They went into another room, this painted with swirling vines and interlinked honeycombs. "I always think of this when we harvest," Korba whispered. She led on to the holy of holies she had pointed out from the main hall. Entering through an elegantly corbelled facade, the innermost room was plain with a simple, unfinished altar carved into the back wall. Upon the rough-hewn altar lay a dark obsidian disc with a hole near one edge like a large pendant. Nuriya polished the disc on her tunic and so finely cut it was that it shone like a mirror. High on the back wall was a protrusion with a hole through it, and responding to the obvious intent, Nuriya found a thong in her bag, looped it through the mirror and hung it. It was pleasing, hanging there, its glassy surface reflecting torchlight about the room.

Nuriya knew that it was time to do what she had come to do and so they made their way back to the central chamber. "Let's put out the torches," Nuriya suggested, wanting to stand again in the room's natural light. With torches extinguished, the women found the doorway to the holy of holies glowing red with the light of the setting sun. As the sun shifted lower and lower, deeper and deeper crept its apex of light toward the inner sanctum. The women were awed by the magnificence of the sun's own ritual.

Nuriya saw the dangling obsidian a moment before the sun met her own reflection within it. Prismatic lights exploded. A fiery shard flashed into Nuriya's eye then more lights began to flash. "No!" she screamed. She knew what was coming. Before she was swept into a seizure, she managed the panicked thought, "Benevolent spirits, help me! Don't let the soldiers get to me!"

Hawk had been lingering in the entryway, fretting over the women as the sun set but loathe to enter the domain of the dead. The moment he heard Nuriya's scream he lit a torch and raced into the darkened cavern. Echoes reverberated around him and he could not tell from where the sounds came. "Where are you?" he shouted, jabbing his torch, slashing skulls and skeletons with frantic light, his own voice echoing and mystifying him further. After an agonizing time of waiting for the echoes to cease, he heard the muffled sound of Korba's voice.

Hawk reached the overlook to the central chamber and raised his torch high, casting bizarre shadows over the walls. "Here, Hawk," Korba pitched her voice low but it carried easily to his ears. He could barely make out the healer kneeling over a shape on the ground. "Nuriya!" he shouted, echoes exploding once more. Miraculously, he found his winding way to the floor of the chamber, his torch illuminating Nuriya's convulsing body. "Demons!" he hissed.

"Not demons, Hawk. This is a seizure—a spirit journey," she added with uncertain hope.

"What do we do?"

"Hold her head and don't let it hit stone."

Korba watched Nuriya with an objective eye. The intensity of the seizure was beginning to calm. "I had hoped..." she broke off, pushing to her feet. "Stay with her. I'll be back." She relit her torch from Hawk's.

"Where are you going?"

"Not far. You'll hear me."

Hawk needed to be strong now among things he did not understand. He held Nuriya's head, watching torchlight flicker across
her otherworldly expressions. Soon came the sound of Korba's
chanting throughout the chamber. The chanting did not calm
him. Nuriya's open unseeing eyes in this temple under the earth
did not calm him. Here he was, under the Cave of Bones, in a
temple no one knew existed, watching over his love, who loved
another, while she journeyed among the dead. Hawk, he
thought, you are an idiot.

The flashing lights became brighter and more continuous until it
seemed that Nuriya had entered a world made entirely of light.
Patterns and shapes pulsed within the phosphorescent luminosity.
The beauty was exquisite, but she remained choked with fear.

"We are not soldiers," Nuriya heard emanating from a shape
within the luminescence. If starlight could speak, this was the
voice it would have. "We have never been soldiers."

"Who are you?"

Before she received an answer, Nuriya saw that which she
most feared—the man with the severed arm, the one who
cawed endlessly, "Atherot, Atherot."

"No!" she shouted, but the soldier didn't even look in her direction. He was gazing toward a pattern of shining light, saying,
"Atherot, you have come." The light shone brighter than bright
and Nuriya saw the man's eyes fill with awe and his face grow
gentle. His bloodied body became engulfed in radiance, and
then he was no more.

There was a moment of utter stillness before other soldiers
began to appear. Two, then three, five, then twenty warrior

ghosts communed with forms in the shining light, calling this one, "Athena," that one "Asherah," this one, "Mother," gazing into magnetic luminosities, until each and every one was engulfed and then seen no more.

A brilliant, silvery light coalesced before Nuriya. She could make out no features but it seemed that the form was female. "What happened to the soldiers?" she asked the shape of light.

"We showed them the way." This was the sound of moonlight on water.

"To where?"

"To their peace."

Nuriya wondered at this, conversing with moonlight—was she dreaming?

"Yes, you are *dreaming*," the sound shimmered with amusement.

"Are you the spirits of the dead?"

"We are spirit, and we have lived before."

"But the soldiers—were dead—and they were so awful." Nuriya had seen the phantoms disappear but the fear of so many days was still with her.

"We died in peace. We were not lost."

"Why do you linger here?"

"Our people bid us remain to watch over our Dreamer. You have returned Her to us at last. Go. She awaits you."

Hawk heard Nuriya murmuring and leaned in to catch the words. When she raised herself to move to the dream chamber, they came face to face and eye to eye. "Hawk," Nuriya acknowledged him. "I'm going to the Dreamer." She crawled toward the chamber, trusting he would understand. She did not want to break her connection to the spirit world with explanations.

◎◎

Hawk had no words to describe what he felt in that moment. Such a brief interlude—such a rare vision—when Nuriya looked at him, it was as if the light of the stars shone through her eyes. And when she acknowledged him, it was as if she named him as a man for the first time, the man he knew himself to be—the steadfast guardian—and fierce protector. He realized that crouching here in the belly of the Earth, watching over Nuriya, was exactly where he wanted to be.

Nuriya kept her focus on what she had been told to do. She climbed into the chamber and curled around the Dreamer. She could make out Korba's warbling chant within the background of humming and it buoyed her, gave her the courage to pray, "Dreamer, heal me."

For a long time nothing happened. Disappointment and anxiety lurked at the edges of Nuriya's awareness. Then her gut lurched, and it felt as if she was moving very fast. She opened her eyes to see a series of images flashing before her, pictures of the recent past: the ship's mate making his offering—her warning Ilobaal of the ambush—their first lovemaking. Each image was fleeting but contained the complete story within it. There was a painful flash of her assault—then Meera was gazing into her eyes—and then the day Hawk fell off Jimi. Time was moving backward. She saw the faces of patients she had assisted Korba in treating. There was her father, and her mother, but even they were gone before she had time to think. She saw Korba as a young woman, arriving on the island for the first time, and it got even stranger after that. A poor fishing folk came ashore to try their hand at farming and Nuriya knew them to be the ancestors of Korba's husband, Davi. An earlier people swept through the island in search of riches, found none and moved on. Time spun faster, glints of bronze, faces, ships—until Nuriya reached the time which seemed to be her destination—for she entered into the image as if she was there, body and soul.

The temple facades stood three times the height they were now, their polished stone exteriors reflecting sunlight like grand beacons, visible from far out at sea. The surrounding land was prosperous, supporting well the caretakers of the temples. In this time and in this place Great Mother Goddess was revered as the Mother of the World. Dreams were considered Her sacred guidance. Pilgrims from all about the Great Sea came to receive healing on this island of peace, where life and worship were joyful expressions of honor to the Divine Mother.

But beyond this oasis in the center of the sea, a change was upon the land. The time of Great Mother was ebbing, and the power of Her Sons, arising. Peoples of the mainland north roamed in increasingly fierce tribes, honoring the mighty sword and neglecting their reverence for the Mother. In the south, the empire of Egypt was arising. The Pharaoh, Son of the Sun God, would become supreme leader of all its people. To the east, in the city states of Akkad, Umma and Lagash, a myriad of Son Gods jockeyed for dominion. The highest honors were given to the Gods of War and their surrogate kings. As Son Gods grew in power, their followers conquered in Their Names to feed them even more power. The Goddess was demoted, divided, raped, and married off.

Soon, the change arrived on Malta's shores. Ships that once brought pilgrims and trade now brought conflict and disrespect. Rather than seeking healing, men sought only brides. There was tension, too, among the temple builders as they grappled with the pressure to conform to the changing world. When their way of life could no longer be maintained without weapons and walls, they made the decision to move on.

The People of the Temples moved north and west, away from

civilization's reign of the Sons, taking their building skills and their spirals with them. The Dreamer was left behind in this secret, sacred place. The People of the Temples said to the spirit of the Dreamer, "As breath moves in and breath moves out, as the seasons turn and turn again, it is time for Great Mother to sleep and for us to go. Until the time when She reawakens to walk the earth in the hearts of Her children, we ask You to remain. Hold our memories and our hopes in Your Dreaming. Wherever we go, we will think of You here, guarded by our ancestors, and safekeeping our dream."

The flow of information finally stilled and Nuriya was awash with images and awe. Reverently she whispered, "I welcome this Dream into my heart."

She heard shimmering moonlight respond, "You, too, are a Dreamer, Nuriya," and she felt proud to be named so.

Then she heard the voice of a blazing fire. "Dreaming is a sacred power. To use power for selfish ends brings darkness into the world. How will you use your Dreaming, daughter?"

Shame burned inside Nuriya. "I don't know—I tried..." She faltered then whispered pleadingly, "I think—I did wrong." All about her lights intensified into flaming spears and the dread of the haunting flooded back in. A sound cracked like thunder and Nuriya shook to the core of herself. From beyond the horizon a great force gathered. It rolled toward her, gathering and gathering, crashing into her chest and imprinting her with these words: "Your Heart Is For Joy And For Sorrow, And For Loving, Always." Waves of the force rolled up to fill her eyes: "Your Eyes Are For Laughing And Crying And For Seeing Clearly." From east and west came a great rushing into her arms: "Your Arms Are For Healing And Holding And Bringing Comfort." Then the brightness of sunfire filled her womb: "Your Loins Are For Pleasure And For Birthing And For Loving, Always." And a tumult of intensity filled both her legs: "Your Legs Are For Standing Strong."

Nuriya's body had become a bright and vibrating beacon of light, each leg rooted deep into the rock of this place. She heard, though she could not tell from within or without, "Be Whole. Be Healed. Be Divided No More." And so it was.

After a time, Moonlight-on-water shimmered: "Remember us, Healer Nuriya, your relations here. We will help you choose wisely." Then the stone and shell necklace was placed about her neck, and Nuriya felt she was crowned queen.

Hawk took note when Korba's chanting stopped. "How is my child?" the healer asked, appearing from the shadows.

"All right, I think. She said, 'I'm going to the dreamer,' then she went to sleep."

Korba observed the calm on Nuri's face and felt her pulses. "It won't be long now." She found a nearby wall to lean against. "Come, Hawk, sit with an old woman."

"Pardon me, Korba, but I'll stay right here."

"As you choose."

Eventually Nuriya opened her eyes to see Hawk's face haloed in torchlight. She squinted past him, into the shadows. "Where am I?"

Hawk reached for a courage he did not feel to say, "Under the Cave of Bones."

"But..." she turned to see the dream chamber behind her, "I thought I was in the chamber..."

"Welcome back, daughter," Korba greeted her. After performing a brief exam, the healer asked Hawk to leave them to speak in private. Reluctantly, he backed away.

"A great being gifted me the shell necklace," Nuriya said touching her chest. Finding copper and silver instead of bone and shell, she was puzzled again.

Korba hobbled over to the bench, picked up the shell necklace and raised it to the ceiling. "We thank you. We honor you," she prayed aloud, then draped it over Nuriya's shoulders saying, "Who am I to object to a Great Being's wishes?"

Nuriya removed the Tanit pendant, staring at it long, then shook her head. "It's not right for me—to vision battles." She put the pendant on the bench where the other necklace had been, saying, "I honor the men of the Tanit who lost lives in the ambush and in the battle. I pray they be guided to their peace." When she turned back to Korba she had tears in her eyes. "It will be hard to say no to him."

The old healer rested a hand on Nuri's shoulder. "You are strong. You will find a way. Are you going to keep the statue?"

"No. She belongs here. But I don't want to leave her so exposed. I don't want to risk she might be taken again."

"I know the place. Bring her, and the pendant."

Korba led to a trilithion marked doorway and pointed down. Nuriya descended an uneven spiraling stair into the deepest recess, and found herself in yet another labyrinth of niches and small chambers. Korba was all business as she and Hawk crowded in behind, telling Hawk to move a stone, positioning the Dreamer, and draping the silver pendant over her as an offering. Then the three stood before the Dreamer in silence, in a moment beyond words.

Finally, they made their way back out into the night. A lazy golden moon, three days past full, hovered over the eastern slope. Korba asked for a bed in the back of the wagon and they started home.

"Thank you for coming, Hawk," Nuriya said as they rolled along in the moon dark. Waking up feeling so deeply cared for had not gone unnoticed.

"You're welcome," he said earnestly. "Anytime you need me, Nuriya."

Feeling a new intimacy with Hawk, Nuriya spoke more freely than she ever had before. "I always thought it was a mistake that my father left me on Malta. All my life I've been waiting to leave, to go to Tyre. But now I don't know. Back there, the spirits spoke to me like they knew me. They showed me," she paused and realized she might never have words for what they showed her, "Many things."

"You belong here, Nuriya," Hawk said emphatically then added so softly that she almost didn't catch the words over the wagon wheels, "I want you to be happy."

"Thank you," she said quietly and they rode on in a companionable silence.

When they were close enough to see the moon-glow reflecting off Ħaġar Qim, Nuriya spoke again. "I'd like to visit Ghoga tomorrow."

Hawk flashed a goodly grin. "How about I bring her to see her new pen?"

Nuriya slept well and in the morning returned to Ħaġar Qim for the first time since that fateful vision, ready to face whatever presented itself—whatever depth of sorrow, or anger, or forgiveness. Alas, what she found when she sat before her cherished spirals, was that holy and exquisite feeling of being embraced by a vast and mighty love.

Nuriya knew the power that allowed her to feel such love was what Ulma called Goddess. But 'Goddess' made Nuriya think of Anat—and an unpleasant sequence of thought that led toward Ilobaal. She tried naming the power, "Great And Generous Presence," or "Great Mysterious Love," but those words were clumsy on her tongue. In the end she yielded to the name she was taught as a child, the name by which Korba addressed her deity and the same which she heard when she journeyed in the Cave of Bones. "Great Mother," she said, slowly, as if she had never before spoken the words, "I'm not sure what it means to pray to You, but I thank You for this, for letting me feel this beautiful love."

Ghoga spent her first night in her new pen. Blaki bawled unceasingly and Sema made Hawk sleep in the field with her so the family could get some rest. The next time they tried it, Hawk brought Blaki to stay with Ghoga, and that went much better for everyone.

Hawk and Nuriya were leading mother and calf back to the cistern when Nuriya spotted Adnan heading to Ħaġar Qim. She handed over Ghoga's rope. "I must speak with him."

Hawk stood at a distance as Adnan announced to Nuriya, "The warriors are returned from their successful campaign. Ilobaal of Tyre will tomorrow seek the Oracle." He could not be cajoled into further news.

Nuriya walked slowly back to Hawk. "I will speak to him tomorrow."

Hawk's face showed his worry. "Should I be with you?"

"No. I have to do it myself. I will tell him..." she looked away, "...that I cannot be what he wants me to be."

"I should come."

"No. Don't. I'll be all right."

"Be careful."

Nuriya excused herself to pray before her altar.

The next morning she rose at dawn to await Ilobaal's arrival. It wasn't until late morning that she heard an unnerving racket. Did Ilobaal bring an army? She forced herself to remain seated until his voice rang out, "I seek audience with the Oracle of Anat." She stepped to the doorway.

A throng of men were arrayed about the Aleppo pine. Rocannon was there, and Hilobaal, and other faces she did not recognize, perhaps ten altogether. She had not envisioned such an audience for this sober meeting.

"We come with gifts of thanks for our victory against the Greek aggressors!" Ilobaal proclaimed. He stepped forward and spoke in a lowered tone, "We sailed from Carthage to strike the dogs late in the day. They had the sun in their eyes and we the advantage. Syracuse sent twenty ships to defend the camp and still they were defeated! The Greeks won't sniff again in the west for a very long time. The Tanit felled three, as you foretold, my Oracle. You knew! You are a true Seer and all my men know it."

Ilobaal's praise touched a powerful craving in Nuriya, yet she clung to a conviction deeper still. She glanced toward the men. "What do they want?"

"They want to know their gifts are acceptable."

"Tell them what they need to hear."

Ilobaal turned to the group and raised his voice, "The Oracle accepts your thanks and proclaims that you are honored by the Goddess Anat for your deeds of valor." A satisfied murmur moved among them.

He organized the gift giving, calling out the name of each man, "Orvid, Hanibaal, Becamel." They brought forth offerings, handed them to Adnan, bowed before Nuriya, and backed away to the wagons. Adnan stacked the goods in the front alcove, prominent among them, a stone anchor from the Tanit and a bowl of hammered silver. One man offered a ruby ring, and another a gold chain. "Trophies from the pillage," they wanted her to know. Nuriya's stomach was sour.

The men were dismissed with flowery words and Ilobaal took Nuriya inside. "They love you, Nurija! And this is only the beginning, only Malta! When I present you in Tyre, all will know that you are gifted with the Sight." Nuriya opened her mouth to speak but Ilobaal raised a hand to stop her. "Wait. There is more to tell. Two warships will remain here until they receive orders from King's council. The envoy speeds there already to discuss plans for a western fleet. This is my ambition bearing fruit! When my father names me to govern Malta none will speak against me. Soon I will build for you the temple at North

Rock, as I promised." He said this last, flourishing a bow. Then he kissed his palms and raised them toward her, as if adoring a statue. "My Goddess, my love, you are so beautiful."

"I do not want this."

"What do you mean?"

She took in the gifts with a wave of her hand. "I do not want any of this."

Ilobaal then observed the wool in place of her fine robe, the crude necklace in place of the silver pendant. "Are my gifts not pleasing?"

"They are lovely."

"Then what is it you do not want?" Annoyance was in his tone.

"I am not an Oracle."

"We have been through this, my love. You may not like it, but it is plain that you are."

"I do not want to be."

"Seeing is a gift from the Gods. Either you use it to honor Them or you disdain Them."

"How can visioning battle honor the Gods?"

"Is that what is troubling you? It is because you do not know your own Gods! I will hire an excellent tutor and then you will not be troubled, my pet. The Gods are honored when their enemies are defeated."

"The Mother suffers when Her children kill each other."

"Dearest," Ilobaal said patronizingly, "the old ways are gone. Look at this temple, crumbling ruins. I will build a temple to Anat and then you will see glory. You cannot help that you were raised in ignorance."

"Ignorance!"

"I am sorry if it offends your ears. Hush." He put his fingers to her lips to quell protest. "I must tell you something." He spoke very seriously now. "There will be more fighting—for Sicily, for Sardinia, even for Carthage. This is a time of new conquests.

Your gift of Sight is beyond the price of rubies. You will be great among our people." He studied his future in the lines of her face and a strange look came over him. "Listen, Nurija. Listen to what Ba'al sings to Anat." He raised his eyes to limestone walls as if gazing to the far distance and in a resonant tone recited,

Hurry, Rush
To me let your feet run
To me let your legs race
For I understand the lightning which the heavens do not
   know
The word which the people do not know
And the earth's multitudes do not understand
Come, and I will reveal it
On the Mount of my Victory.

"Do you see how He honors Her? Anat must be by Ba'al's side to share His victory." He took both Nuriya's hands and kissed them. "You will travel with me all around the Great Sea. I will show you the markets of Africa, the Great Sphinx of Kush, the Acropolis of Tyre, and by night," he pulled her close, "you will rest in these sturdy arms."

Nuriya turned her head from him. "I do not want this."

"What now, my love? Am I so easy to turn away?" He cupped her face and with exaggerated restraint, brushed his lips across hers. "Can you get love like mine from shepherd boys?" At the stoniness of her silence, Ilobaal raised an eyebrow.

Nuriya placed her hands firmly against his chest. "I do not want this."

"I love you, Nurija."

"Clearly you love your ambition more."

"You are one with my ambition, don't you see? You are the fulfillment of my prophesy."

"I am not clay to be molded to your liking, your mistress, or your Oracle, or your Anat. I do not want this. I cannot do it."

"Do you not want me?

Nuriya was caught off guard by the directness of his question. She gazed up into his handsome face, and despite her intention to be hard, she yearned for his touch. Yet her soul cried out fiercely inside her: Do not toss me again into the wake of this man's ambition! She gathered together body and soul, and looking into his eyes, shook her head, No.

Ilobaal stared at her, taking long measure of the situation. He had risked his life in the name of NurijaAnat and the ecstasy he envisioned on his return had filled him for days. That he would be denied made no sense, and the senselessness infuriated him. He spoke with deliberate dispassion, "Not even my father says *no* to me." He reached for the collar of Nuriya's shift and with a wrench, tore it to the waist. "I want you." He leaned her back over the altar, ignoring her head banging into stone. He covered her breast with his mouth and sucked. He had been ready for her since his sword first tasted the violent lure of Greek flesh. He felt fire in his loins then and it had not abated. With another wrench he tore her tunic to the hem. With her wild beauty magnifying his desire, he pushed into her. Heavenly. He pushed again and swept his gaze up her voluptuous form, up to those exquisite eyes—when it struck him like thunder!—the same blank fear, the same white shock, the same eyes as when she first woke to him on that long ago night.

Ilobaal reeled away, fumbling with his tunic, desire evaporating and confusion crowding his mind. This did not celebrate his victory. This did not honor his love for the Goddess Anat. He grabbed a length of cloth from the gift pile and threw it at her.

"Cover yourself, woman!" He retied his tunic and began to pace, his heels pounding stone, his hands raking his hair. Eventually he stopped before the mound of lapis linen heaped upon the woman's body and spoke as a superior officer, "When the temple is built, you will be its priestess. You are the Oracle of Malta whether or not it appeals to your notion of religiosity. I will inform you when your services are needed."

Nuriya did not watch him go. She heard footsteps, a curt word with Adnan, then hoof beats fading into the distance. She let the cloth fall to the ground and lay with her body exposed upon the altar. Tears washed her face, but there were no shattering sobs. While she had been hurt by Ilobaal before, today he had stepped beyond the pale. But the journey in the Cave had changed her—she knew she could live without him. She didn't know the way forward, but somehow she would find a truer path, and the courage to walk it. She breathed deeply and slowly, and let the knowledge sink into her bones.

After a long while she thought of Ghoga and of having her own cart. Perhaps she would be a traveling healer as Korba had been, staying out for days at a time. Maybe she would buy passage on a ship and start a new life in a new place, like Kepi had. Her mind wandered here and there, to Egypt, to Tyre, but her mind did not leave her. For that she was grateful.

When the sun dropped toward the sea, Nuriya wrapped the blue cloth around her torn tunic and climbed the hill. She did not see the lone ox-herd who had sat in the shadow of the oaks since early morn. He, too, got up stiffly and turned for home.

11.

Blessings

☯☯

Nuriya felt correct in her decision about Ilobaal but that did not mean she was calm about it. At the next honey harvest, she was stung five times for her trouble and had to alternate clay packs with plantain poultices for the rest of the day. When Korba pressed her to talk, she shared only the part she was willing to tell, "I told him, no. He was angry, but I'll be all right." But she was not all right. She felt bruised, and vulnerable, and raw. She appreciated that Hawk continued to bring Ghoga for visits, but his awkward silence had returned, and that suited her fine.

Nuriya wished she could be a child again—to not have to decide anything of importance, and be taken care of by someone older and wiser. She told Korba that she didn't want to go on calls by herself for the time being. Her worried teacher welcomed her request.

At the full moon of the summer fruit, news reached them of welcome festivities for Lady Johara's arrival. Naturally, Nuriya was determined to avoid port but she could not always avoid her own wandering mind. While pondering the Lady's rumored beauty up at the cistern one day, she spied Ilobaal passing below. Without stopping to think, she began to walk toward him.

Ilobaal turned his horse across the slope until the path became too treacherous then dismounted and gave his lead to Adnan who followed at a distance.

They stood face to face, several long paces between them, an annoyingly confident smile playing about Ilobaal's lips. "I wish to speak to you, dear Lady."

"What about?" She put no welcome in her tone.

"I need your help."

A reflexive thought popped into her mind. "Is your wife ill?"

He made a motion as if brushing away a gnat. "She arrived fat and healthy. This is another matter. I just received word from the envoy. The Tanit has been commissioned to the Navy of Carthage until the end of the season. We're ready to leave on the morrow." He spoke with a pride he seemed to expect her to share.

"But your wife just arrived..."

"She will be cared for." He took two steps closer and spoke in a conspiratorial tone. "Consider, Nurija. Come to Carthage with me. You could be my escort there without question. I will hire a servant for you and finally get you off this rock."

The shock of his audacity racked her like thorns. "Of course I will not go with you!"

Ilobaal shrugged. "You will see it my way in time." Stepping back, he resumed formality. "I am here for the Oracle's vision. A special task was given me by the envoy. My role must be," he searched for the proper word, "subtle."

Nuriya gasped. "You go as spy!"

"Hush. Rocannon even knows nothing of this."

"I will not do it."

"There is no treason to learn the intention of Carthage toward the house of Elulaios. In this way I make myself indispensable to my King."

"You do not understand. I am a healer, not an oracle. You do not honor that skill, but it is enough for me. I will not do it."

"I am not asking, Lady Nurija. I am commanding you." Ilobaal glanced toward Adnan who stepped forward, resting a hand on his sword hilt. It was the first time Nuriya had seen the boy armed and she shook her head at the display. "Don't be a child," Ilobaal snapped. "This is an important opportunity. As my star rises, so does yours."

"I gave you my answer."

Ilobaal changed strategy. "You asked something of me, Nurija, when we met. Do you remember it?" He let her think, and suddenly she felt five years old. "I have found what you asked."

Nuriya swallowed before she could speak. "Where is my father? What did you find?"

"You would deny me what I want and yet expect me to give you something of such great import?"

Nuriya stared at him long and despairingly. It was evil, him dangling before her this precious news. And yet, in a terrible irony, she couldn't help but see how elegant he looked in his long cloak and armored vest, couldn't help that her body trembled to be near him. She tried to reel in her flailing heart and asked feebly, "Won't you tell me?"

"After you assist me."

Her eyes darted, seeking a solution. Finally she said, "I will ask blessing for your journey. If the Mother deems I should see something of your fortunes, I will tell you. Then," she pleaded, "you will tell me of my father?"

"Agreed." He motioned her to proceed to the temple.

They went through the back of Ħaġar Qim, Adnan taking the animals around front and positioning himself at the entry. Ilobaal waited for Nuriya to settle herself. "Great Mother," she said out loud, "I ask the blessing of Your love on Ilobaal's journey to Carthage," and she lowered her gaze.

Scarcely had her lids closed when four scenes flashed before her:

–Ilobaal and his warriors sparring alongside the warrior crews of Carthage.

–A Carthaginian soldier colluding with his mate. He turned, revealing the ghastly scar along one cheek, wrapping his eye.

–A dagger sliding from a waist band, and thrusting through the dark.

–Ilobaal bleeding into iron-bound planks.

Her eyes flew open. "You go to your death, Ilobaal!"

"That cannot be. It is against the prophesy."

"The man..." She leaned onto her hands, trying to speak, shaking with horror. "The man—with the scar—he will kill you."

"I do not accept!" Ilobaal bellowed. He, too, was shaking. He pointed toward Nuriya. "Shunned woman, you have tricked me. You have tricked me because of your spite! Take back your curse!"

"I would not curse you, Ilobaal!"

He grabbed her by the shoulders. "Take back what you said." Anger twisted his features into a stranger's face and Nuriya's fear magnified. Her senses began to dim. There was a commotion outside, but Ilobaal did not turn his attention to it. He shook her again, commanding, "Get hold of yourself, woman," and when her lids began to flutter, he slapped her hard. Her neck snapped back.

In the next moment Hawk hurtled through the entryway and threw himself upon Ilobaal. Adnan screamed in behind, jumped Hawk's back, and grabbed him around the throat. Ilobaal rolled from under his attacker and sprang to his feet, drawing his sword. Hawk stopped struggling in deference to the weapon. Every man was breathing hard.

"Shepherd boy, do you know who I am?" Ilobaal shouted in Canaanite.

Hawk spat to the ground.

Ilobaal pointed the sword to his throat. "Rotten peasant!"

An eerie mewl sounded and they turned to see Nuriya crumpling to the ground. Hawk lurched from Adnan's grip, ignoring the sword and caught Nuriya as her body began slow, then faster, and faster convulsions. He cradled her head while her body jerked, her eyes wide and unseeing, her hands twisting into strange designs.

Adnan fled. Ilobaal stood by helpless and horrified. Never had he seen Nuriya in a grand mal seizure, only in the relatively calm twilight state. The convulsions seemed to go on for an interminable time. Gradually, the seizure diminished and Nuriya began to mutter. Hawk murmured in response, "It's all right, Nuriya. I'm here. It's all right."

"What does she say?" Ilobaal yelled in Maltese.

Hawk ignored him.

"How long does this take?"

Hawk padded Nuriya's head, and watched random tremors course her body. After a while he looked up to see the grim Ilobaal towering over them. "We wait," Hawk said.

"Unacceptable!" Ilobaal bellowed. "Adnan!" The shaken boy reappeared. "Bring the Lady to me when she recovers. I will be at port preparing for departure." He stormed out, and left at a gallop.

Nuriya came into wakefulness with Hawk stroking her hair and murmuring as he might console a baby animal. She smiled. Then she remembered the last image she had seen before she went into blackness, and forced her eyes open. "Have they gone?" An ache pulsed at the back of her head.

"The boy is here. I should have been with you, Nuriya." She touched his arm to reply, but could find no words.

Adnan entered, his eyes wary and his expression sickly, yet making the effort to fulfill his duty with firmness. "Lady Nurija, you are to come with me and report to Ilobaal of Tyre."

"Not today, Adnan."

"Those are my orders."

"I'm sorry. Will you help me, Hawk? I want to go home." Hawk helped her up and they stepped around the boy.

Hawk left Nuriya in Korba's care and went to find where Ghoga had wandered when he dropped her lead. He stayed that evening until both women slept and came again at first light. As the sun rose from the sea, the Magistrate's wagon appeared on the hillside. Adnan sat up front with a guard; another guard sat in back.

An unfamiliar soldier climbed the path. "The presence of Lady Nurija is requested at port," he announced.

Hawk stood along with Nuriya. "I'm going with you," he said. Nuriya gave him a small smile and Korba said, "Thank you, Hawk."

The port was brimming with commotion as men prepared three warships to sail on short notice. Warriors in full regalia stomped up and down gangways alongside teams of dockworkers passing kegs of water and wine. The wagon was stopped half-way down the alley. Nuriya and Hawk dismounted and were led to the Astarte shrine. Upon its altar was the offering of a ram, its dissected innards splayed for examination.

Ilobaal could be seen conferring with his captain aboard the Tanit. After a time he came down the gangway flanked by two warriors. He glanced toward Hawk with a look of disgust, and said a word of command to his guard. The warriors stepped back.

Ilobaal spoke to Nuriya in a low, clipped tone. "The auger reads success for our commission. I brought you here, Lady Oracle Nurija, before the shrine of Astarte, to remove your curse and make your blessing for our successful journey."

"I made no curse."

"Then you have no reason not to command that any curse be lifted and to bless these ships and my mission." He nodded her to the shrine.

Just then an announcement was proclaimed from up the alleyway and all turned to see a male servant preceding a woman, covered in a shawl and wearing beautiful white robes, with two handmaidens at her sides. Ilobaal motioned for the servant to halt and Nuriya to proceed.

She raised her hands toward the shrine and spoke in Maltese so the guard would not know her words. She had prepared herself on the ride out. "Power of the Great Mother, Your ways are beyond my understanding. Life to death and death to life unfold within your Being. Today, Ilobaal of Tyre embarks on a journey. He follows his dream though I have seen danger. If this danger may be taken from him, I pray it be so. If it is in the balance of life, and the will of his Gods, that he drink of this cup, I pray he meet his challenge with honor and dignity. Ilobaal of Tyre, go with your Gods. May your ships travel safely."

Ilobaal looked stricken. He barked out an order, turned on his heel, and marched off.

The guard went to the entourage of Lady Johara and led them to the foot of the gangway. Nuriya bowed her head when she passed as others did, though she tried to glimpse the face hidden within the folds of her shawl.

The Lady's entourage waited at the edge of the dock. Eventually, Ilobaal descended the gangway, took Johara's hands and spoke to her, witnessed but unheard by all present. The Lady bowed as Ilobaal reboarded the ship then she was led back up the alleyway and the throng of men preparing departure sprang back into action. When Adnan and the guard disappeared into the commotion, Nuriya and Hawk began the long walk home.

One moon after Ilobaal sailed on his mission to Carthage, Nuriya woke from sleep with a start, knowing the assassin's dagger had found its mark. At that dark hour, Ilobaal was calling to Anat, and thinking of her, his plea reverberating inside her mind, desperate and relentless. She dared not go back to sleep. Alone, she had no power to help him. By the light of the stars Nuriya made her way to Girgenti Valley and waited, nervously, on the hill above Tul's farm. With the first stirrings below she went to find Hawk and humbly begged him to take her to the Cave of Bones.

Hawk insisted on going inside with her. Nuriya explained that she did not intend to journey with the spirits, only to speak to them in her heart but Hawk said whether she journeyed with spirits or no, she would not be going in alone.

They went through the burial cave into the temple chamber and there she beseeched the ancestor spirits to help her fallen warrior find his way to peace. For Hawk's sake she kept her emotions in check, remaining conscious of him, the room, and her body, the whole while she prayed, with the spirits' gentle hum thrumming about her, and Ilobaal's distant plea droning on and on. She beseeched the spirits over and over, until for one unforgettable moment, she felt him with her—Ilobaal— knew his presence, smelled his scent. And then he was gone, his voice, silenced.

Her eyes opened of their own accord and she found herself standing with Hawk in the temple of the Cave, her face damp, and her heart in disarray.

Despite the anguish of the day, she went down to visit the Dreamer in her deep chamber, knowing she might not have the chance again for a long time to come. She stood before her, speaking in her heart: I carry your memories and your holy dream. She imagined the Dreamer asking her: What memories? and what dream? And so she answered: I carry memories of the

time when the Mother of the World was honored by the world. I
carry the dream that She will be remembered again, in the hearts
of Her children.

Nuriya looked around the space then, taking in the makeshift
altar and the curving stair. There was a spiral carved into the
stone the Dreamer rested upon and interlinking spirals painted
on the wall. She registered the glyphs with a dawning insight.
"Korba's incessant spirals" was what she used to think as she
pounded ochre to powder for the healer's paint. Even when she
chose her own altar she did not think of the spirals as symbols
of meaning—they were eyes that saw into her, and portals for
love. But in this moment Nuriya saw differently. Like coiling
tendrils of vine that circle as they climb, coming again and
again to the same place, only higher or wider each time, they
brought to mind the cycle of the Dreamer's dream: the Mother,
moving from honor, to memory, and one day, reawakening to
honor in the hearts of Her children. The spirals reflected
Nuriya's own journey even, as she embraced teachings she once
rejected, in new ways.

The day was full and the heat oppressive when they emerged
from the Cave. Nuriya faced the entrance and acknowledged
her gratitude to the ancestor spirits for the gift she had been
given, of knowing that Ilobaal had found his peace. She asked
Hawk to return with Borg and seal the Cave as before, without
mortar, so that those who sought would find, but the unwary
would not wander in and disturb the spirits there.

When Hawk dropped her in front of Ħaġar Qim, he asked if
she wanted company. Nuriya felt his disappointment that she
turned him away, but she needed to be alone.

At last she sat before her own altar and allowed the grief
she'd held at bay to crash over her, battering her, as rocks are
battered by the winter storm sea. She cried for her dead warri-
or, she gasped at senseless longing, she rued ever their meeting

and then she cried again, until it was finished, for now. Then she sat, tucked under the corbelled roofline in the heat of the afternoon, dazed by her tears and baking with the stones.

Later, when Hawk called that he brought water and berries, she did not begrudge him. She went out to say, "I'm almost done. Will you wait?"

"I will," he said.

Nuriya sat once more before the altar. Though her head felt stuffed with fresh pulled wool, her heart was as calm as the air after a storm has passed. She spoke out loud in her native tongue, "Great Mother, I thank you for life, though I do not understand it." She smiled, even as the sting came again to her eyes. "I thank you for love, though it also brings pain. I dedicate myself to You, and to healing, and to love."

Ilobaal's body was returned for burial. A tomb was carved into the rock below Ta' Silġ and a sarcophagus was sent from Carthage. Bon saw it carried from the dock in a solemn procession and described it in detail. It was fashioned out of clay in the likeness of a man and hollow in the center for the body to lie. Bon told them about a stand-off between Ilobaal's father and the officials in Carthage, and rumors of retaliation from Tyre. Although the funeral rites were private, they were also a much discussed affair, for the islanders had never heard of burying a man with food and wine and silver ingots.

A deep heaviness descended upon Nuriya after Ilobaal's death and she moved dully, save when she was tending a healing or at her altar. Korba tried to get her to spill her heart, but the way her teacher accepted her own life at the edge of the island, on the outskirts of society, told Nuriya that she could not help her with this. Not only was Ilobaal dead, with the turmoil of their painful and misguided affair reverberating inside, but her lingering hope that she would one day sail with him to Tyre was extinguished. What could she hope for now? What kind of future dared she dream of?

When, on occasion, Nuriya arose from melancholy long enough to observe Korba's acceptance of her mute brooding, she might thrash about until she found a reason to shout. But that was rare. Most days she spent in dutiful service or in silent staring toward the sea.

For Korba's part, she found her apprentice's work without flaw and therefore, if Nuri chose to grieve in silence, she was willing to wait. She did observe that Nuri cheered briefly when Hawk brought Ghoga for visits and so Korba would cajole him into staying for supper. Alas, those meals were only slightly more conversational than with the two women alone.

Besides the burial, the most important thing to happen that late summer was Jila's emancipation. Secretly she asked Sky to help her escape her ever more violent husband. In exchange for a ruby ring and a gold chain, a shrewd merchant promised passage to Jila's Sicilian homeland for her and her young children. Leaving Jaron behind caused Jila great anguish and Josep promised that he would look out for him.

Nuriya was not at port to see Jila off. Because Jaro already slandered against her as a witch that troubled his family, Sky counseled her not to go. She would do her best to not let him discover Nuriya's part in his wife's escape.

On the day of the autumn equinox Korba sacrificed an old hen, and when Hawk brought Ghoga for a visit, she invited him to their picnic. Soon Hawk's friends came looking for him, begging him come to port and join the running relay; the festival would be subdued this year but there would be prizes after all. "I've promised my company to these ladies and their fine chicken," Hawk replied jauntily as he walked them off.

"There'll be plenty of food at port, or is there something about this particular chicken that has your mouth watering?"

"Be off, my friends."

"You're not tethered yet, Hawk," they called.

It was a gorgeous day with fanciful clouds shape-changing before them. Nuriya found pleasure in the ease of Hawk's laughter and the strength of his movement as he played with Ghoga. It made her think of a certain kiss they once shared, and she smiled—maybe her heaviness was finally lifting.

After supper, Korba left them to enjoy the sunset. The Beauty Star glowed brilliant in the sapphire twilight when Hawk turned to Nuriya, and with a tumble of words, asked her to marry him. "I've always loved you, Nuriya. I want to care for you and make you happy. I promise to honor your work even when I don't understand it, and I will defend you with my life."

Nuriya was caught off guard. She struggled to not look away. She took a slow breath, gathering her thoughts, and put her hand over his. "Thank you, Hawk. I mean it. But I'm not ready for this. I need more time."

Just then a shooting star soared above them through the path of the Eagle and they raised their faces to its light. Hawk squeezed her hand, painfully hard, and let it go gently. They sat apart then, and spoke of other things. Nuriya hurt for Hawk, but she couldn't rush herself, nor make him an empty promise.

Nuriya continued to listen with half an ear to the news from port. There was talk that a new magistrate would arrive the next summer. Formal negotiations between Jaro's brothers and the council had been initiated. The Tanit was home for the winter, would any of the men think to visit Ilobaal's "Oracle," and what would she say if they did? There was news from patients as well. Rom visited, gifting the healers with a basket he wove himself in an elegant design of black and brown squares. And the cousins, Cara and Bela, both flourished. Nuriya found even the good news confusing— reminding her of magic she had known, but also of the horrors. She understood, now, that what people called her *gift* was the way power moved through her, that sometimes, in response to need or request, took the form of visions. But her ignorance still made her dangerous. The ancestor spirits in the Cave of Bones had named her a *dreamer* yet she remained burdened with a potent gift she was afraid to use.

Sometimes Nuriya daydreamed seeking passage to Tyre come spring, though traveling alone to a foreign land to look for her father would be shockingly reckless. She wondered vaguely how long Hawk would wait for a response from her before he offered his affections elsewhere. She could conjure the memory of their kiss, and feel the urging of her body toward what more it prom- ised, but if she opened her heart to Hawk, would she forever regret giving up the chance to find a place in her father's world? If she prayed for anything these days, it was, "Show me the way."

One afternoon, as Nuriya vainly longed for someone to tell her what to do, she came to a decision. She went home for a waterskin and bowl and headed to Ħaġar Qim.

Raising the snake necklace before her altar, Nuriya prayed aloud, "If you hear me, Mother, I need your help. I don't know what these symbols mean, but I trust you meant them for me." She poured water, rubbing the symbols as if polishing them. Then trembling before the unknown, she drank every drop from the bowl. She felt a confidence in taking this action that she had not felt for a long time. She pulled off the shell neck- lace and performed the same ritual, for although the central stone had no markings, it was, to her, a thing of power. She poured water, rubbing and polishing the stone, and again, drank every drop.

As the autumn cooled toward winter, Nuriya settled into a pat- tern at treatment calls that seemed to work: if she felt tingling on her skin, she would allow it, knowing that healing power was moving through her, but if she felt spinning, or dizziness or head pain, she would walk away and take deep breaths until the sensations abated. At last, she felt ready to work by herself again; she sought to relieve Korba of the overnight calls, allowing her beloved teacher her early bedtimes and her more and more necessary naps.

There were a few scattered rain showers at the end of autumn, but no heavy rains yet. Several days after winter solstice, Nuriya traveled, without Korba, past mid-island, to treat a child with a fever and swollen glands. On the way home she asked the family to take her to Ulma's. As the cart passed the outer fields, she waved to the men of Sky's clan repairing the rubble field walls. Rike, a handsome young man with thick, wavy hair and engaging brown eyes, peeled away from the group and sauntered over to intercept the cart's path. "Hello, Nuriya," he called.

"Hello, Rike."

"I hope you're spending the night. I promised to teach you the stones game. I can show you after supper."

"I won't be staying that long. I just came to check on Ulma."

"That's a shame. Wait here. I'll see if the men can manage without me." He hastened away before Nuriya could protest and then ran back, jumping up to the cart bench. "I'll teach you now."

The girls of Sky's clan, as well as of those of the neighboring clans, kept track of Rike's activities and indeed, several heads turned as the cart entered the compound, their eyes to Rike rather than the visiting healer.

Ulma was sitting in the sun and received Nuriya warmly. It was the quiet of early afternoon, with the men out in the fields and the women in the grinding hut, gathering wood, or sitting with Ulma, mending in their laps. The matriarch had made good progress in regaining the use of her arm, though Lili complained that she resisted working her leg. The young healers discussed therapy strategies then Lili asked Nuriya to join her collecting mushrooms.

Rike skillfully intercepted, showing Nuriya where he set up the game behind his family hut, near the walled garden and out of sight of gossiping women. He guided Nuriya to the play mat, an ox hide marked with lines, a pile of dark stones on one side, and light stones on the other. "You pick, Nuri," Lili's cousin, Ren, called, emerging from between two huts, flanked by neighbor girls and her younger sister. Nuriya picked the light stones and sank before her pile, the girls plopping down beside her, turning over stones to find the two etched with signs, giggling into their hands and turning the stones back over. They all proceeded to teach her the game at once.

Rike flirted and the girls tittered and Nuriya was amused to find her attention wandering—comparing Rike's self-assured manner to Hawk's restrained affection, Rike's slight build to Hawk's sturdy shoulders. She was thinking, that maybe it was time to surprise Hawk by walking over to visit him for once, when they all heard someone scream, "Fox fell in! Fox fell in!" Ren gasped and the girls flew away between the dwellings. Rike and Nuriya quickly followed as the women poured out of the grinding hut and someone wheeled Ulma around to face the well.

"Are you sure?!" Ren was screaming.

"Who was watching him?"

Heads turned toward Ren. "Are you sure?" she screamed.

"Where's Ara?"

"Gathering wood."

"I don't hear anything."

"I was in the hut. I saw his feet go in."

Bete was heaving at the cap stones, two heavy cut stones that narrowed the well opening to the width of a bucket. Rike pushed forward, and pried the stones off. He had one leg over the rim before Ren threw her leg over the other side saying, "You might land on him. I'll go." She put teeth and nails into untying the bucket from its rope. Rike drew his knife and cut it off.

"Go. I'll lower you." Ren grabbed the rope and went over the side. The rope cut against the well lip as it lowered her weight. "Get a heavy rope from the animal pen," Rike yelled. Once Ren's splash was heard, the courtyard was dead silent but for the splashing, Ren's gasps, and her worried cries, "Oh. Oh."

Soon, Ara's scream pierced the quiet. There was more splashing then finally, "I've got him! Pull me up!"

"Where's the rope?" Rike roared, his head bobbing like a wounded animal, judging that the frayed bucket rope wouldn't hold. Bete thrust a thick hemp coil into his hands and Rike immediately lowered it. "Hold on. I've got you." He and several women hauled Ren up clutching the unconscious toddler between her arms. His lips were blue, his skin the purple of dusk. Ara grabbed her baby. "Fox!" she screamed, shaking him. She whacked him hard between the shoulders, a dull thud to his limp body. "Fox, Fox," she cried, rubbing and pounding, and becoming ever more frantic. She held him before her, shouting, "Breathe!" She put her mouth over his, blew, and shouted again, "Breathe!"

Ulma caught Nuriya's eye. With a powerful yet unspoken intention, the matriarch demanded of her, *You must do something!*

Nuriya's racing heart stopped. The image of Bela's spirit misting among phantoms flashed before her, then the venomous fist exploding in Rdum. For an instant she saw her own mother's dying eyes. She felt paralyzed by all these things she did not understand. Then she heard in the echo of a memory, the spirit of the Cave of Bones saying, "Remember us, Healer Nuriya. We will help you choose wisely." She willed the spirits be with her as she stepped forward. She knew what to do. She slipped one hand between mother and child and put the other on Fox's back. With strength and will and assisted by spirits of light, Nuriya pushed in and up under Fox's ribs. Vomit and water burped out over Ara's back. Fox hacked, then he breathed! His color became pink and he reached for his mother. Ulma nodded, and Nuriya, dazed, slipped back into the crowd.

She worked her way toward the walled garden, shaken, but with an astounding realization taking shape. Fox had been unconscious for too long—but when Nuriya thought of the ancestor spirits, she knew he would be well. The spirits had the power to help and they wanted to help. Nuriya could feel them with her even now. "Thank you," she breathed, trembling with relief. "Thank you so very much."

Lili came into the garden to say, "Ulma sends for you." As the young healers passed the hearth, Ara's mate, back from the fields, for news of the near-drowning traveled fast, intercepted Nuriya with a huge bear hug. "Thank you, little sister!" he whooped and set her back on her feet. Others called out or reached to touch her as she passed. Lili opened Ulma's door flap then took off in another direction.

The matriarch had been brought inside after the commotion over Fox quieted. "Thank you for saving the life of my great-grandson," Ulma said, her good eye as piercing as ever. "I saw power move through you, child. I don't think the old Ulma would have seen, but this one-eyed invalid saw. The others will know that you pressed the right place for Fox to vomit, but you and I know something more." They were silent a moment before Ulma continued, "It has been less than a year since our paths crossed and you have matured more in that time than some of my clan do in a lifetime." Nuriya heard praise but the words also made her want to cry; she felt so aged and ancient from all she'd been grappling with. "I need your help," Ulma said, jarring her out of self-pity.

Lili stepped inside the dwelling with a girl, a few years younger, following. "This is Leeta, my granddaughter. Do you know each other?" Nuriya nodded; she'd met Leeta along with the rest of the clan. She noticed that the girl was squinting in the darkened room, and that sections of her lower eyelids were discolored and puckered. Lili explained. Last summer Leeta came to Ulma saying she got dirt in her eyes. They treated her with a soothing eyewash and at first, the redness and swelling had gone. But ever since, the light hurt Leeta's eyes. Her mother complained she'd become clumsy with her weaving and she couldn't tell her colors. "I want you to treat her," Ulma said. "Now."

Nuriya did not hesitate. She closed her eyes and called on the ancestor spirits to help. She asked Lili for the herbs she wanted, "Would you bring storksbill and borage?" She heard something else inside and repeated it out loud, "And I need fresh milk."

Leeta lay down while Lili rummaged in bags and started a pot to heat. Nuriya showed Lili the quantity of each herb she wanted then sat at Leeta's head, listening inwardly. The spirits communicated, without words, that shock needed to be released from Leeta's eyes. Nuriya cupped her hands over the girl's eyes and called out whatever it was. A feeling like sparks flew into her palms and a scene flashed in her mind. She saw Leni, Jila's daughter, cowering behind an amphora pile, her tunic dirty and torn. Jaro stepped into view. "Git Leeta. I said, leave her be." He picked up a handful of dirt and gravel and pulled back to throw. "Git out of here, I said."

Guide me, help me, Nuriya prayed as the scene unfolded in her mind. She was told by the spirits that she need not follow the vision, but she must drain Leeta's eyes until no shock remained. Sparks flew into her palms so hot it felt like her hands would blister, but only when the heat ebbed did Nuriya lift them. She picked up the bowl of milk, saying, "Open your eyes, Leeta. I'm going to wash them clean." She dripped milk at the outer edge of each eye. Leeta blinked. "I'm washing fear from your eyes," Nuriya said. She dripped and said again, "I'm washing the fear from your eyes."

She poured the herbed water through a cloth and while waiting for it to cool, she cleaned Leeta's face, dabbing the milk from her cheeks, smoothing her hair, and speaking in a casual manner. "Is Leni your friend?" Leeta nodded gravely. "Do you know where Leni is now?"

"Far away?"

"She's with her mother, in a good place. They're in Sicily, where Jila grew up." Leeta studied Nuriya's face as she spoke. "It's probably a lot like your home, with cousins and aunties and babies. She's safe now, Leeta." Nuriya paused again, listening inwardly. "Leni misses you and wants you to be happy. She wants you to be healthy. Come to sit. Every day for twenty days, you will come to Ulma's hut. Lili will make an eye wash. You'll put your eyes into the bowl, open and close them three times, and say, 'I wash the fear from my eyes.' You'll put your eyes in the bowl, open and close them three more times and say, 'Leni is safe with her mother.' And one more time put your eyes in the bowl and say, 'My family will keep me safe.' Will you do that?" Leeta nodded. "Let's do it together. I'll remind you what to say."

Later, after Lili and Leeta had gone, Ulma said, "I understand now. Thank you. Leeta will tell Lili what really happened." Nuriya felt confident that Ulma would know what to do about Jaro. "I've someone else I want you to treat," the matriarch added. "Come at new moon. I'll have her waiting."

"I will."

As she walked out into the afternoon, Nuriya realized that she hadn't been afraid working with Leeta. And she didn't feel afraid to come back and work with whomever Ulma lined up. She hungered, in fact, to work under the watchful eye of Ulma, who could "see power." More than that, the ancestor spirits had shown that they wanted to help. How extraordinary! Nuriya felt as happy as she had when power first moved through her more than a year before, the day she worked on Hawk's ribs. How naïve she had been. She was still naïve, but she had a guide now, and helpers.

Two of Lili's aunties drove her home and taught her rhyming songs the whole way. They stayed for a delightfully and surprisingly, animated supper.

A few cold days later, before she had the chance to get over to visit Hawk, Adnan came to Mnajdra and announced, "The Lady Johara requests Lady Nurija's presence." Nuriya joined him in the familiar wagon, making a great effort to not anticipate the meeting.

Nothing could have prepared her for the grandeur of the Magistrate's residence. From outside it was similar to the other buildings of quarried limestone, but what a marvel it held within. Arched interior doorways hung with embroidered drapery, elaborate torch sconces lined the walls and hanging lamps dangled overhead. There were chests of cedar with latches of gold and a table of African ebony. Carved ivory plaques were set at intervals along the walls, telling a story. Adnan took Nuriya into a courtyard lined with potted plants. The floor was a tile mosaic of ships under full sail. How could such splendor be here on tiny Malta? Was this the life she might have known with Ilobaal? Nuriya's heart crackled with emotion that would wait to be untangled in private. Lady Johara came into the courtyard dressed in white linen clasped with silver pins and wearing a necklace of coral and silver that Nuriya had once seen in a fabric-lined box. The Lady's countenance was indeed lovely though she scarcely met Nuriya's eyes. She beckoned Nuriya through a doorway and bid her sit on a low couch covered with sleek fur. A servant followed with an infant in her arms. Johara sat in a tall chair, carved with a scene of hunters and lions. She looked tiny in the elaborate chair, like a child playacting at the role of authority. "Greetings, Lady Nurija," she said in a diminutive voice. "Thank you for coming."

"Greetings, Lady Johara. I am honored."

"Before my husband left for Carthage," Johara paused, took a breath, and continued, "he told me—if he did not survive—his journey—I was to seek the Oracle."

"I beg your pardon, Lady," Nuriya cut in, "I am a healer, not an Oracle..."

Johara's face reddened. "Are you not the Oracle Nurija?"

"I am Nuriya."

Ilobaal's widow frowned and Nuriya felt contrite for confusing her, but she was determined to refuse any request for prophesy. Lady Johara composed herself and began again, rushing her words this time, "My husband told me if he did not survive I was to seek the Oracle to ask a blessing for our son."

Nuriya let her defenses ebb. She had no reason to refuse this humble request. "I will ask a blessing for your son."

The serving woman placed the infant into Nuriya's arms and she smiled into his dreaming, drowsing face, with his father's brows and his mother's sweet mouth. She bent close and breathed in angelic perfume. Then she turned her eyes skyward. "I ask the Great Power which you call by the names of Astarte and Anat, Ba'al and Melquart; and the Power which I know as Great Mother; I ask the ancestors of this child; and the ancestors of this land, to bless this son of Tyre, to guide him in health and wisdom all the days of his life."

"Thank you," Johara murmured, her mother's pride glowing strong. "Your kindness will be rewarded." She took her son from

Nuriya and settled him to her breast then spoke to the servant who bowed and went out of the room.

She is so young, Nuriya thought, and probably lonely. She asked her, woman to woman, "What are your plans for you and your son? Will you stay on Malta?"

"Next summer we will return to Tyre. King Elulaios, my great uncle, has offered to raise my son in his court. It is an honorable position for us."

Nuriya imagined befriending Ilobaal's widow in order to accompany her to Tyre, but in the next moment she was astounded to realize that she no longer wanted to leave Malta. It was here she wanted to be, working with patients and working with Ulma, learning about the spirits of this place and how they wanted to help. Then the full import of Johara's words washed over her. "The prophesy is fulfilled," she exclaimed. She quoted to Johara as Ilobaal had quoted to her from the Oracle Priest of Melquart: "'And one day, your son will return to Tyre to live in the House of the King.' You go with the blessing of your Gods, Lady Johara."

The young woman's eyes shone and she bowed her head. "Thank you, Oracle."

The whole of Ilobaal's prophesy washed through Nuriya's mind: "When the Star of Gold and the red Star of the Warrior ride with the Lion through the long night, you will meet an ally. In the next turning of the season, you will soar toward your ambition like a shooting star. And one day, your son will return to Tyre to live in the House of the King." Nuriya perceived these words anew and her heart squeezed tight. My quick, bright flame, she thought, my shooting star...

An older man with a flowing, white beard and dark bushy brows bustled into the room, interrupting the moment. "I am sorry, Lady, I did not know you had company," he muttered, backing away with an armload of scrolls. Then he stopped abruptly to stare at

Nuriya. After a moment he bowed then turned to Lady Johara. "Forgive me," he said.

There was an awkward pause before Johara took up her role. "Lady Nurija, this is Master Ghali, of the council. Master Ghali, this is Lady Nurija."

Ghali bowed again. "If I may say, Lady, you do so look like your mother."

Like a seabird rising into headwind, Nuriya's heart lurched and churned, taking flight. "You knew her?" she asked breathlessly.

"Not well, but one could never forget the eyes." He turned to Johara and said again, "Forgive me."

Johara tilted her head, unsure how to respond.

"Oh, sir, please... Could you tell me about her?" Nuriya begged.

Ghali turned to the daughter-in-law of his Magistrate and suggested, "Perhaps Lady Johara could arrange a more appropriate meeting for Lady Nurija and myself to speak?"

"Of course," Johara replied.

Feeling the crush of disappointment at seeing the man step through the doorway, Nuriya cried, "Wait, Master Ghali." He turned back and she took a breath for courage. "Do you know my father, Master Ghali?"

The man's expression softened. "I did. I am sorry for your loss."

"My loss?"

Ghali looked to Johara, but finding her expression blank, cleared his throat and replied, "It was I who traced your father. I reported to Eshebaal's son," he nodded to Johara, "that your father died when his ship sank off the coast of Ras Shamra. He left behind a wife and two children. I am sorry for your loss."

"When was that?" Nuriya stammered.

"Four years ago, I believe."

"No. When did you tell Ilobaal?" she demanded. Both Ghali and Johara jumped at her naming the dead, but Nuriya ignored them, intent on an answer.

"I stayed in Tyre some days after the wedding. I told Eshebaal's son as soon as I returned to Malta," he assured her.

Nuriya stared at him, and then at Johara who was trying to fathom the significance of the exchange. Abruptly Nuriya rose from the couch. "Thank you for your hospitality. I must go."

"Please wait. My servant is bringing an offering."

"Send it to Mnajdra, and tell Adnan I will walk. I must go."

She stepped stiffly from the residence but before she reached the fork, she was running. She ran the path toward the village, puffing her breath in and out, watching the stones fly past. She skirted the village and gradually slowed to a stop. When she leaned, panting, against her knees, her mind revealed to her a surprise. She thought she would hate Ilobaal for withholding this news—but she did not. She thought she would be devastated to hear of her father's death—but she was not. She felt only—freedom! She stood and let the wintry sun pour through her eyelids, feeling her world shift and rearrange, as if she closed her eyes on the constellation of the Bull of Heaven and would blink them open to find the Sign of the Scales before her. She had wanted for so long to be a part of her father's world, to make him proud, when he was not even alive to judge or care! She started to laugh, the last remnants of her yearning for a kingdom she'd never seen falling away like chaff from the grain.

Hearing a noise, Nuriya opened her eyes. Ghoga's dam was emerging from the oaks below. She watched Hawk halt Blaki, dismount and begin walking up the gentle slope. A shiver moved through her body. She had seen this moment before—on that long ago day when she sat by Hawk's side puzzling over a wondrous new gift and a strange vision. She had seen Hawk in this future time—this same face, and gesture, and smile that said, "I greet you, cherished one. I welcome you from wherever you have journeyed this day."

Hawk was standing before her, without awkwardness now. He was remembering, too, it seemed. A feeling bubbled inside Nuriya, flaring up as ember to a flame. The feeling was joy—unbound and free—joy that wanted to embrace the sky above, the land beneath her feet, and this man before her. With a movement as natural as taking a breath, Nuriya offered her hand. And matching her smile with his own, Hawk twirled her gracefully into the circle of his arms.

Glossary

Ba'al—pronounced "Ball" or "Ba-al," the Canaanite Storm God.

Ghoga—pronounced "**O**-ga" a name I created from "Ghogal," the Maltese word for calf. The Maltese language contains Phoenician, Arabic and Italian influences.

Ħaġar Qim—pronounced "**Ha**-jar **Eem**," meaning sacred stones or standing stones.

Ilobaal—pronounced "**Ee**-lo-ball," a Phoenician name patterned after the King names of Tyre.

Iva—pronounced "**Ee**-va," meaning "Okay."

Mnajdra—pronounced "Im-**Nai**-dra," meaning a place of observation.

Trilithion—the arrangement of two tall stone blocks, capped by a lintel slab, used to designate a sacred place. (Malta, Stonehenge)

Wied—a river valley

About The Author

© James Tucker

Catherine Veritas is a writer, painter, and Holistic Chiropractor living with her husband on the Big Island of Hawaii. Interest in the sacred temples of Malta inspired her pilgrimage to the archipelago. Ancient Malta became her passion, leading to two more research trips, culminating in the novel you now hold in your hands.

More information may be found at:
www.themaltesedreamer.com.
www.catherineveritas.com